"Chung-Cha belongs to C
you destroy me, God will s

The agent chuckled.

"And what if I destroy her?"

Praise for *The Beloved Daughter* by Alana Terry

Grace Awards, First Place
IndieFab Finalist, Religious Fiction
Women of Faith Writing Contest, Second Place
Book Club Network Book of the Month, First Place
Reader's Favorite Gold Medal, Christian Fiction

"...an engaging plot that reads like a story out of today's headlines..." ~ *Women of Faith Writing Contest*

"In this meticulously researched novel, Terry gives readers everything a good novel should have — a gripping story, an uplifting theme, encouragement in their own faith, and exquisite writing." ~ *Grace Awards Judges' Panel*

"The Beloved Daughter is a beautifully written story." ~
Sarah Palmer, Liberty in North Korea

Slave Again

a novel by Alana Terry

Slave Again
Copyright © 2014 Alana Terry
1941735282

Cover design by Damonza. Cover image elwynn/Shutterstock.com.

www.alanaterry.com

PART 1

CHAPTER 1

"Kick me again, and I swear I'll kill you," Mee-Kyong growled.

She fell backward, exposing the small swell of her abdomen. Pang didn't miss his opportunity. As soon as his heel connected with the underside of her belly, a warm gush streamed down her leg. "What did you do?" Her voice faltered. "What were you thinking?" She gawked at the puddle beneath her.

Pang shook his head. "You shouldn't provoke me like that." He sank down beside her. "You know how hard it is for me to keep my temper." Mee-Kyong didn't try to stand. She stared at the blood-tinged liquid on the floor. He groaned. "I asked you to help me not get so angry anymore." He scooped her up, and a smaller leak cascaded down to the ground. "You're bleeding." He brushed her cheek with his lips as he laid her on the bed. She was too nauseated to open her eyes. Pang curled down beside her on the mattress, wrapping his arms around her and stroking her hair. "Next time, try not to make me so upset. At least not until our child is born."

She intertwined her legs with his, wincing as her nerves shot fire through her belly in protest. He pressed himself up against her back and ran his fingers around her navel. "I would never do anything to hurt either of you." His hot breath tickled her ear. "You are my family now." A shiver started at the tip of Mee-Kyong's tailbone and scurried all the way up her back, finally erupting into goose bumps across her shoulders.

He buried his face into the curve of her neck. "All I want to do is love you." Her whole body shuddered.

Half an hour later, she stood still and focused on his snoring. *Not yet. Wait a few more minutes.* She held her breath. Invisible iron fingers clamped down on her uterus. Her discharge was now mostly blood instead of clear liquid. *He'll be sleeping soundly soon enough. Don't be an impatient fool. Wait a little bit longer.* A contraction forced the breath out of her, and Pang shifted on the bed. She froze. He couldn't wake up. Not yet.

She held her abdomen, pressing her fingers against the hard swell. *You can do this.* She stared at her bruised belly. Pang twitched in his sleep. Mee-Kyong rose slowly, keeping her hand over her midsection. She tiptoed to the far side of the cabin and turned around long enough to study her lover. She had endured so much as a prisoner in Camp 22. She could make it without Pang. But did she really want to? He was the father of her child. He had purchased her freedom with his own. He gave up everything — his job, his standing with the Party, his personal safety — just to help her escape the gulag. *You owe it to him to stay with him.*

Pang grimaced and let out a loud snore.

Mee-Kyong wrinkled her nose. *I hate snoring.* She reached into Pang's traveling bag and pulled out his knife. *Do it now, or you'll never have the courage, you coward.* She wished Pang weren't asleep, but it had to be this way. If he was awake, she would never follow through. He would thwart her just as easily as he would swat a mosquito. Whether with his fists or his kisses, he could always find a way to stop her.

She grimaced when a contraction seized her abdomen. More blood oozed down her leg as she studied the former prison guard. Scratch lines ran across one side of his chest. She stood above him, etching his muscular frame into her memory. Even in his sleep, he made a fist.

The contraction tapered off, but she still hesitated. *You've always been too pathetic to do anything.* She should just take a nap like Pang and sleep off her worries. That night, the broker would come and hustle them into China. Once they were out of North Korea, Pang wouldn't be so tense. He wouldn't get so angry. She put her hand protectively over her abdomen. Her other hand trembled, almost dropping the weapon. "Maybe we should stay," she whispered to her womb.

Pang choked on his own snore. His mouth hung open as he lay splayed on the bed. Mee-Kyong gripped the steel handle. *He looks so pathetic when he drools.* She breathed in and plunged the knife into Pang's chest.

CHAPTER 2

Mee-Kyong slid down against the wall, clutching her abdomen and gaping at the blood on her arm. *What are you sitting down for?* She shivered and refused to look toward the bed. She hadn't expected Pang to wake up. She had imagined it would be easy. Quick and painless. Merciful, even. She leaned over and vomited. *Quit acting like a baby.* She spat and wiped her mouth on her shirt. *You need to leave, or you'll end up even worse off than him.*

She staggered to her feet and leaned against the wall for support. Her eyes caught the blood-stained blanket on the bed, and she retched again. Mee-Kyong picked up the knife and wiped it clean. At least if she had to use it again, she'd learn from her mistake and angle it right. She thought about Pang, held her stomach, and groaned once more. *Nice planning, you idiot. Now you've got to find your way to the border by yourself.* How was she supposed to make it to China without him? She could have put up with a few more days of his assaults, couldn't she?

It's only nerves, you wimp. Of course her stomach was a little upset. She put one hand on her abdomen and steadied herself with the other. *It's only nerves.* Nerves that she would have to overcome if she was going to escape North Korea with her hard-earned freedom.

Pang had never mentioned the name of the broker who would lead them into China, but Mee-Kyong had to decide what to do before he showed up. She either needed to get away from the cabin before he arrived, or she'd have to find a hiding place for the body, clean up the entire mess, and think of a compelling lie to convince the man to help her escape without Pang.

Right now, it looked like her only real option was to run away. She couldn't move the body by herself, not with the continuous cramping in her uterus and searing pain in the small of her back. She didn't have the fortitude to even look at the corpse, let alone clean away the filth of death. She wasn't about to check to confirm her suspicions, but the odor from the bedside made her guess the blanket was soiled with more than just blood. And even if she hid the body, she had no money to pay the broker.

Money. *You fool. Why didn't you think of the money?* She bit down on her fist. Pang always kept his money in his pocket.

She willed her body to turn toward the bed and swallowed down another rush of bile. Even Pang's pants were filthy. *Now look at what you have to do.* She straightened her spine as best she could with her swollen abdomen. She had persevered through an entire childhood in a North Korean prison camp, relying on her own wits and strength. The gulag raised her. She was born behind a barbed electric fence, but she endured. She had eaten raw rodents. She had lanced a boil with her teeth when no better medical care was available. She had survived her relationship with Pang, even though he always threatened to be the one to kill her. If Camp 22 had taught her anything, it was how to survive.

And right now, what Mee-Kyong needed to survive was an envelope full of cash.

She trudged to the bed, averting her gaze. She didn't want to face her lover's eyes again. The stench of death's final humiliation assaulting her nostrils, she grimaced and crept her hand toward Pang's pocket. She felt her way, finger after finger, until she found the cash. She snatched it out and then doubled over gagging. She tried to twist her body away, but a stitching pain in her side stole her breath instead, and she stumbled to the ground. *Clumsy dolt.*

Propped up on one elbow, she pressed down on her waist. Her uterus was as hard as the cement floor of the dorm back at Camp 22. Mee-Kyong shut her eyes. Her whole body felt like it was orbiting around a point just above her head. After vomiting once more, she fumbled toward the door, wondering what she had to do to forget the corpse that lay on the mattress, defiling her senses and her memory.

She didn't even make it out of the cabin before she staggered again to the ground. *Get off this cursed floor.* As she rocked back and forth on her elbows and knees, anguish from her abdomen radiated through the rest of her body. Her arms trembled as she struggled to hold herself up.

The baby wasn't supposed to come for another six or eight weeks. That's what the nurse Pang brought from Onsong had said. Mee-Kyong planned to be safe in the Chinese interior by her due date, not stuck in this cabin next to Pang's corpse. What was she supposed to do if her child was born here? She couldn't bring it with her to China. She would have a hard enough time surviving by herself. How could she expect to take care of a newborn? Pang never mentioned it, but she always assumed he would whisk the baby away and get rid of it somehow. They had both hoped the Onsong nurse would take care of the problem for them, but it was too late into the pregnancy for that.

By nightfall, she was still on the floor. Her body had decided to expel the child with or without Mee-Kyong's consent. She closed her eyes and clenched her teeth. *Don't be such a sniveling wimp.* In the prison camp, she had endured all of Pang's violent outbursts; she could endure something as universal as childbirth. Like Pang's temper, this delivery wouldn't last forever. At some point, it had to end. The only problem was that when it was over, instead of having a lover to comfort and soothe her wounds, she would have a baby she didn't know how to care for, a baby she didn't even want.

No matter what happened, it had to end soon. Either she would die, or her body would evict Pang's baby from her womb. There would be no more waiting. Mee-Kyong gritted her teeth. Drenched with sweat, she barely had time to inhale before she needed to bear down again.

Her skin burned. She clenched her eyes shut, and with one more push, she stretched wider than she thought was physically possible. Another small squeeze, almost an afterthought, brought her child into the world.

Soft fuzzy down covered near-translucent eyelids. Perfectly formed nails tipped the ends of ten wrinkled fingers. It was a boy. Mee-Kyong held him up in detached scrutiny.

Pang's baby was dead. At least she wouldn't have to figure out what to do with their bastard son. She struggled to clean herself up, using the already bloody blanket to wipe off as much of her filth as she could.

Repulsed by the sight of the child, she wrapped the corpse in Pang's undershirt and shoved it away in a corner of the cabin. Her legs trembled as she dressed. *You are not going to give up now.* She had to survive. Who cared if she had just delivered a baby? So had every other mother in the course of all human history.

She lifted her chin, steadied herself with her hand against the wall, and staggered out the cabin door. She only made it a few steps before she collapsed. *Don't stop moving, you lazy idiot!*

She got up and counted her steps until no degree of self-degradation could coax her body farther. She was bleeding even more heavily than she had been before the delivery. She was still within sight of the cabin when an aftershock gripped her uterus so tight she a sob escaped.

Stand up. Her body refused to respond. She tried to blink away the blurry lights in her field of vision, but her sight didn't clear. *Forget the pain.* Another contraction, the byproduct of labor, made the ground spin around her. She wouldn't be going anywhere.

Suddenly chilled, she curled up into a ball and tried to warm up by hugging herself. *If you lie down, you'll never get back up again.* She tried to resist the drowsiness that encircled her shivering, aching body, but right now she only had the will to sleep.

Tomorrow, she would continue on her journey.

CHAPTER 3

Min-Ho had already examined the young girl from head to toe and then all the way back up again. Now he focused on the way the bottom of her throat trembled when she spoke. "My teacher said you could help me get a job." She swept her bangs across her forehead.

"You're kind of young, aren't you?" Min-Ho smiled to calm the girl's nerves. He wasn't about to scare away a catch like this.

Sun focused on her hands. "My family needs the money."

He didn't ask for any more details. Details didn't matter. He hadn't met a girl like Sun in years. Numbers and figures raced through his mind. "You'll need some new clothes." His fingertip grazed the sleeve of her sweater, and he gauged her reaction when his knuckle brushed the back of her hand. "Much prettier clothes. Wouldn't that be nice?"

She glanced down. He was pleased to note the red creeping into her cheeks. He pursed his lips. "You know, I could get you a job here in North Korea, but there's no guarantee you'll earn a single won. If the Dear Leader doesn't pay your boss, you can't expect your boss to pay you. You understand how it all works." Sun blinked a few times but said nothing. She didn't understand at all. Another good sign. "How old are you?" He wasn't sure if the child was wise enough to lie, but he guessed not.

"Fifteen," she whispered. No, not very wise at all.

"You know, I've helped girls even younger than that find jobs across the border."

She touched her smooth, olive cheek. He picked at one of his pimples and shuffled closer to her on the park bench, watching her expression as his leg brushed against hers. "You're smart enough that I won't lie to you. It's risky. Lots of people would take advantage of a young girl if she doesn't have someone looking out for her, you know." Her eyes grew wide. He put his hand on Sun's knee, making sure not to touch the skin underneath the skirt of her school uniform. "I could help you find a good job in China, though. A better job than what you could find here."

"And you'd help me get there?"

He nodded. "Of course. It's too dangerous for you to cross the river alone. I'd be there to help you. I even know most of the border guards." He paused to let her suck in a little breath. "We have certain … arrangements. In fact, several of them are my friends. They'll let you cross."

"And when I want to come back home?"

His hand was still on Sun's knee, but his thumb brushed her skin. "You just let me know, and I'll come and bring you back to your family, safe and unharmed."

"With all the money I earned?"

Min-Ho scratched away at his chin. "Exactly." His other palm now rested completely on Sun's warm leg. They sat for several moments in silence. He finally cleared his throat. "You'll need to be very brave when we travel. I have some medicine that will help you sleep." He stroked her skin. "You won't wake up until we're across the border. Can you do that?"

Sun nodded and hugged her arms across her chest. Min-Ho coughed. "You might also be asked to do other kinds of things. Scary things, for example, that you've never done before."

She turned to meet his gaze. "I'm old enough."

Min-Ho grinned. "Of course you are, child." He stood up and took her by the arm. "One more thing. We need to make it look like we're a couple, or people might get suspicious. When we walk, put your arm through mine like this." The promise of a large steak dinner whetting his palate, Min-Ho paraded with Sun through the park. "Stand tall. Nobody should be able to guess your real age." She hadn't stopped blushing since he took her elbow. "We'll toss out that school uniform, too. Anyone who sees you dressed that way will know you're just a child." Sun frowned, but Min-Ho prattled on, scratching his cheek with his free hand. "Don't worry about a thing, though. I told you I'd take care of everything, didn't I? I have some new clothes that will fit you. You can try them on at my apartment."

"Your apartment?"

Min-Ho patted Sun's shoulder. "I have everything we need there. Remember, I've helped lots of girls do this before. It couldn't be easier. But first you need new clothes, or else everyone over the border will see you're an illegal alien. Do you know what happens to runaways if the police catch them in China?" Sun shook her head. "They get sent home." Min-Ho picked at a second pimple, pausing so Sun could feel the weight of his words. Then he smiled. "Come on. It'll only take us a few minutes to get there."

He watched the nape of her neck constrict. She looked up at him with wide eyes. "You mean right now?"

He continued to lead Sun forward but slowed his step. "For this to work, we need to move fast. We can't afford to sit around and wait. Unless you've changed your mind, that is."

"I didn't change my mind." She clutched Min-Ho's arm. "It's just ... tonight?"

He stopped walking long enough to brush her flushed cheek with the back of his finger. "These things happen fast. People have already seen us together at the park." He tilted her chin up until she looked at him. Winter was still a month or two away, but she was shivering. "There are people here that know who I am. They know what kind of work I do." She winced, and he tightened his grip on her arm. "I've got the contacts to keep me out of trouble. No one around here will bother me. But you ..." He sighed. "The police will know we were together. They'll track you down.

They'll find out who you are, you know. It's not hard for them. Then they'll be angry with you for talking to me. And angry with your family, too." Sun didn't make any noise. Min-Ho couldn't force his eyes away from the small indent of her neck. "Now you see why we need to get ready right away."

She nodded and leaned against him as he led her out of the park. Back at Min-Ho's apartment, the girl started to calm down a little. The red dress he had bought across the border fit perfectly. It had cost him four months' savings, and he had squirreled it away, certain he'd eventually find the right one to wear it. The thin straps accentuated Sun's dainty shoulders. The low cut made it hard for him to focus on anything besides the little hollow in her neck that quivered so provocatively while she swallowed.

The only problem came up when he mentioned they'd be leaving right away.

"You mean I can't even hug my mother good-bye?" Sun's voice trembled nearly as much as her chin. He frowned to hide his pleasure. Even while she was fighting tears, she didn't suffer from the blotchy eyes and puffy cheeks that made average girls look so pathetic when they simpered.

He passed her a handkerchief. "If your mother discovers where we're going, she'll only worry about you, right?" She nodded and sniffed. "How could you put your mother through that just for one last hug? You do love her, don't you?" He wiped one of her tears with his thumb. "Just think how happy she'll be when you come home with your first paycheck." He had already done the math. If Mr. Lee agreed to his price — and only a fool wouldn't — Min-Ho would earn back four times what he had spent on the red dress.

Sun brushed her bangs aside. "Jae wouldn't approve if he knew about it."

"Jae?"

"My brother." She looked down.

He sat beside her, close enough he could feel the goose bumps on her bare flesh. "Jae won't complain when you come home with enough rice to last all winter, will he?" She didn't react when he drew little circles with his thumb around her elbow. He stretched his free arm and pulled her in tight. "You should try to take a little nap. You'll need your energy for the trip tonight."

She kept her eyes to the floor. "I don't know how I can ever repay you for your kindness."

Min-Ho had to swallow down his anticipation. His payment would come soon enough.

CHAPTER 4

Even underneath the blanket, Sun shivered in her new red dress. She had never seen anything so fine or even imagined such beautiful clothing existed. Min-Ho told her she looked old enough to work in Pyongyang itself. She wanted to obey Min-Ho and get some rest, but she couldn't stop thinking about how brave he was to risk his own safety to help her find a job in China. She was young, but she'd work hard once he led her across the border.

Her arms tingled, not just from the cold but from the excitement. She felt so grown-up in her new clothes. She hugged herself, wondering what life would be like in China, where she'd have a real job, with a real employer who could pay her real money. She pictured how surprised Mother would be when she returned home with a whole envelope full of cash. And her brother, Jae. Sun smiled and envisioned him beaming at her with so much pride. Min-Ho was right. It would be selfish to stop by home first and say good-bye. Better not to let Mother know where she was going. Besides, if she did tell her family, Jae would try to stop her. Her brother never thought she was old enough to do anything important. He'd be so impressed now if he saw her in Min-Ho's red dress. Then he'd have to admit she wasn't a child any longer.

The door to her room opened slowly. She shut her eyes and pretended to sleep. Grinning in spite of herself, she hoped Min-Ho would think she was just dreaming pleasantly. Her arms tingled as she heard him approach her bed. It was a real bed with tall posts on each corner — proof he knew all kinds of wealthy patrons in China. How else could he afford such a soft mattress, such a puffy pillow?

"Are you awake, young one?" At his whisper, tingles raced up Sun's bare shoulders and prickled the base of her neck. How could someone as influential and brave as Min-Ho notice such a poor, provincial girl? Why was he willing to sacrifice his own safety for her? She never felt so lucky before. She hated displeasing him, but she also knew that a giggle would soon give her away if her words didn't. She tucked her bangs behind one ear. "Yes, I'm awake."

"I thought you might be." His tone was amused, not disappointed. He sat on the edge of the bed and put his hand on the section of blanket covering her leg. Her first instinct was to pull away, but she forced herself to relax. He was doing so much to help her. She had to show him how grateful she was. Min-Ho cleared his throat. "I'm actually glad you're awake. We need to talk about something."

She made a move to sit up, but she was more comfortable lying down, covered by that big, fluffy quilt. Min-Ho scratched his cheek and frowned at the wall. "I have friends who patrol the border. We have a certain understanding, them and me."

"So they'll let us cross safely because they trust you?" Sun was pleased she could grasp such a mature concept and hoped Min-Ho would be impressed, but he didn't return her smile.

"My friends tell me crossing into China is more dangerous these days than ever before."

She clutched the blanket and hoped he didn't notice her anxiety. What was he saying? Did that mean he couldn't help her?

"Don't worry." He squeezed her leg. "We'll still be able to go. It's just that my friends will want to be paid even more than usual. And I spent almost all of my extra money to buy your dress. I'm afraid I'll need to ask for my payment now instead of once we get to your employer's."

"Payment?" The back of Sun's throat tightened. She tried to swallow away the dryness. "I thought … I didn't realize …"

He furrowed his eyebrows. "You mean you weren't planning to pay me?"

Sun begged herself not to cry. She looked up into his acne-scarred face. "I'm sorry. I didn't know. When my teacher told me about you, when she said you could find me work ... She didn't mention that I would ... She didn't say ..."

Min-Ho wiped away one of her tears. "I didn't mean to upset you, little one. I'd love to take you to China for free, but I have expenses to worry about. They don't let people cross over for nothing, of course."

She lowered her head. "I don't know about these things. My mother and father ... They don't teach me. We don't talk about China or going across the river." She wiped her nose with the back of her hand. "My family doesn't have any money at all. Nothing. That's why I came to you." She sat up in bed, her bare shoulders heaving with each tiny sob.

"I don't want to see you cry, little one." He reached over and stroked her hair. "But it's too dangerous to try to cross the border empty-handed. As much as I want to help you, if the guards stop me, I'll need some money to keep me and you both out of trouble."

Sun's lip quivered. Now nothing would come of her plans. Her parents would still struggle. She would never make her family proud. She would have to give the red dress back. She exhaled deeply and looked around the room. She didn't know where Min-Ho put her school uniform, but she needed to get dressed and get home by nightfall.

Min-Ho glanced at her, his hand still resting on her leg. He put one finger up to his chin and picked at one of his pimple heads. "You know, I might have a way to make this all work out." Sun sucked in her breath but tried to keep her expression neutral as he continued. "I just remembered a friend of mine loaned me some extra money the other day. It might be enough to help get us across."

She clasped her hand over her mouth to hide her excitement. "You would be willing? You'd do that for me?" Her voice squeaked in spite of her best efforts.

He rubbed his chin, and his eyes narrowed. "My weakness is I can never deny a pretty woman anything." A smile spread across his face. "Besides, it's not your fault you didn't know about the fee."

Sun reached out and clutched his hand in hers. "Thank you, sir. Thank you. And you have my word that as soon as I get paid, I'll send you whatever money I owe you."

He shook his head and held up a hand. "No, little one. I've already made up my mind. Your family is poor. You've all struggled enough. It wouldn't be right for me to take a single won from you. You're young but courageous. You deserve to be treated well. I won't take food out of your mother and father's mouths. Work hard, little one. The money you earn will be yours to keep."

Sun tried to slow her heartbeat and held the blanket up to her face to cover her grin. Her eyes scanned his cluttered floor, and she quickly turned back to Min-Ho. "May I serve you?"

He frowned. "What did you say?"

"Cleaning. Cooking. There must be something I can do before it's time to leave." She didn't mention she never learned to cook anything but gruel and roots.

"You want to do me a favor?" He laughed outright. "As I said, I could never deny anything of a woman as beautiful as you."

Sun wiped her cheek. At least her mother had taught her the importance of a good cleaning. And Min-Ho's house certainly needed it. "Where's your bucket? I can wash the floors."

He reached over and took her hand in his. She hoped he didn't notice the way her arm hairs stood up on end. Min-Ho caressed her palms. "You don't want to ruin those delicate hands by scrubbing. Besides, you might dirty your new dress."

"Then how can I ever work off my debt?"

Min-Ho smiled, and even with his face covered in acne, Sun couldn't help but notice how handsome he was.

CHAPTER 5

It took longer than Min-Ho expected for his concoction to work on the young girl, but at last she slept solidly. Her body was heavier than her petite frame suggested as he hoisted her into the trunk of his car.

Most of Min-Ho's money as a broker came from girls, but since the younger ones weren't always willing to follow him into China, he supplemented his income by working as an ordinary border broker, escorting families, couples, stragglers, and anyone willing to pay to get out of North Korea and into the relative prosperity of China. Tonight, he had a pickup scheduled near Onsong, less than an hour's drive away. A couple was waiting in the cabin he used for that very purpose. He needed to hurry. He had to get Sun away from her hometown as soon as possible. The last thing he wanted was for the girl to change her mind and run back to her family in Chongsong. Not only would he lose the yuan he knew Mr. Lee would pay for his find, but he might have to face whatever father, brother, uncle, or cousin would challenge him for trying to whisk Sun away.

Once he left, Min-Ho doubted he'd be returning to Chongsong — or any of the neighboring villages — for a long time. It was fortuitous the teacher had told him about this rare beauty. His contacts knew just what to look for, which is why Min-Ho paid them so well. With Sun sound asleep in the trunk and not due to wake up for at least another twelve hours, Min-Ho checked his rearview mirror and headed toward Onsong, where he hoped the couple was ready.

If they weren't, he wasn't about to wait for them. He pulled his car up alongside the cabin and shut off the engine. He had lost track of how many trips like this he had made. As long as his clients paid, he had no reason to remember their faces, their names, their stories.

He knocked on the cabin door. The couple was supposed to be ready. In fact, Min-Ho was a little late. When nobody answered the door, he let himself in.

From the moment he stepped into the cabin, the silence hung ominously around him like a fog. He held his breath. It wasn't a set-up. He would have heard if there were men hiding to arrest him. He would have sensed their presence. But this … it wasn't just the silence of night. Clenching his flashlight, he made his way to the bedroom.

Min-Ho had seen death before, but never like this. A knife stab, several by the looks of it. Near the far wall was a puddle of blood with drops leading toward the door.

Under ordinary circumstances, he might regret the loss of a paying client. But with Sun sleeping soundly in the trunk, he didn't worry about a couple hundred yuan. Still, he grew even more resolute to leave the region for good. He wasn't about to be linked to a murder.

Before turning, he scanned the room — a suitcase on the floor, a cloth bundle folded up in the corner, probably just a wad of clothes. There was nothing for him here, unless the man died with some treasure hidden in his pockets. Min-Ho spun on his heel and left the cabin without looking back. He didn't need to prod around, hunting in pockets for aluminum when he had gold tucked safely away in the back of his car.

He heard the muffled screams as soon as he was out of the cabin. Cursing, he jogged to the trunk and forced it open. Sun's foot flew out and barely missed his face. He frowned. His mixture was guaranteed to maintain its potency for twelve hours. It should work even longer on a girl as small as Sun. His supplier must have mixed something inert in the supply. He was glad he opened the trunk when he did. With the child hyperventilating like that, who knew how long it would be before she ran out of oxygen completely, especially once he got the car running again?

He vowed vengeance on his supplier but didn't take the time to plot the fine details. He already had his hand on the backup in his pocket and forced a smile to his lips. Fingering Sun's cheek, he crooned, "It's all right, little one. You need to stay hidden for a while longer. It's just like we talked about, remember?"

Her breathing didn't slow. Min-Ho had to hurry to the border if he was going to make the exchange before morning. "This will help you rest." Before Sun could protest, he pulled out the extra syringe and injected it into her arm in one smooth, practiced motion.

He sauntered back to the driver's seat, kicking an old sandal that lay in his way, and had only rolled the car a few feet before his headlights captured an animal huddled in the road. He slammed on his breaks. The figure scampered away in slow motion, and Min-Ho saw the creature was human. "What do you think you're doing?" He got out and stomped toward it, his fists clenched. "What's wrong with you?"

The woman stumbled to her feet and eyed his car. Placing her hand on her side, she formed her lips into a slight pout. "I need help," she confessed with a little tremor in her voice.

Min-Ho eyed the stranger. Her pants were steeped in blood. She could barely stand on her own. He couldn't afford to waste any more time. Nothing could jeopardize his meeting with Mr. Lee. The woman steadied herself against the hood of his car. "You need to help me." He didn't respond. She reached into her pocket. "I have money. Lots of it." Her voice was stronger than she first intimated.

Min-Ho raised an eyebrow. "How much?"

"Three hundred yuan."

He snorted. Under normal circumstances, that amount would be enough to at least pique his interest. Tonight, with a once-in-a-lifetime investment sedated in his trunk, he wasn't so easily swayed. He opened the car door and lowered himself into the driver's seat. He had wasted enough time in Onsong already. He turned the key in the ignition and rolled the car slowly toward the road that would take him to the border, to riches. The woman took a faltering step. Min-Ho expected her to stumble off the path and out of his way. Instead, she staggered into the middle of the street, collapsing against his car as he slammed his boot down on the breaks.

He lowered his window and flung out his head. "Are you crazy?"

The woman lay with her chest on top of the hood but finally managed to slide over and open the passenger door. "I'm going across the border with you." She slunk into the seat next to his.

"What makes you think I'm crossing the border?"

"I know what kind of business you do."

Min-Ho shrugged. "Lots of folks think they know somebody else's business."

The woman narrowed her eyebrows. "You're taking me with you."

"Listen, lady …"

"My name's Mee-Kyong. And I told you, I have money." She pulled a thick envelope out of her pocket. Min-Ho eyed it and then squinted to see if he could detect a bluff. She held his gaze without blinking. "I know who you are, and I know what you do. My husband hired you to come and take us across the border. I've got your payment here. Now let's go."

Min-Ho frowned and picked at a pimple. There was no reason at this point to deny her assessment. "And where is your husband?"

She crossed her arms. "We were attacked. The assailants left us both for dead. Turns out they were only half right."

Min-Ho noted the twitch in the woman's eye. "So they beat you up, killed your husband, and left?" he asked. She lifted her chin and nodded. "And they didn't take your money with them?"

She pursed her lips together. "It was hidden. Now, are you going to honor my late husband's arrangement? Here's double the payment since now I'm the only one you have to transport."

Min-Ho picked at his cheek. Could this woman somehow ruin his plans for the girl from Chongsong? He peeked in the envelope. There was enough money to cover bribes for an extra passenger. She wasn't as young and fresh as Sun, but he could probably even get a little from Mr. Lee for her as well. Min-Ho sighed and put the car into drive. The stranger said nothing, but he noticed her smile out of the corner of his eye.

They had only been driving ten or fifteen minutes before something pounded in the back of the car. For the second time that night, Min-Ho cursed his fraudulent supplier. He watched his passenger out of the corner of his eye to determine if she had noticed anything. Sun was supposed to be comatose by now, and he didn't have to time to stop.

A kilometer or two later, there was no way to keep ignoring it. The girl in the trunk was screaming loudly enough for her voice to carry over the engine's sounds.

"What are you hiding back there?" Mee-Kyong sneered. "A pack of wild cats?"

"I'll check on her a little later. This isn't a safe place to stop." If he was lucky, she'd fall back to sleep. Why wasn't the medicine working?

Mee-Kyong crossed her arms. "Her? You sure you haven't got more than one back there?" Her voice dripped with disdain.

"We're not stopping now."

Her body tensed up in the passenger seat. "You are stopping now, or I'm getting out of this car. You won't see a single won of my money."

He chuckled. "Nice try. But you've forgotten that I'm the one holding the cash."

"Not anymore."

Min-Ho glanced at the envelope in her hand and tried to hide his amusement. He knew plenty of moves that would disarm her in an instant, but for now he would humor her. After all, Sun wouldn't bring him any income if she suffocated back there. With the concoction behaving so erratically, he probably didn't have much choice. He drove for another minute with his jaw set, and then he pulled the car over to the side of the road. "Have it your way."

He took the keys out with him and headed to the back. When he opened the trunk, Sun blinked up at him, the skin pulling against her collarbone with each shallow breath she took. He removed the tape from her mouth as gently as he could, and then he leaned down and scooped her up. "I'm so sorry I had to do that, little one. You know why, though, right? You've been so brave for a girl."

"My shoe. It flew off my foot when you opened the trunk the last time."

"I'll get you another one," Min-Ho promised absently.

"Are we across the border yet?" Sun's voice was hoarse.

He shook his head as he carried her to the back seat. "We have a little longer to go still. But I thought you'd be more comfortable in here. You promise to be good back here, don't you, and not to cry or make much noise?"

Sun nodded with wide eyes. "I'll be good."

CHAPTER 6

Mee-Kyong twisted around in her seat and examined the girl as best she could. She was a tiny wisp of a thing, even younger than Mee-Kyong had been when she first met Pang. "What's your name?"

The girl didn't raise her eyes. "Sun."

"I'm Mee-Kyong." She pressed against her abdomen, which protested in pain each time the broker's tiny car sped over a bump in the road. "Have you ever been to China, little cousin?" Sun shook her head. "That's a pretty dress," Mee-Kyong remarked.

"Thank you," the child croaked pitifully. How long had she been screaming in the back before Mee-Kyong and Min-Ho heard her?

Mee-Kyong winced and faced forward again, sitting carefully with one hip propped up to keep the weight off her sensitive areas. *Don't get attached to her, you sentimental wimp. You know exactly what the broker plans to do with her.* Still, she couldn't keep herself from wondering about the child. Where was her family? She was too innocent not to have one. Did they know she was here? Did they suspect what was about to happen to her?

"You'll need to be ready soon." It was the first time Min-Ho spoke since letting Sun out of the trunk.

Mee-Kyong grimaced and shifted her weight onto her other hip. "Aren't you going to untie her hands?"

Min-Ho shrugged. "Do it quick. We cross the border in less than ten minutes."

***

26

Sun liked Mee-Kyong from the very beginning. She didn't know where Min-Ho found her, but she was glad she wasn't traveling alone. She already missed her family more than she wanted to admit. She wished Jae were here to tell her one of his fantastical bedtime stories about lands where food grows on trees and the fields are filled with the leftovers that fall to the ground. She swallowed away the dryness in her throat. What had she been thinking to leave her family?

Just a few minutes had passed since Min-Ho handed a large roll of bills to the patrolmen on the bridge and drove across to the Chinese side of the border. Everything was so bright and colorful. Electric signs and bright street lamps illuminated the night. Sun had to squint her eyes to shield out some of the brilliance. "Is this where we'll be working?"

Min-Ho shook his head. "Nah, this is just Tumen. It's more like a town, really. I'm taking you on to Yanji. It's even bigger."

Nothing could have prepared Sun for the sights when Min-Ho's car finally sped its way into the interior of Yanji about an hour later. She had never seen so many people gathered in one place before. Even in the middle of the night, young men and women scurried down one street and up the next. The women wore shoes with spikes on their heels, making Sun wonder how they kept from falling. The pedestrians were mostly Korean, with a few ethnic Chinese joining the throngs. Now Sun realized why Min-Ho told her she needed new clothes. Women and girls paraded by, some only a few years older than Sun, dressed in every color of the spectrum: flashy pink, bright teal, deep maroon. Their faces were just as vibrant, with glittery eyelids and red painted lips.

Sun put her hand to her throat and held her breath. She could hear her heartbeat all the way up to her ears. She squirmed in her new dress and stared out the window as Min-Ho rolled past one side street after another. Sun had never seen so many lights in one place and wondered how the Chinese could afford to keep them on all through the night.

Yanji itself stretched on and on. Each time Sun thought they must be through the heart of the city, Min-Ho would turn down another road, each one even more dazzling than the last. Eventually, he slowed down in front of a tall building. She counted the windows. It had five levels, and almost all of the lights were on inside. The sign in front was written in Korean, illuminated by a spotlight coming from the ground. *Round Robin Inn.*

Min-Ho parked. "We're here. Get out." It was Sun's first time in a car, and she didn't know how to open the door. She watched the way he pulled against the handle. "Not you," Min-Ho barked at Mee-Kyong. Sun jumped at his stern voice. Had Mee-Kyong done something wrong? "You stay here," Min-Ho ordered. "I just need the girl."

Mee-Kyong turned back to face Sun. "Hope it goes well for you, little cousin." Her words were kind, but her face was contorted like she was in pain.

Min-Ho came around and opened Sun's door, his acne-scarred face softening. "We made it." His voice was back to normal now, friendly and considerate. As nervous as she was, Sun managed to return his grin. He offered her his arm, and she took it like they practiced at the park. After smoothing out the skirt of her red dress, she swept her bangs out of her eyes and behind her ear. He brushed her bare arm. The light touch tickled. "Mr. Lee is going to love you. I just know it."

Sun turned when she heard Mee-Kyong make a noise from the front seat. It sounded almost like a snort, but she couldn't tell for sure. During the ride, she had assumed she and Mee-Kyong would be working together. So why did Mee-Kyong have to stay in the car? Sun felt flattered, but also a little guilty, that Min-Ho was going to escort her into the inn all by herself. "Will you be all right here?" she asked.

Mee-Kyong nodded and flashed a smile. "Of course, little cousin. Now go make a good impression." Sun tried to read the expression on Mee-Kyong's face, but the blinding lights all around made it difficult.

Min-Ho wrapped his arm around her waist. The protective gesture warmed her entire face. Had his sleeping medicine made her dizzy? "Come on, little one. Let's go introduce you to Mr. Lee." She leaned heavily on Min-Ho's arm as they paraded up to the front doors of the Round Robin Inn.

***

Mee-Kyong watched as Sun sashayed away. The child glided over the concrete sidewalk as she held on to the broker's arm. Min-Ho stood with his chest puffed out, stretching his spine as if an extra centimeter might conceal his short stature. Mee-Kyong adjusted her weight once more, groaning from the discomfort. The self-assured broker wouldn't remain so happy, she suspected, when he saw all that blood on the seat of his car.

She shut her eyes. She just needed another minute to regain some of her strength. The pimpled man and his buyer would haggle over money, and then they would be back for her. She could tell by his swagger the broker intended to come out rich. Mee-Kyong was just an afterthought. That's probably why he hadn't wanted to bring her inside for the first meeting.

It was just as well. Mee-Kyong didn't intend to let anybody sell her into the underground market of human flesh. It was time to make her escape. She wasn't even sure her legs would hold her up to stand, but she would crawl one meter at a time if she had to. After spending almost two decades of her life at Camp 22, she wasn't about to walk into captivity again.

She studied the building where Min-Ho took the girl and

thought about the child's beaming face. "Good luck, little cousin," she whispered. She shut her eyes for a moment, wondering which was worse — to grow up in the prison camp and never have a childhood to speak of, or to grow up with a family that loved you and have your childhood ripped away in a single night.

Gritting her teeth against her own exhaustion and discomfort, Mee-Kyong reached for the handle of the car. The door was locked. *What did you expect, fool? Did you think he was just going to let you run off unnoticed?* She fumbled with the gadgets around her. She had only been in a car once before, a week earlier when Pang found them a ride for part of their journey from Camp 22 to the cabin in Onsong. At the time, she had been too excited at the prospect of a free life with Pang to pay attention to doors and mechanisms. *You idiot. You killed off the only good thing that ever happened to you, and now look where you've ended up.*

Mee-Kyong scowled at the windows of the Round Robin Inn. She had suffered worse, but still she didn't plan to stick around. She would find a way to escape. She fingered the knife in her pocket. She remembered the sight of Pang's blood on the blade and imagined returning with it to Camp 22. Which of the guards would she approach first if she had the opportunity? She brushed the handle of her weapon and fumbled at the door with her other hand until she finally found the lock. She fell outside, gasping with pain, and stumbled out into the night. Her bare feet splashed in an icy puddle beneath her, and she almost doubled over from the burning sensation in her gut. She was too weak to even cry out in frustration.

"Going somewhere?" The pimple-faced broker was right above her. Next to him towered a man wearing a suit. His stomach was so massive it bulged out not only in front but also to either side of him. Mee-Kyong reached into her pocket for the knife, and then she saw the girl. Sun stood behind the broker in that flimsy

30

dress. Her bangs fell in front of her eyes and she opened her mouth in the shape of a little ring. Mee-Kyong froze.

Min-Ho gestured toward her. "Here's the other one."

The fat man grunted but said nothing.

Sun rushed to Mee-Kyong's side. "Are you all right? Were you afraid we forgot you?"

Mee-Kyong looked up and noted the hint of guilt in the child's face. She tried to smile, but it felt more like a grimace. "I'm fine, little cousin." She stood up as straight as she could and glared at the two men. "I just needed some fresh air."

CHAPTER 7

"What's taking them so long?" Sun sat on the side of her new bed in the Round Robin Inn, swinging her legs back and forth over the side. Mee-Kyong lay down, thankful for the chance to finally recline. Everything below her waist felt like old, shredded meat. The fat man had posted two of his guards outside the bedroom door. She still had her knife, but she was too tired to even think about escape. She wasn't foolish enough to hope her new owner would spare her since she had just delivered a child, and she wanted to rest before she had to worry about what the remainder of the night held. Unfortunately, Sun didn't seem to share Mee-Kyong's desire for sleep. "They've been in there forever," the child complained.

"They're just discussing payment. The usual. It can take hours and half a dozen glasses of soju before they come to any sort of agreement."

"I hope Mr. Lee won't send me away."

Mee-Kyong couldn't keep from chortling when Sun turned to her with wide, hopeful eyes. "You don't have anything to worry about there, little cousin. You're just the kind of worker he wants."

"And Min-Ho said he could probably get you a job here, too."

Mee-Kyong kneaded her bruised abdomen, welcoming the pain. She let out a dark laugh. "I've done this kind of work before. Well, close to it, anyway."

"Really?" Sun scooted over closer to Mee-Kyong. "Did you like it?"

Mee-Kyong stared up at the dark brown stains on the ceiling. "Money is money, right?"

"Oh, I'm not here to make money for myself. It's all to take back to my family when I'm done."

"Yeah, about that …" Mee-Kyong wondered just how much she should divulge. She could tell the girl everything, but what would be the point? The child would start working at the inn whether she was prepared for it or not. Maybe it was more merciful to let the poor soul savor her last minutes of youth with a little gaiety and optimism.

Sun twirled her hair around with a finger. "About what?"

"Never mind."

"No, you were going to tell me something. Something about going home."

Mee-Kyong sighed. "I just wanted to warn you it might take a little bit longer than you thought before you get paid. That's all."

"How long?" Sun leaned in so close her dark hair fell forward and brushed down against Mee-Kyong's arm.

"Oh, you know. These men, they talk. And it takes a while for them to agree. Don't worry about it too much. Just get some rest, and when they've figured out the details, I'm sure they'll come and let us know."

It only took a few more minutes before Sun dropped into the innocent sleep of the unsuspecting. Mee-Kyong fingered her knife and decided it was a good thing she was too exhausted to sit up, or she might have been tempted to let the poor child die happy right then.

***

That night, Min-Ho dined in the restaurant across the street from the Round Robin. Mr. Lee had haggled like the finest but eventually agreed to Min-Ho's asking price and paid him up front in cash. Min-Ho scratched one of his infected pimples and savored his first bite of steak. He would probably always remember the little beauty in the red dress, wondering sometimes what it would have been like to keep her for himself. But the thick pile of bills in his pocket was enough to keep his mind from vain sentimentality.

The other woman, the bleeding one from Onsong, brought him in only a fraction of Sun's price. She was older, much less feminine, and obviously more experienced, but she was no longer his concern. Half an hour later, Min-Ho was so full from his steak he couldn't even take another sip of soju. After he paid his bill, he checked one more time to make sure he still had the money and then walked out of the restaurant, ready to enjoy the pleasures of the Yanji nightlife for himself.

He deserved that much at least.

***

"Take me to the man in charge. The fat one." Mee-Kyong looked the guard square in the eyes.

He grunted. "Mr. Lee will summon you when he pleases."

She lowered her voice. "You don't want a hysterical woman on your hands. Trust me. There's no telling what damage I could do to that little hotel room you've got us locked up in."

The guard's expression didn't change. "Like I said, when the boss ..."

At that moment the door at the end of the hallway opened. Mee-Kyong saw a set of stairs behind the fat proprietor, who waddled into the hallway panting from exertion. He furrowed his brow and glared at her. "What are you doing out of your room?"

"It's about the girl. I need to talk to you."

The security guard shifted his weight. "I'm sorry, Mr. Lee. She just came out a few seconds ago."

Mr. Lee ignored him. "Say what you want to say and don't waste my time again. Quick."

"The girl I came with isn't ready to start work right away. She needs a few days to rest." Mee-Kyong's leg muscles were about as solid as cooked noodles, but she managed not to buckle over as she faced him.

Mr. Lee eyed her pants. "You're in no position to bargain with anyone right now."

She lowered her voice. "I don't want you to start Sun. Not tonight. She needs time to adjust."

"*Adjust?*" Mr. Lee spat out the word like it was the punchline of a joke. Mee-Kyong wiped drops of his saliva off her cheek. He put his hands on his expansive hips. "Whether she's adjusted or not, she's got a job to do here. There's no choice in the matter."

She locked her knees so her legs wouldn't collapse. She wasn't frightened, just so weak that she could hardly stand. She couldn't let Mr. Lee know it, however. He had to think she was strong. He had to think she was ready. "I can teach her." The laugh she expected never came. Emboldened, she continued. "I can prepare her for what's going to happen. I can tell her what she should do."

Mr. Lee stroked one of his chins. "You could do that in ten minutes. Besides, I already have a customer in mind for her."

She recalled the child's hopeful eyes. "Yes, but if you give her another week, you would have more time to find a higher payer. Maybe even start a bidding war."

Mr. Lee furrowed his brow. "What do you know about it?"

She matched his stoic expression, clenching her teeth so they wouldn't chatter. "I spent eighteen years in the gulag. I didn't feed myself by hunting roaches that whole time."

"And you'd be willing to work double while the girl's in training? To make up for her lost time?" Mr. Lee scratched at his largest belly roll.

"I wouldn't have brought the idea up if I wasn't prepared to do just that."

Mr. Lee eyed her pants. "You think you're capable?"

"It's no worse than what I endured in prison camp, is it?" Mee-Kyong clenched her jaw and fought against her dizziness.

One corner of Mr. Lee's lip curved upward. "I'm sure I wouldn't know."

***

Mee-Kyong limped into Sun's hotel room, hoping the young girl was finally asleep. "I was wondering where you were!" At the child's birdlike voice, Mee-Kyong sighed wearily and tried not to wince as she shuffled over to Sun's bed. "I went to have a chat with Mr. Lee." Mr. Lee agreed to delay Sun's introduction but didn't waste any time putting Mee-Kyong to work.

Sun tugged at the bangs that fell over her eyes and leaned toward Mee-Kyong. "So when do we start our new jobs?"

Mee-Kyong's body swayed slightly from exhaustion as she sat down on Sun's bed. "Mr. Lee said he wants you to wait a few more days."

"Why not sooner?"

Mee-Kyong licked her upper lip. She still wasn't sure what to tell Sun, or how postponing her introduction would benefit the child in the end. When her training period ran its course, she would still fall victim to the same fate as all the other girls at the Round Robin. What did it matter if her introduction came now or later? "It's all about the money," Mee-Kyong bluffed. Maybe by the end of the week she'd have a plan to get them both out. "I warned you. These things take time."

"So we'll both just stay here and wait?"

Mee-Kyong took a deep breath. "Actually, I'll be in and out. Sometimes I'll be next door. It's just one of Mr. Lee's preferences. He thinks we need some time alone, I guess."

"So what now? What do we do while we wait to start working?"

Mee-Kyong curled up on the bed in Sun's room. It would be at least several hours before Mr. Lee needed her services again next door. "For now, we rest." She situated her head on the pillow and covered up with the blanket.

CHAPTER 8

Jae realized something was wrong as soon as he walked into the house. "What happened?" He didn't bother addressing Father, who sat staring out the kitchen window, but went straight to Mother's bed. He knelt down and placed his hand on her heaving shoulder. "What's wrong, Mother?"

"She's left us." She grabbed Jae's arm in both of hers and sobbed into his bicep. "Our Sun's gone."

His heart constricted in his chest. He smoothed out Mother's graying hair and clucked his tongue the same way he used to soothe his little sister when she was still a baby. "We don't know that. She might have gone visiting. Maybe she missed curfew and decided to spend the night with one of her friends. You know how forgetful girls get when they're together gossiping like geese."

Mother didn't stop rocking on her mattress. Jae stood up. "If she doesn't come home after school tomorrow, I'll go to her friends' houses and see if I can find her."

"You are a good son," she muttered.

"Stop worrying. Wherever she is, I'll bring Sun back safe and unharmed. I promise."

An hour later, Jae rolled over fitfully on his cot. Mother muttered in her sleep, and Father sat snoring at the table. Jae silenced his own breathing until all he heard were echoes of his sister's voice. She was several years younger now, the traces of her budding womanhood erased in his memories.

"Another story, Brother."
Jae wrapped both their blankets tight around her skeletal

*frame and then sat her on his lap. The blankets were thin enough
he felt the sharpness of her shoulder blades jut into his chest as he
held her in his arms.*

*"Another story, you say?" Jae felt the wisps of her bangs and
swept them out of her face. "A story for my little sister?" Sun
wiggled in excitement. Jae took in a deep breath. "Once upon a
time, there was a beautiful maiden." Sun giggled, but Jae didn't
stop. "She was prettier than all the other girls in her village, and
one day a king from a faraway land decided he must behold her
loveliness for himself. The maiden was brought to him in a
carriage made out of gold and pearls, drawn by four horses with
their braided manes reaching all the way down to their hooves."*

*Jae waited for Sun to suck in her breath in awe. Her shivering
subsided. Her teeth stopped chattering. "When the maiden arrived
at the river bordering his empire, the king was there to meet her.
He instantly fell in love with her and declared his eternal devotion.
He took the horses' reins and drove her himself across the bridge
into his realm, a paradise where the streams are made of syrup,
and the rocks are sweetened candy. The trees grow fruit all year
round, and it's never, ever winter. Birds fly overhead day and
night, dropping donuts and pastries for all the citizens to enjoy.
Everyone there is fat and happy, and all the little girls wear
colored ribbons in their hair."*

*Jae was getting ready to tell her the part about the wedding
celebration, in which the royal newlyweds ride on two ponies with
wings like eagles, but he didn't need to.*

Sun was already asleep.

Jae clenched his eyes closed, grinding his teeth until his jaw
felt partially numb. He clamped his mouth shut even tighter to
contain the groan that welled up from somewhere deep in his gut.

Sun. Where was she? Didn't his sister know how much he'd
done for her, how much he'd already sacrificed for her? Jae

thought over the past few days, racking his brain for any clues about his missing sister. Had she taken up with any new friends recently? Had anybody been paying her special attention? He tried to recall her behavior. All he could think of was the glow of her broad, smiling cheeks, the hair that never stayed in place but cascaded down her face like unruly streams of water.

He counted back the months. How long had it been since the river swept Sun away from him? He had jumped in after her, disregarding the ice and chill. She shouted his name, kept on shouting it in a throaty little shriek even after he reached her. They were swept downstream together before he finally led them to shore. He was thankful that by then he was already wet; his sister had never seen him cry before.

Jae sighed and thought about what he had told his mother just a few hours earlier. *A friend's house.* She must have gone to a friend's house. He didn't realize he was gripping his sheets until a muscle spasm shot pain up from the side of his smallest finger, racing all the way up his forearm. He shook his hand out and then held his blanket against his body once more. The accident at the water's edge wasn't the first time he had risked his life for Sun. The other times she didn't even know about. Nobody did. Jae sighed.

Tomorrow he would find Sun.

And he would kill anyone who hurt her.

CHAPTER 9

"You swear it was my sister you saw with this man?" Jae lowered his face toward Sun's schoolmate and balled both his hands into fists. The crisp morning air might have felt cold against his skin if he weren't so angry.

The teen nodded so fast Jae wondered if he was jostling his brains out of place. "He's the one, I tell you. Short. Ugly face. Lots of pimples. Maybe your age or a little older."

Jae figured a swift blow to the boy's head would stop it from bobbing up and down so much, but he needed more information first. "And it was my sister you saw talking to him last night?"

He nodded more vigorously. "Yes, your sister, Sun. Everyone knows Sun."

Jae's blood pressure rose even higher at the sound of this sniveling boy speaking his sister's name. He grabbed his collar and lifted him off the ground. "What do you mean, 'everyone knows her'?"

The boy fluttered his legs and held his hands up in a position of surrender. "No, no. Nothing bad. Nothing wrong. Your sister … she's a good girl. She's … I only meant we all know each other. Every one of us. Including your sister."

Jae lowered the boy back to the ground. "And it was my sister you saw speaking with this man?"

"Yes, sir. At least I think so." He adjusted his shirt and backed away several steps from Jae. "Now that I think about it, though, maybe not. It was evening. The sun was setting. It was hard to see."

"I hope you're right," Jae snarled and dismissed him with a wave. Sun's classmate ran off in the direction of the school. Jae squinted in the early morning light until the boy was out of sight and then headed home.

"Mother?" He crouched down by her lopsided bedside. "Mother?" Jae repeated. The wispy woman stirred in bed. Jae held her hand in his. "It's time to wake up."

She grabbed his wrist with her leathery, gnarled fingers. "Is Sun home?"

"Not yet. But I found one of her friends on his way to school. He said he saw her just last night at the park."

"The park?"

"She was probably there with the kids she knows. You know how those teens like to go and play together. She probably stayed out too late and went to her friend's house to keep from breaking curfew. I'm sure she'll be in school today. You don't need to worry about her."

Mother patted his cheek. "You'll check for me?"

Jae hadn't slept more than a few hours, but he pressed Mother's hands and nodded. "Of course. I'll go check this afternoon. I'm sure she's there already."

Father slouched at the table, and Jae couldn't tell if he had overheard their conversation or not. Jae strode by and headed off in the direction of the police station. His boss had files of all the vagabonds who showed up in Chongsong. Jae would have to swallow down the remnants of his family pride and confide in the captain.

That afternoon, after fulfilling some of his duties for the day, Jae left the station and headed to the park to talk to one of the men there. "What can you tell me about this man?" Jae passed the photograph to the leather-faced beggar. Jae's co-workers at the police office nicknamed the man Tip and often relied on his acute memory and watchful eye. A few feet away, a bronze statue of North Korea's deceased Great Leader gaped down on the pair. Tip shrugged. "Yeah, I've seen him."

"He lives here?"

Tip shook his head. "Here and there. He only comes around occasionally from what I can tell. Why do you want to know?"

Jae reached into his pocket and pulled out a small pouch of uncooked rice. Tip shrugged again but took the bag, bouncing it in his hand. "Like I said, he comes and goes."

"Goes where?"

Tip put the rice in his pocket. "Wherever do any of those young fools go who want to make some money?"

"He crosses the border?"

Tip's leg bounced, and he stared at the bronze statue. "That's not what I said."

Jae leaned forward. "But you don't deny it?"

"Listen, I like rice, but it's a little bag. Got anything else?"

"Just this." In one swift movement, Jae spun the man around and wrapped his arm around Tip's neck. He didn't want to injure him — not yet — but he hoped the surprise might loosen Tip's tongue. "The last time my sister was seen in Chongsong was here at this park, talking to this man," he snarled into Tip's ear. "She's been missing since last night. And you're either going to help me find out where he's taken my sister, or I'll show you first-hand what I intend to do once I find him. Understand?"

Tip nodded and shrugged once more when Jae loosened his hold. "I could tell you what the car looks like."

"Then do it."

As Tip described the vehicle, Jae forced himself to remember each and every detail, refusing to imagine what this pimple-faced punk in the photograph might have done to his little sister once he got her alone in there. "Did you see him in his car yesterday afternoon or evening?" he demanded. "Was anyone with him?"

Tip tilted his head to the side. "I was sick last night." Jae didn't know whether to believe him or not. He debated whether he should lead him to a less public area and jostle his memory. "He usually heads northeast."

"So you did see him?"

Tip shook his head. "Nah, I already told you I was sick yesterday. But when I do see him come, it's usually to talk to some ..." He faltered for a moment and glanced over Jae's shoulder. "He usually comes and talks to some young girl and then takes her east in his car."

"And you don't know what he does from there?"

"Healthy young man alone with an innocent little girl?" Tip cackled. "Let's just say I don't think they sit around sipping tea."

Jae lowered his face until his nose pressed up against Tip's. "Do you realize that's my sister you're talking about?"

For a moment, Tip's eyes widened, but then he softened his expression and shrugged both shoulders again. "Hey, I'm just telling you what I know. That's what you wanted, right?"

Jae sighed. "Right. That's what I wanted." He turned on his heel and strode to the police station. It was time to have another talk with his boss.

It wasn't hard to convince the police captain to let him track down Sun's abductor, but it did cost Jae his entire savings. He had stored away some of his black-market profits for the past two years to give Sun something of a wedding celebration when her time came. Knowing his sister's best prospect in life was to find a wealthy husband, Jae had saved up his money in hopes of one day helping her woo him. Now, unless Jae got to her in time, Sun would never catch a man of any kind, so he handed over his savings and convinced his boss to help him.

The police captain had been watching the broker for some time. Two other girls had disappeared from Chongsong over the past nine months, including his wife's young cousin, which probably explained his willingness to aid Jae on his way. With all of Jae's savings in his pocket, the captain signed the travel papers

Jae needed and agreed to grant him an undocumented leave of absence from police duty.

His intel would take Jae as far as Onsong. There weren't any checkpoints, the captain assured him. "He's been followed before to this cabin." The captain wrote some directions on a piece of paper and slipped it into Jae's hand. "We think he uses it as a hideout for his customers while he gets his travel plans in order."

The captain was just as cooperative, although less direct, when Jae asked how he should get to Onsong. "I've noticed the officer on night duty leaves the keys on the peg in my office. It's quite foolish of him. Anyone with access to my room could just walk in and take the car."

Jae had to work late at the police office but went right to Mother's bedside when he returned home that evening.

"Let her rest," Father grumbled.

Jae ignored him. Mother opened her eyes, and her expression changed in an instant. "She's gone." It wasn't a question.

Jae lowered his voice. "I know. But I found out some things. I met a man at the park who knows where she might be."

Mother made a move to sit up in bed, but Jae pressed gently down on her bony shoulders. "I'm going out to find her, Mother. You just rest and go to work tomorrow like normal. It might take me a few days."

Mother whispered something in a gravelly voice. Jae had to lean forward to hear. "Curfew."

"I'll be all right, Mother. I know what I'm doing." He stood to leave.

She clasped his hand and didn't release her grip until he turned around to look at her. "Bring back my daughter."

Jae bowed his head. "I will, Mother. I promise."

Father let out a grunt as Jae strode out the front door into the darkness of night.

He found the cabin about an hour later. Sun had been gone for an entire night and day already, but he still hoped against reason she would be there. He pulled the police car up in front and fingered his rope.

He was a few steps away from the car when his flashlight beam landed on something in the road. He dropped down and clutched the thread-bare shoe, which his sister had outgrown years ago but still offered scant protection from the elements.

Sun. His heart repeated her named with each quickening pulse.

After slinking around to a window, he peeked inside the small wooden building. The moon offered up only a thin sliver of light, but he could make out the shape of a person on the bed. Only one. It was too big to be Sun, Jae noted with disappointment. Perhaps the broker himself? He took out the rope he had brought with him. If the broker was asleep, his job would be easy. He peered in the window again and tugged on two ends of the weapon, testing its strength. He would find out exactly where his sister was. And then he would mangle the man who stole her away.

Jae cracked the door open and listened. The only thing he could hear was his own pulse pounding in his ears. He clenched the rope and entered the dark cabin. In some way, he blamed himself. He should have warned Sun. He should have told her what these men were like. It was a conversation Father certainly never had with her, and Mother was too busy keeping the family from starving to notice how Sun had blossomed and matured over the past six months. Mother had no idea how beautiful Sun had grown.

Poverty and beauty were a deadly combination for someone like his sister.

He tiptoed like a tiger stalking its prey. The stench inside was moist and earthy. He crept up to the bed and nearly vomited. It wasn't the broker. The suspect in the photograph was ugly, with pimpled scars across an angular face. Even though the dead man's mouth hung open and his muscled chest and abdomen were covered in blood, he had obviously been desirable — the kind of specimen that could easily turn a young girl's head. Jae clenched his jaw shut. He didn't want to look but couldn't turn away from the mangled corpse. It had been stabbed multiple times. But who would have killed him? The broker? Anyone who lured young women away from their families, for whatever purpose, must also be capable of murder.

Jae shone his flashlight around the room, looking for any clues. On the floor against the far wall he noticed a pool of blood, nearly dried but not quite. Next to it was a bundle wrapped up in some kind of cloth and propped up in the corner. Jae clenched his fist, strode toward the object, and turned down the top of the rag.

Less than a minute later, he was back in the police car, swallowing down his bile as he raced back home. He couldn't focus on anything but the two bodies from the broker's cabin. Whenever he tried to think about anything else, his mind conjured up the grotesque images with merciless clarity. The drive back to Chongsong gave Jae time to make sense of what he saw. No matter how hard he tried to explain things, there was only one conclusion. It nauseated him even more than the carnage he witnessed in the cabin.

Sun had deceived them all. She wasn't the innocent, pristine little sister he had set out to rescue. The dead baby bore witness. If the child was Sun's, she had been carousing around behind her family's back long before the broker found her in the park. She hadn't been kidnapped or coerced away at all. Jae clenched his fists and remembered the infant's pale blue skin.

Sun had conceived a child.

Jae hadn't recognized the dead man on the bed. Was he the one who convinced Sun to leave with the broker? Was he the one who ruined his sister's honor? His throat was clenched, ready to let out the roar that any moment might well up from deep within. However the scenario had played itself out, Sun wasn't victimized. She willingly left with the broker. She wanted to leave with him.

It was still dark when he arrived back in Chongsong. Jae parked the car behind the police building and had no problem returning the keys to the captain's office. Once he got home, he spent a quarter of an hour washing himself. When his arms and hands were numb with cold, he leaned over and rinsed out his mouth. Could he ever bear the taste of food again? He spit the water out, leaned over, and retched. His baby sister ... pregnant? She was only a child herself, just beginning to mature. He thought about Sun's apparent coming of age over the past several months, the budding figure, the developing confidence.

Now he could explain it.

And what about the broker? Jae had planned to seek him out, to punish him for deceiving his little sister and threatening her purity. He spat on the floor. What purity? His sister had already experienced the ways of lust and passion before she met with that acne-covered trash in the park. She was already corrupted, already pregnant, already living a lie and hiding her shame from the family that cherished her. And when she found out she couldn't keep living under her parents' roof without exposing that lie? She sought out a broker and arranged to escape.

Something in the plans went wrong, though. Jae recalled the bloody corpse on the bed, the mangled chest that probably knew the softness of his little sister's hair as she embraced her lover in the dark. Who had killed him? Perhaps the broker, driven by lust, had wanted Sun for himself. Jae rinsed his mouth out one last time. He recalled his mother's tears when Sun first disappeared. Had the harlot even thought about what shame her behavior would bring to her family? Mother already toiled relentlessly to feed everyone. How could she be expected to carry the additional burden of her daughter's shame?

Jae glared down at the water bucket. He remembered last

spring when he rescued Sun from the thawing creek. He should have let the river sweep her away to her death.

Jae didn't care what future Sun chose. With her lover dead, she would have no respectable way to provide for herself. So be it. Girls like that deserved far worse than a brothel. She could rot away in some shabby Chinese inn until she died, and Jae wouldn't shed a single tear on her behalf. She was no sister of his. Jae heaved the water bucket outside.

"Sun?"

Jae unclenched his fists and took several breaths to calm himself as he approached Mother's bedside. "No, it's me." He gripped the hand that reached out toward him.

"Did you find your sister?"

Jae swallowed down the pain in his throat and hid his sister's shoe under his mattress. "Sun is dead."

CHAPTER 10

"I'm so glad you're home tonight. Do you know where Sun is?" Jae glared down at his sister's schoolmate who stood outside his front door chattering like a squirrel in springtime. "They say she's been taken across the border. Kidnapped."

Jae set his jaw. "You should know better than to go around spreading rumors."

She didn't flinch. "You have to find her. You have to get her out of there and bring her back home." She lowered her voice. "Some of my friends told me what kinds of things happen over there. What they make the girls do."

Jae stepped outside and scowled down. "Shouldn't you be getting home before curfew?"

She shook her head. "Sun's so naïve. She's … inexperienced." The girl flushed. "If what the other kids are saying is true, she won't know how to defend herself. She's …" Sun's friend covered her red cheeks with her hands. "She's young."

Jae cleared his throat. "You don't need to worry about Sun anymore." He slammed the door and strode to his bed, digging his fingernails into the flesh of his palms. He swallowed down a furious growl and resisted the urge to tug out his hair by the roots. No sister of his would play the part of an innocent, loving child while hiding a shameful pregnancy from her family and her friends.

Jae pictured the man in the cabin. The corpse lay with his eyes open, his expression indecipherable, neither anguished nor at rest. Was he the one who stole her away from her home and threatened to drown her family in shame? Jae regretted the man was already dead. If Jae had reached him first, it wouldn't just be his torso that ended up butchered. Jae clenched his teeth. What had the smooth-complexioned, muscular man said to entice his sister to her ruin?

He hung his head in his hands, sank down on Sun's bed, and fingered her discarded shoe. Sun ... his own baby sister. His precious baby girl. How often had he sat up, telling her stories until she fell asleep? How often, during the worst of the famine so many years ago, did Jae whisper to Sun about the great life beyond, where happiness waited and feasts were held in abundance? They were lies, but they were merciful lies, and he fed Sun's empty stomach with words and images of gluttonous plenty.

Sun ... with that soft black hair, those unruly bangs, the rounded cheeks that remained plump even during the most extreme months of hunger. Sun didn't know it, but Jae had twice risked his life by rushing over the frozen Tumen River into China to find food for her. Getting caught was a more bearable fate than watching his sister starve to death.

He squeezed his eyes shut. How he had loved that child! He would have done anything for her, would have faced hunger or danger or even the gulags to ensure Sun's protection. Didn't she know Jae cherished her over anything else in the world? Didn't she know it would kill Jae if she ever fell into harm? Could he really turn his back on her? Could he cut her out of his heart that flippantly? From her little corner in the cabin, Mother let out a pitiful moan.

Jae threw his coat over his back. He would need it across the border.

There was only one thought in Jae's mind as he walked away from his parents' home. He needed money. An awful lot of money. The captain at the police station was a rich man, probably the wealthiest in the entire village. Jae liked his boss, but he was on a nearly impossible mission. He couldn't just walk across the border without a single won to his name and expect to find his sister. Waiting for complete darkness, he paced the woods near the captain's house for what felt like hours. He didn't know where the captain stored his cash, but he didn't have the time to snoop around for a few days in hopes of catching him make a deposit. Sun and the broker already had a two-day lead on him. His sister wasn't going to rescue herself while Jae sat around playing thief.

When it finally grew dark, Jae pulled his hood over his hair and reached into his pocket for his makeshift mask. Whatever happened, he didn't want to be recognized. He wasn't sure how much time he had left to reach his sister, but the night wouldn't tarry forever, and neither could he.

He lowered the mask over his face and crept through the window into the captain's house. He made his way through the main living room, but by the time Jae realized the captain was waiting for him in the bedroom, it was too late. Jae grunted and stumbled as his boss' ceramic jug cracked against his skull. A fist sped toward his head. Jae ducked. The captain reached for the mask but missed. Jae straightened up, flinging the full weight of his body against the captain's shoulder. Both men fell to the ground, their mixes of curses and grunts awakening the captain's wife and child. The woman held out her arms and called to her son. He scurried across the floor but Jae grabbed him before he reached his mother.

The boy kicked and struggled in Jae's arms. "Father!"

The captain froze. His wife screamed again. In a swift motion, Jae pulled out the rope from his pocket and wrapped it around the boy's neck. He kept it slack and put his lips close to the child's ear. "Tell him I need two thousand won," Jae whispered. The boy shuddered. "Tell him," Jae repeated in a low snarl.

"He wants two thousand won, Father."

The captain nodded at his wife. She scurried under the bed. Jae kept his eyes to the ground. A moment later, she emerged with a bundle of bills.

"Count it out," the captain demanded.

CHAPTER 11

No matter how bad it gets, it still beats life in the prison camp. The food was better, for one thing. Mee-Kyong didn't have to eat bugs anymore. The pain sometimes threatened to knock her unconscious, but it probably wasn't any worse than what Pang would have put her through if he were still alive.

Why did it always come back to Pang? Why couldn't she forget the soothing power of his voice or the silky touch of his skin? There was a time when his irresistible charm, even his possessive insanity, exhilarated her. When else in the gulag had she felt so alive? She couldn't allow herself the luxury of missing him. He had been useful for one thing, and one thing only — survival. Pang's extra rations got her through prison camp. And his jealous passion for her eventually got her out of it.

Because of Pang, Mee-Kyong was free. At least, she would be once she found a way to leave the Round Robin. Having Sun there complicated things. Mee-Kyong couldn't articulate why she cared about the unfortunate girl. If it weren't for Sun, there was no way she would have agreed to work a double shift. And what good had it done? Sun would still have to go through her introduction as soon as Mr. Lee found a patron wealthy enough to purchase the child's innocence.

You should find a way to escape, fool, not waste your energy worrying about some pathetic child. Once she regained some of her strength, she could flee. But that would mean leaving Sun behind without anyone to stand between her and Mr. Lee's hungry customers. *Why do you care about her so much, anyway?* Sun had never done anything for her. If Mr. Lee started working Sun right away like he initially planned, Mee-Kyong would only have half the customers to trouble over. Why should she worry so much about a little girl, a girl who had brought her nothing but torment?

She couldn't answer that question, even though it kept her awake at the end of each shift.

One day you'll thank me, little cousin.

She jumped up when Mr. Lee barged into her room. Red splotches stained his fleshy face, and drops of sweat beaded on his bulging forehead. "I hope your friend is worth ten thousand yuan."

She forced all expression off her face. "So your little bidding war worked out in your favor?" Mee-Kyong sat up slowly and tied her bathrobe around her waist.

Mr. Lee ignored the question. "She's been adequately prepared, I assume?"

Mee-Kyong fingered the nylon sash of her robe. "She'll be ready in a few more days."

"She'll be ready this afternoon."

She reached over for her comb and brushed her hair, taking pride in the way she could deliberately keep her hands from trembling. How many times had she lied to Pang? This would be no different. "You should let me have a little time with her first."

Mr. Lee chuckled mirthlessly. His entire midsection jiggled, and his lungs wheezed with the effort. "I gave you two whole days."

She shrugged. "Two days or two weeks, she's still only a child."

"What do you think I'm getting paid for? An old hag dripping blood?"

Mee-Kyong ignored the insult and fidgeted with her collar. "She'll be nervous. She might make a mistake."

"That would not be so fortunate for you, *Teacher*." Mr. Lee spat out the last word like a curse.

Mee-Kyong imagined the expression on his adipose face if she plunged a knife into his heart. "Of course, I'll continue to coach her so she'll be ready for her meeting."

"Good," Mr. Lee grunted, passing gas as he maneuvered his overburdened frame out the door. "I just hope her customers are more satisfied than yours."

She lost track of how long she spent vacillating between her bed and the door once Mr. Lee left. What good had she done by giving Sun extra time before her introduction? None at all. Two days. A mere two extra days of childhood, but her fate was still the same. Mr. Lee was the only one who benefitted at all from Mee-Kyong's plan, which gave him extra time to find the highest bidder.

Mee-Kyong's legs were as stiff as a statue of the Dear Leader himself, and just as heavy, as she made her way to Sun's room, liquor flask in hand, sick with the realization that she had no way to help Sun escape. She couldn't even help herself. In better health, she could probably sneak past Mr. Lee's guards, but she wasn't strong enough yet. She couldn't run, and she certainly couldn't fight her way out. One kick to the abdomen would drop her in an instant. In a month or two, she could run away. But what about Sun? The girl was nothing more than a child. She was a head shorter than Mee-Kyong, and just as skinny and malnourished as the sickliest of girls from the gulag. Mee-Kyong was only a few years older, but when it came to life experience, the difference could have been measured in decades.

She couldn't get Sun out, not yet anyway. The child would have to go through with her introduction. She eyed the small flask in her hand. At least she could help Sun forget for a few hours. But Mr. Lee would get his money's worth out of the child after all. There was no other choice. At least not with Mee-Kyong still so weak from the delivery. She took a deep breath. She hadn't told Sun anything yet. She had tried once or twice but always changed her mind out of pity. The girl had no idea what was about to happen to her. Mee-Kyong had been waiting, refusing to squelch

Sun's enthusiasm and naiveté until the very last moment.

That moment was here.

Her hand felt like it was weighed down with an iron chain as she lifted it to Sun's door. She knocked even more loudly when there was no response. The poor soul was probably taking a nap, oblivious to her danger, dreaming about home and all the money she'd bring back to her adoring family.

Go in there and get this over with, you stupid coward. Mee-Kyong couldn't wait any longer. In just a short time, Mr. Lee's bidder would come and claim his prize. There was no way to spare Sun from the fear and the pain, but at least Mee-Kyong could tell her the truth. The child deserved that much. She deserved to know what was about to happen to her. And the liquor could help her relax. Would Sun hate her after tonight? Mee-Kyong took a deep breath and lifted her chin. It was time to tell her everything. Beyond that, there was nothing else she could do. Not yet, at least. She cracked the door open and heard the child's stifled sobs.

She was too late.

CHAPTER 12

Sun curled up on the mattress and bit her lip to keep from crying out loud. The bitter drink Mr. Lee had given her made her legs heavy. Her head was spinning. How could this have happened to her? How could she have let everyone deceive her? It had only been two days since she crossed the border with Min-Ho. Two days waiting in a filthy hotel room, eating no better than she had at her parents' home. Two days spent locked up because her fat and blotchy new boss told her it wasn't safe to venture out until he got her the appropriate identification papers. She had been so eager to start earning money to help her family back home. Then tonight Mr. Lee sauntered in, heaving around his enormous swell of a belly, and told her everything was in order. She was now a working woman.

Sun scratched her cheeks until her fingernails were bloody. Maybe if she were disfigured ...

"Horrible, isn't it?"

Sun jumped. She hadn't heard Mee-Kyong enter. Before tonight, she had wondered why Mr. Lee gave them each their own room when they easily could have shared one large bed. Now she understood.

"Mr. Lee told me you were starting." Mee-Kyong covered Sun up with a heavy blanket but didn't actually touch her. "It won't always hurt that bad." The words were so quiet Sun could barely hear them. She shut her eyes. She didn't want to look at anyone. She didn't want to face another human being for the rest of her life. Mee-Kyong lowered her face closer to Sun's. "I got my bath tub ready for you. I thought you might want to wash yourself off." She handed Sun a small flask. The acrid drink brought stinging tears to her eyes.

Sun swallowed. Mee-Kyong reached out her hand, but Sun didn't take it. Clutching the blanket around her shoulders, she staggered on uneven legs, certain a bath would never wash away her filth.

***

Mee-Kyong knocked softly on the bathroom door as her mind blared accusations. *It's your fault she wasn't prepared for this. You should have at least warned her.* For a moment, she felt like she was at one of the nightly self-criticism sessions back at Camp 22. When there was no answer, Mee-Kyong considered just walking in. After all, privacy wasn't a luxury Mr. Lee granted to his workers. Sun knew that now. Before long, anyone with money to spare could see her nakedness. Why should it matter if Mee-Kyong beheld the same?

How had she felt after her introduction in the prison camp? It was so long ago she could scarcely remember the guard or the circumstances surrounding their union. What she did remember, however, was the taste of the rice she ate afterward.

She had never been in Sun's situation. She had been conceived in Camp 22, never stepping foot outside its electric fence until she escaped with Pang just a few weeks earlier. For most of her life, she lived like an orphan with dozens of other girls. Her friends from the dorm were the closest thing she had to a family. She always knew her body was not her own; her school teachers and overseers from the gulag could strike or abuse her whenever they saw fit. Many girls just withered away. They grew weak. They couldn't handle the suffering, and so they eventually died. The methods varied remarkably, but in the end it didn't matter. They died just the same. Mee-Kyong had vowed to survive, and so far she had. Her spirit was toughened by a lifetime of calluses, calluses Sun had never needed to develop. Mee-Kyong wondered what she should say to ease the child's mind. She knocked on the door once more and finally opened it.

Sun lay face-down in the bathtub, her black hair billowing up on top of the water. Mee-Kyong ran to the body. *She's dead, and it's your fault.*

Mee-Kyong tried to ignore the angry shrieks of her conscience. She was only trying to help, and she would have continued to do so. The wimpy child just wasn't patient enough. Mee-Kyong was hardly to blame. *Stupid girl.* Yes, of course she was hurt. Of course she was ashamed. But hadn't Mee-Kyong told her it would get easier?

Mee-Kyong glared at Sun's narrow shoulders. Her bones were as brittle as sand. The girl couldn't even withstand her introduction. And Mee-Kyong had been seeing one customer after another, taking on extra men to give Sun a chance to be broken in easily. She had done so, despite being still torn and injured from childbirth. And Sun couldn't even manage to live through her first customer.

Pitiful.

Mee-Kyong pulled the girl's face out of the water and could still smell the liquor on her breath. *Stupid child. Stupid, ignorant, naïve child.* If Sun couldn't survive an introduction, how did she think she'd ever make it to adulthood? *Pathetic baby.* Whatever puny mistreatment Sun suffered in one night was nothing compared to the lifetime of horror and despair Mee-Kyong endured in Camp 22. Had she flung herself into the bathtub as soon as things got painful? Ignoring the hot tears that spilled down her cheeks, she slapped Sun's face.

Sun opened her eyes, turned her face, and vomited into the water. Mee-Kyong wanted to hug the girl and hated herself for it. "I told you it would get better. Why didn't you listen to me?"

Sun's lip quivered, but Mee-Kyong was thankful that the child didn't cry. "I slipped in the tub. It was an accident." She lowered her eyes.

Mee-Kyong raised an eyebrow, but she wasn't going to argue. It wouldn't kill anyone to let Sun keep at least a shred of dignity after all she had been through. There wouldn't be much dignity in the days and weeks to follow. "It gets easier," Mee-Kyong breathed. "I promise."

Sun turned her head but didn't look at her. "It was kind of you to save me."

Mee-Kyong studied Sun and decided the girl deserved some honesty for once. "I didn't think you were still alive." She looked at Sun until the girl met her gaze. "Otherwise, I might not have."

PART 2

CHAPTER 13

Juliette Stern ran the brush through the young woman's hair. "Are you nervous?" She could barely ask the question without her voice squeaking.

"If God's will is for me to leave, how could I be worried?" Hannah's image in the mirror reminded Juliette of the Met's sculpture of Saint Margaret, the sixteenth-century martyr. She wondered how someone so young could know what was coming and remain so serene. After growing up in Seoul as the American ambassador's daughter, Juliette's Korean was nearly impeccable. Tonight, however, she couldn't even express in English her love for Hannah and the other students she was sending off.

"You know you'll be missed." Juliette lowered her voice. "By more than just Mr. Stern and me."

Hannah didn't blush, but Juliette noticed her bite the corner of her lip. Eve, the Sterns' housekeeper, slipped her head into the room. "I'm sorry for interrupting, but Mr. Stern just called from the office. He said he's a little late. He expects to be home in twenty minutes or less."

Juliette nodded, both in thanks and in dismissal. "Thank you. We'll start when he gets here." Eve shut the door, and Juliette thought about the students they would commission as soon as Roger got home. Would she ever know what happened to them ... which were to experience a full life of ministry and impact, and which were doomed to imprisonment and death? The Sterns wouldn't have any contact with the students once they returned to North Korea. There was a finality to this farewell that made it even more poignant than sending her college-bound daughter back to the States a few weeks earlier.

Crossing her arms, she sighed. "I'll get your robe from the closet." Her husband had scoffed at the idea, but Juliette purchased caps and gowns for the Secret Seminary students. After the uncounted hours of labor these young people had poured into their training, Juliette insisted on providing this special touch. She also hired two extra workers to help Eve prepare a send-off feast, since God alone knew how the students would manage to feed themselves once they crossed the border and returned to North Korea. But she would think about more positive things tonight. She forced herself to smile at Hannah, whose hands were folded in her lap as if in perpetual prayer. Juliette cleared her throat and forced chipper confidence into her tone. "Let's finish getting you ready."

***

Roger Stern steeled himself against the breeze and hurried past the lane of houses. His neighborhood was peopled almost exclusively with expats, mostly European or American businessmen like himself. He tightened his beige pea coat against his chest and pressed on.

Of all the days for one of his printers to fry on him, it had to be today. Not only was his wife planning a huge ceremony and elaborate buffet to send the Secret Seminary students off, but he needed to ship out his largest order of the quarter by tomorrow for it to arrive in New York on schedule. Roger would have to go back to the office right after the graduation ended and probably pull an all-nighter to guarantee the books got out in time.

What a day. Of course, Juliette had to get herself so wrapped up in this ceremony she went so far as to order caps and gowns for the students they were sending out. Caps and gowns — as if the graduates' decision to return to the most hostile mission field on the globe was a reason to celebrate. On the other hand, it was exactly something his wife would dream up. She was never one to do things small-scale. When their daughter Kennedy asked to ride a horse a decade earlier, Juliette didn't take her to the kiddie corral for a five-minute spin on the pony-go-round. No, Juliette made arrangements for their eight-year-old to take riding lessons for the entire school year, and that summer would have convinced Roger to buy Kennedy a horse of her own if they hadn't already been packing up their things to move to China.

Roger waved to his security man, Benjamin, who lately had been doubling as a landscaper, and strode into his house. The scent of soy sauce and ginger wafted through the entryway in greeting, along with the tantalizing sound of meat sizzling in the kitchen. He wondered at the irony of this feast even as his mouth watered. Wasn't it cruel in a way to stuff the graduates with such fine cooking just hours before they crossed the border into a land ravaged by famine and scarcity? He inhaled deeply and wondered if all cultures had a last-meal tradition for their condemned.

"Hello, Eve." Roger handed his hat and scarf to the housekeeper. "Is Mrs. Stern already in the den?" Eve nodded, and he headed upstairs. Since he was late, he expected to find the students already in their ridiculous graduation get-ups and was surprised to find the den empty except for Simon. Upon entry to the Secret Seminary, each refugee was given a new name. Their christening served as a reflection of their new identity as Christian believers as well as a safeguard for those who had illegally crossed the border into China.

"Hello, Mr. Stern." Simon bowed his head, and the tassel on his graduation cap toppled into his eye.

Roger grinned as the young man fiddled with the mess of strings. "Here, let me straighten that up for you."

Simon thanked him and shrugged his shoulders. "I think Mrs. Stern ordered these in American sizes." He held up his arms to show his sleeves, which hung so far down they covered his hands completely.

Roger patted him on the back. "A tradition. When a student works hard enough to earn his degree, the people in charge want to make sure he's as uncomfortable as possible so he doesn't sleep through his own graduation."

Simon returned the smile, but his eyes were fixed on the door. Roger glanced behind him. "Are you expecting someone?" A deep, almost maroon blush crept up the sides of Simon's face. "I take it then that you haven't talked with her?" Roger asked.

Simon rubbed his forehead. "Who?"

Roger wondered how much redder the man's face could grow. "I think we both know who we're talking about. Or do you want me to force that blush all the way up to your eyebrows by saying her name?"

"Don't!" Simon let out an awkward chuckle, but his stare never wavered.

"Fine," Roger agreed. "I'm sorry. But tell me now. Did you have a chance to talk with … with a certain graduate we've discussed before at length?"

Simon's head wagged from side to side like the tail of that little yippy Schnauzer Juliette bought for their daughter so many years ago. Roger put his hand on Simon's shoulder. "You're running out of time, don't you think? Are you going to wait until after the ceremony to talk to her?" Simon's head continued on its horizontal track. Roger felt dizzy just trying to maintain eye contact. "You'll never know if you never ask."

Simon lowered his eyes. "It's not that. I asked her already."

Roger raised his eyebrows. "And?"

Simon sighed. "She's got her heart set on going home."

"She's a very brave young woman."

"The bravest."

Roger stared straight at Simon. "You don't want to leave, do you?"

Simon didn't meet his gaze. "I hate to think of what might happen to her. She's so young. So innocent. And she's going out all by herself ..."

Roger didn't feel like rehashing all the reasons it was safer to send the graduates out solo instead of in groups. "So she won't change her mind, then? Even after you talked with her?"

"No."

"And you told her everything? Including how you feel?"

Simon lowered his gaze until Roger could only see his eyelids. "I told her I didn't want to see her hurt."

"But did you tell her how you feel about her?" Roger pressed.

Simon threw both hands up. His sleeves cascaded down to his shoulders. "She must know it by now."

Roger shook his head. He would have smiled at the young man's fears if the issue weren't far more complicated than a simple crush. Lives were at stake. And once the graduates left tonight, they wouldn't be coming back. Roger thought about when he first met Juliette, how terrified he had been, how convinced he was that a girl so confident and beautiful and sophisticated deserved to find someone well-off and well-bred, someone exactly the opposite of him. It had taken him three months just to work up the nerve to invite her to the movies. Sometimes Roger wondered what might have happened if he had never found his courage. He was about to respond to Simon when two other graduates entered the den, their tasseled caps painfully askew and their limbs completely swallowed up by their billowy gowns.

"Well, I guess it's time," Roger sighed.

"Yeah," Simon agreed. "I guess it is."

***

After the ceremony, Juliette handed the graduate a small envelope. "I can't even begin to describe how proud I am of you, Brother Simon." He lowered his head. Although he was only in his mid-twenties, Simon was one of the oldest students graduating tonight. Juliette studied his features one last time. She had grown used to him knocking on their bedroom door at all hours of the night, impatient to ask her husband some deep theological question that couldn't wait for morning. Simon was bright and quite skilled, so skilled the Sterns had even offered to help him relocate to the States and pastor a Korean-American church. He had refused.

Juliette tried to give him a parting smile, but she had to bite down to keep her chin from quivering. He bowed to her as he accepted the money. "May God bless you for your generosity," he whispered.

She squeezed her eyes shut. She had already shed enough tears during the ceremony itself. She didn't want the graduates' last memory of her to be maudlin. After all, she was the one staying here in the relative safety of Yanji. She took a deep, quivering breath.

"It's been an honor and a joy to see you grow," she finally managed to murmur, but he wasn't looking at her. He stood with his hands limp by his side, gaping at Hannah, whose singing during the ceremony was what had set off Juliette's tears in the first place. Juliette observed him discreetly as he walked up to the young woman, who stood by the window that overlooked the Sterns' garden.

He stood behind her for an awkward moment and then cleared his throat. "So I suppose this is good-bye."

Juliette lowered her gaze but still heard Hannah's sweet soprano in reply. "There are no good-byes in the kingdom of heaven."

Juliette turned away to give them some privacy. This wasn't

the kingdom of heaven yet, but she wasn't about to break the news to the young couple.

***

Roger's belly threatened to pop the button right off his pants, but he put on his overcoat and leaned over to kiss his wife on the cheek. "That was a wonderful feast, Baby Cakes."

She pouted. "You going already?"

"Yeah," he sighed, "I've got to get that order ready to go out tomorrow." He pecked her once more on the other cheek and then left before she could voice any more arguments. It was chilly, and Roger thought about the graduates who would be crossing the Tumen River into North Korea.

Roger waved good-bye to his security guard who was raking the front lawn. Benjamin was a whole head taller than the other refugees, which is why he worked security. It wasn't necessarily the thugs and thieves Roger worried about. Most of them didn't bother with the high-end neighborhoods. But the Sterns' work with North Korean refugees was technically illegal and not something the Chinese would approve of if they caught wind of it.

So far, the Sterns had done what they could to remain in the good graces of the Chinese bureaucrats. They submitted all their paperwork on time and took excessive pains to make sure everything stayed in impeccable order. Still, Roger was grateful he didn't have to leave his wife and young housekeeper unprotected. He lifted the collar of his coat up against the breeze and headed back to work.

***

Juliette ran the vacuum mindlessly over the leftover confetti from the graduation party. Eve would have done it later, but she was busy cleaning up the kitchen. Besides, Juliette welcomed the physical activity to keep her mind off her worries.

Simon left just a few minutes earlier. The other young men had departed one by one after dinner, taking various routes to the Tumen River. From now on, they were on their own, with only the Holy Spirit for guidance and companionship. Juliette hoped that would be enough.

Hannah hadn't moved from her position at the window since Simon's departure. There had been no tearful parting, no intense farewell. Juliette recalled the angle of Simon's shoulders as he walked out of the den, the glint of a tear she had pretended not to notice shining in his eye. Juliette turned off the vacuum. She walked up to Hannah and touched her gently on the shoulder. "You have everything packed and ready?"

Hannah squeezed her eyes shut for a moment before turning from the garden view. "Yes." Her voice betrayed more emotion than her face revealed. Hannah cleared her throat. "I'll be ready in a minute," she replied more steadily and turned back to her vigil over the flowerbeds and herbs that were showing signs of the cooling autumn weather.

"Take your time." Juliette secretly hoped the young woman would change her mind. When she straightened after picking up a fallen string from a tassel, Hannah stood by her, clutching her envelope in a steady hand. She stared at the floor and shifted her weight from one leg to the other. Had the girl's courage failed her? How could someone in Juliette's position possibly blame her? Hannah was only nineteen years old. Of all the girls who enrolled in the Sterns' Secret Seminary twelve months ago, Hannah was the only one who lasted through the crisis training. The others dropped out of the program, opting instead for safe passage to South Korea, which the Sterns helped arrange with some of the funds from Roger's printing business.

"Have you changed your mind, then?" Her husband would be

upset, but Juliette would sleep better tonight knowing Hannah was far from her homeland, where raids, undercover spies, and starvation were only the beginning of a young missionary's worries.

Hannah nodded and fingered the envelope. In an instant, Juliette understood the awkward dilemma. Upon graduation from the Secret Seminary, the students each received a sum of money to survive their first few months back in North Korea. "It's the money, isn't it?" Juliette tried to make things as painless for the young girl as possible. She didn't want Hannah to feel ashamed for choosing the less dangerous route. Even in South Korea, Hannah could find meaningful work to put her discipleship training to use.

"I'm sorry, Mrs. Stern." She bowed and held the envelope out with both hands.

"I understand." Juliette took the money. "Will you want to stay here for a while longer, then?" Hannah furrowed her brow at her benefactress. Juliette tried to reassure her with a smile. "I could talk to Mr. Stern about hiring you in his factory."

Hannah widened her eyes. "Are you saying I'm not ready to return home?"

In spite of her grasp on the Korean language, predicaments like these still frustrated Juliette on a regular basis. "I thought you had changed your mind about crossing the border."

Hannah recoiled slightly. "No. Not at all."

"Well then, if you're returning to North Korea, this money is for your expenses. It's part of the agreement. You've earned it. Besides, you'll need it to complete your first mission." Juliette offered the envelope back.

"I just don't think I should take it."

Juliette tried to hide her exasperation. "You're going to need this, honey. Trust me."

Hannah bit her lip but kept her hands clasped together. "When Jesus sent out his disciples, he told them not to take a money bag with them."

Juliette adjusted her Prada glasses. A dozen arguments ran through her mind, but she doubted any of them would change Hannah's resolve. Juliette slipped the envelope into her pocket. "If you won't take the money, at least let me put some extra snacks in your pack, then." She picked up the backpack, led Hannah into the kitchen, and placed some granola bars in the front zipper pouch. "There." Juliette cleared her throat, which had started to constrict.

Hannah wrapped her arms around her mistress. "I will never stop praying for you."

Juliette hid her surprise. Since she arrived at the Sterns', Hannah had always shied away from intense displays of emotion. Juliette hugged the young woman back. "God bless you," she whispered in Korean.

After she cleared her throat once more, she added in English, "I love you."

***

The special agent pulled out the government-issued cell phone and dialed the secure number. "This is Agent Ko. I need the director."

The slightest trace of static popped in Ko's ear as the operator transferred the call. "What's going on there, Ko?" The director's voice was as tense and rushed as always.

"The students left Yanji this evening."

The following silence bore witness to the director's unease. Ko knew better than to blow this assignment. The director wasn't forgiving. Neither was the Party. "What else did you find out?"

"The itinerary of one of the students. Goes by the name Levi. He's crossing at Tumen then going directly to Hoeryong. Meeting with a pastor there." Ko gave a thorough physical description.

"If your information is correct, the Party thanks you." The director's voice was a low growl. *If you fail, you're as good as dead.* He didn't say these last words, but he didn't need to. Ko already knew.

ALANA TERRY

CHAPTER 14

Juliette rummaged through her kitchen cupboards.

"Can I make something for you, Mrs. Stern?" Startled, Juliette sucked in her breath and saw Eve.

"It's late. What are you doing awake?"

Eve lowered her gaze. She wasn't even in her nightclothes yet. "I heard you out here and wondered if you needed anything."

"Tea would be lovely." Juliette didn't want to admit she was only looking for chocolate. "Something decaf, please."

While Eve got the water boiling, Juliette clicked on the lamp at her writing desk and booted up her computer. With as busy as she had been getting the Secret Seminary students ready to cross the border, she hadn't taken the time yet to respond to her daughter's most recent email.

Kennedy had only been back in the States for two months. Juliette felt her daughter's loss more keenly than any homesickness she'd experienced during her past ten years in China. Mingled with her anxieties over Kennedy's well-being was a deep sense of guilt for having a daughter safe at Harvard. What opportunities would the Secret Seminary students have when they returned to their homeland? What future could they look forward to, except one of constant fear and danger?

"Would you like honey in your tea tonight?" Eve placed two mugs on the table. Juliette took off her designer glasses and massaged her temples. Would Hannah and the other students taste honey again before they died? No one spoke it, but everyone involved understood the future for a Secret Seminary graduate wasn't very promising, at least not when gauged by life expectancy.

73

"Not tonight." Juliette sighed. "Thank you for asking."

Eve placed the honey jar back on the cupboard shelf.

An hour later, Juliette plopped on her bed and stared at the ceiling and wondered if her husband would be coming home at all. Sometimes when things got busy, Roger would work through the night and stay on the next day to oversee another twelve-hour shift.

The Sterns never planned to become missionaries. When they moved to China, the decision was strictly based on good business. Roger could do the same work he had been doing in New York City for a small fraction of the cost. Even the extra expenses for international shipping didn't compare to the money they saved on labor and supplies by relocating overseas. Having grown up in eastern Asia, Juliette considered herself better adjusted and equipped than most of the other expat wives in her husband's business circle.

Juliette and Roger eased into life in Yanji, and business boomed. They could afford to send Kennedy to the All Girls American School, where test averages were twelve points higher than those from the public schools back in New York. When it came time for her to graduate, Kennedy had her pick of top-tier colleges. She finally settled on Harvard when they invited her into their early-admissions medical school program. She'd spend the next four years in the library or some science lab, and once she got her bachelor's degree, she'd transition right on to Harvard Medical School. Juliette was proud of her daughter but still found it hard to be so far away. Was Kennedy eating well? Was she getting along with her roommate? How was she settling in to the States after spending almost half her life on foreign soil? Was she making friends?

Juliette sighed and adjusted the blankets on her bed. She felt guilty she wasn't praying for Hannah and the other Secret Seminary graduates. She tried to focus her mind on prayer but wondered all the more about her only child.

A timid knock sounded on the bedroom door. Eve poked her head in even before Juliette could respond. "Benjamin sent me to tell you there's someone outside."

Juliette reached for her robe. "Did he let them in?"

Eve shook her head, keeping her eyes toward the floor. "No. It's past ten, and Mr. Stern's out."

Juliette tied her sash around her waist and sighed. Roger was a policy man. He created regulations for everything, including when the security guard could or couldn't open the door. What if it was a refugee? What if it was one of the Secret Seminary students? Juliette hurried downstairs, forgetting to put on her slippers.

She heard Benjamin's booming voice even before she saw his towering frame. "No one's awake. Go away." He stood in front of the closed door, his arms crossed impassive, his feet spread apart.

Juliette hurried up behind him, careful that her footsteps wouldn't be heard outside, and placed her hand on his arm. She was a tall woman but had to tilt her face up to reach Benjamin's ear. "What if it's about one of the graduates?"

The door rattled. Someone outside was trying the knob. "Get out of here," Benjamin bellowed.

"How do you know it's not one of ours?" Juliette strained to see through the tiny peep hole, but Benjamin's sturdy girth was firmly planted in her way.

"Trust me." Benjamin's voice was low like a snarl. "They're not with us."

She put a hand up to the top of her robe. "How many are out there?" Benjamin held up three fingers. This was the part of ministry Juliette hated the most. With the Chinese police scurrying around to catch North Korean refugees, the Sterns always had to be on guard. That was one reason they hired Benjamin to take care of security in the first place. That's also why her husband said they couldn't open the door at night, not unless he was home. Juliette had argued the rule was ridiculous. As long as Benjamin was around, they were safe from just about any threat. Besides, what if a truly needy person did come looking for help? But Roger was adamant. On nights like this, it seemed, perhaps he had reason to be.

"What are they doing?" Juliette asked.

Benjamin shrugged. "Don't know. But they're not doing it here." She made a move toward the peep hole, but Benjamin stretched his arm out, blocking her way.

"You're sure they're not refugees?" she questioned again. He nodded. She would feel better if she could get a fair look herself, but Benjamin was immovable.

Eve fluttered up to her side and gripped her arm. "Is everything all right?"

Juliette peeled her eyes away from the door. "Probably just some trouble-makers. Right?" Benjamin grunted his assent. "Go on upstairs, sweetie," Juliette prompted Eve. "I'll be up in just a few minutes." She gave the girl's hand an assuring squeeze and shut her eyes for a moment.

Benjamin stretched his neck up to the peep hole. "They're going now."

Juliette finally managed to make her way to the door. From the porch light, she saw the backs of three young men. One of them pointed to another house down the street, and the gang headed toward it. She squinted. No, they weren't dressed like refugees. She straightened her hair. "What do you think they want here?"

"Trouble." Benjamin flicked some invisible dust off his shirt. "Would've got it, too."

Juliette gave him one more pat on the shoulder. "Thank you for being so diligent."

Benjamin turned down the small hall that led to his bedroom. "That's my job."

***

Back in his bedroom, Benjamin kept his ears strained just in case the hooligans decided to come back. He wasn't about to let thugs in. He heard a quiet knock on his door and grunted, putting down his training weights. "Mrs. Stern?"

"No, just me."

He reached for a shirt to throw on and propped open the door. "Yeah?" He wondered what Eve was doing here. Probably Mrs. Stern sent her down to deliver a message or something. He stepped out into the hall, careful to shut the door behind him. "What?"

Eve nibbled the tip of her little finger. "I don't know." She turned and glanced toward the front door. "Think Mr. Stern will be home soon?"

He crossed his arms. "You worried?"

She shrugged. "I don't know. Maybe. I mean, they were kind of loud at the door. Like they weren't going to leave."

"They left."

Eve turned one shoulder, her teeth still working on what was left of her nail. She paused once and then looked back at Benjamin. "All right. Well, guess I'll go upstairs."

He was already back in his room, his door half closed by the time she could say good-night.

***

Juliette laid her glasses on her nightstand and pressed her throbbing temples. It had been a long day. She knew Benjamin was right to send the men outside away, but she hated the idea of refusing anyone who might genuinely be in need. She took deep breaths, telling herself that the young men were nothing but riff-raff, probably coming up to the expat neighborhoods to see if anyone was foolish enough to keep a window or car door unlocked, not refugees from across the border looking for shelter. Still, they might need help. Should Juliette have ordered Benjamin to open the door? What if they were hungry? At the very least, she could have given them some of the spending money she always kept squirreled away. Roger refused to give cash out at the door; it would only cause more headaches down the road, he insisted. But sometimes a few wads of bills found their way out of the Sterns' house, nevertheless. Juliette rolled her neck in slow circles, rubbing her shoulders to ease the tension. At the very least, she didn't plan to tell Roger about the visitors. Benjamin would probably mention them tomorrow, but if he forgot, there was no reason to give her husband an additional cause for stress.

She heard footsteps on the stairs and saw Eve flit past the open door. The girl's bare feet fell soft as velvet on the carpet. Eve glanced up for just a moment and caught Juliette's eye. She looked down, the barest trace of a blush coloring her face. "Everything all right?" Juliette asked.

Eve bit her nail and stood in the doorway. "I was just getting ready for bed." She sounded the same way Juliette's daughter did when she made up excuses for coming home late from a school dance. "But would you like me to make you tea?"

Juliette studied her quizzically. "I don't need anything. I just wanted to make sure you weren't too shook up. From those guys downstairs, I mean."

Eve let out a tiny giggle. "I've been working here long enough to not get worried."

Juliette put her glasses back on to study Eve's features better. "Well, then I guess it's time for bed, isn't it?"

Eve's tense shoulders relaxed. "If you're sure you don't need tea. Good-night," she sang out, a little faster than etiquette demanded. Once Juliette heard her light footsteps recede down the hallway, she shut her bedroom door and headed straight to her walk-in closet. If she ever deserved a treat, it was tonight. Where was her stash? She wasn't afraid her house staff would steal from her, but she certainly didn't want to feel compelled to share, nor did she care to have everyone realize just how deeply her habit ran. Juliette's hands trembled as she rummaged through old journals and boxes of books that never made it onto the shelves in the den. She needed to calm down.

"There it is." Ever since sending Kennedy off to Harvard, Juliette had started talking to herself. She heard her daughter's voice in her head, teasing her for her late-night cravings. *"You're going to split that with me, aren't you?"*

Juliette opened up the white-chocolate Godiva bar. It was almost a full pound. Of course there would be enough to share if Kennedy were still here. Juliette sat on her bed, breaking off dainty bites of bliss and wondering what Roger would do if he knew she was eating chocolate alone on their Egyptian cotton sheets. She thought about the nights she and Kennedy stayed up in bed while Roger worked late. They watched classic black-and-white films together, laughing at the wimpy heroines and swooning mockingly over the characters' love interests. Juliette hadn't watched a single movie since Kennedy returned to the States.

Her hands were steadier now. She looked at the bar, easily large enough for two to split, and heard rustling from the next room over. Eve was still up. She called the young housekeeper in.

"Yes, ma'am? Did you decide to have some more tea after all?"

"No, thank you." Juliette held out half of the chocolate bar. "I just thought you might like some of this."

CHAPTER 15

Roger walked into his bedroom in time to see his wife shove a cream-colored wrapper under the pillow. "That kind of night, huh?" Roger winked.

"You don't even want to know." Juliette smiled and scooted herself over in the bed. "How did everything go at the office?"

Roger slid into his pajamas, his limbs heavy from the day's work. "Looks like we'll probably get things out on time." He slipped in bed next to Juliette and put his arm around her robust frame, softened and rounded by decades of late-night snacking. He could tell by the way she positioned herself something was wrong. "You worried about the graduates?"

Juliette shifted her weight. "I should be."

"What's keeping you up then? I mean, besides Mr. Godiva?"

She paused but didn't smile. "Just thinking of Kennedy."

Roger rolled his eyes, careful she wouldn't notice. North Korea could cross the Demilitarized Zone, World War Three could break out next door, and his wife would worry herself sick about whether or not Kennedy was brushing her teeth every night before bed. He massaged Juliette's shoulder. "So did anything exciting happen while I was out?"

Even after he tried to curl himself around her like a spoon, she wouldn't relax. "What kind of excitement are you talking about?"

Roger let out a mix between a humorous snort and a sigh. "The typical, I guess. Ragged refugees hunted down by the Chinese police, banging on the door, seeking asylum. You know … the usual."

Juliette's laugh would have been more convincing if she

weren't so tense. Roger closed his eyes and breathed in heavily. It was nice to finally lie down, even though he'd have to get up in just a few hours to check on the printing order. He thought about the Secret Seminary graduates and wondered how they were managing their first night out on their own. When Roger and Juliette started the training program for North Korean refugees, they prayed together nearly every night, begging God to anoint and protect their students. A year ago, they started classes with eleven trainees. Today they sent out the six that completed the entire program. With their daughter away at college and the Secret Seminary students gone to whatever fate awaited them, Roger figured the house would feel pretty empty in the days to come. He wouldn't be surprised to see his wife gain a few more pounds, either. Boredom and loneliness were not friends to her figure, as Juliette herself liked to joke. Roger kissed her and rolled over, remembering to say a silent prayer for the graduates before he fell asleep.

***

Juliette closed her eyes. She frowned in concentration, trying to recall the last song the Secret Seminary students sang before they left. Was it *How Great Thou Art? The Old Rugged Cross?* She hated not remembering. Why hadn't she paid more attention? Juliette took a deep breath. She couldn't think about the graduates at this time of the day. Tomorrow she could wake up and begin a whole new sixteen-hour worry session anew. For now, she had to focus on happier things.

Like Kennedy. Juliette had gotten an email from her daughter just a few hours earlier. She was off to take her first midterm. It was chemistry, one of Kennedy's strongest subjects. She wasn't too nervous, or if she was she didn't show it in her note. Juliette wished they could talk more by phone. She could hear in Kennedy's voice what she couldn't always read between the lines of her emails. But with the time difference, catching her daughter in her dorm was like playing a Vegas slot machine. The Sterns always had to be careful on their home phone, too. With the Chinese government, you could never be sure if your lines were tapped. Juliette couldn't talk to Kennedy about the graduates. She couldn't refer to them directly in her emails, even though Kennedy had known them all before she flew out to Massachusetts.

There Juliette went again, thinking about the Secret Seminary students. What was happening to Hannah right now? Was she still safe? Juliette and Roger had discussed Hannah's fate over the course of many a late night. She was the youngest of all the graduates, but she proved to be an amazing Bible scholar. She was as innocent as the gentlest of doves, but she certainly hadn't attained the shrewdness of a serpent.

"I just don't know if she's going to be able to make it out there," Roger had told Juliette several weeks before graduation. "She's got this notion that everything is so black and white. I'm just not sure it's safe sending her out with the rest of them."

"You know it would tear her up to stay behind." It was true, but there was just no telling what kind of horrible suffering the National Security Agency would put a young, inexperienced girl through if she were caught. Even now, Juliette wondered if letting Hannah return was really the right choice. Hannah and Kennedy were about the same age, and there's no way she would have considered sending her own daughter across the border. Why had she agreed to let Hannah go?

Juliette readjusted under her sheets and tried to think about what she would do the next day. Roger's office needed some serious organizing, but she would have to wake up feeling a lot more rested to make much difference. She didn't roll over when Roger wrapped his arms around her. Even after he fell asleep, she stayed awake and listened to his quiet snoring for over an hour.

***

Roger had already left by the time Juliette woke up the next morning. She turned over on her side and slipped her hand under the pillow. There were a few pieces of Godiva left. She didn't need them right now, but just knowing where they were brought an added level of comfort. She thought about the day ahead of her. For the first time in almost a year, there would be no Secret Seminary classes. No prayer meetings after breakfast. No Bible study over lunch. Juliette would miss the sound of the hymns the students sang in the den. She would miss the inspiration and boldness she gleaned from the refugees and their stalwart faith.

She tried to figure out what time it was on the East Coast. Would Kennedy be asleep? Getting ready for bed? Juliette didn't even know when her daughter went to sleep anymore. She hadn't talked to Kennedy in almost a week. Was she eating properly? How were her classes going?

She knew it was silly to worry about her daughter. Kennedy was safe in her dorm. Juliette's head ached when she thought about the strangers who came to the house the night before. She would have to tell Roger, but then he would only worry more. She wasn't ready to think about that quite yet. She stayed in bed for almost another hour. Her excuse was that it would give her a chance to pray for the Secret Seminary students. By the time she emerged for breakfast, her entire Godiva stash was gone.

Eve didn't say anything when Juliette came downstairs, but she scurried to prepare a late breakfast. Sometimes Juliette wished she didn't have a house staff to wait on her. She couldn't even divert her mind by cooking. She wasn't hungry, but she figured her system could use a little protein this morning. She watched Eve working and finally asked, "Do you know how to make fudge?"

Eve stood over a pan of eggs and frowned. "Fudge?"

Juliette tried to think of the phrase in Korean, but didn't even know if the word had a translation. "It's a dessert. Made out of chocolate."

Eve shook her head. "I don't think so."

Juliette beamed. "I'll make a shopping list."

Six hours later Juliette sat in front of an empty plate, but her taste buds weren't as satisfied as she had hoped. Somehow, it just didn't seem right to be eating fudge in the middle of the afternoon when the Secret Seminary graduates were back in North Korea, where sweets and delicacies were reserved for the wealthy in Pyongyang, for the Dear Leader and his cadre of loyal assistants. Juliette reassured herself that her students would be in North Korea whether she ate fudge or not, but that only assuaged the guilt a little.

She and Roger had argued back and forth for weeks about his plan to cut off all contact with the graduates once they returned home. In Roger's mind, keeping communication lines open would only make things more dangerous for everyone involved. Juliette imagined facing a lifetime of uncertainty, never knowing what happened to Hannah, Simon, and the others, and sometimes had to shut her eyes and deliberately force the air in and out of her constricting lungs.

She carried another piece of fudge to her desk and read that day's email from her daughter. It was newsy and characteristically chipper in tone. Kennedy talked about her schedule and her impression of her professors and classmates. Her roommate was a thespian and was rehearsing like crazy for a modernized version of Shakespeare's *Twelfth Night* set in Times Square on New Year's Eve. Her resident advisor had a boyfriend from Qatar, and Kennedy's lab partner in chemistry was an international student from Kenya. Chemistry was a cinch compared to the Advanced Placement class she took at the Girls Academy in Yanji, but calculus was — in Kennedy's own words — a "beast." Her teacher's aide was from Seoul, and sometimes Kennedy thought she'd do better in class if he actually spoke Korean so she didn't have to decipher his accented English. Juliette smiled at her daughter's descriptions. Kennedy had spent over half her life living in China, went to a school where the classes were all taught in British English, and came home to speak Korean with the Secret Seminary students. In some ways, Kennedy's childhood as the daughter of an American businessman in Yanji was quite similar to Juliette's own upbringing in South Korea as the ambassador's daughter.

Juliette dabbed her mouth with an embroidered napkin and smiled. No mention of boys, besides the RA's foreign love interest. Staring at each word over the top of her Prada frames, Juliette tried to determine if her daughter was lonely. It was hard to tell. Wherever she was, Kennedy drew people to her like flowers attract bees. She was always popular, whether in the States or at the All Girls Academy. But in all her time in Yanji, Kennedy never had a best friend. Juliette hoped and waited for her to find a compatible spirit, a soul mate of sorts, but her daughter seemed to enjoy a plethora of superficial friendships without letting any take root, deepen, and grow.

Juliette sighed. In her head, she heard Roger's voice telling her to stop worrying so much. Kennedy was a good girl. No, a great girl. She was a model student, and the years she spent in Yanji gave her a depth uncharacteristic of most American college freshmen. Juliette was proud of her daughter and missed her fiercely. She and Roger had talked about bringing Kennedy back to Yanji for Christmas break, but it was a long and expensive flight. Kennedy had a standing invitation to spend summers and holidays with her aunt in Maryland, but Juliette still wished her daughter didn't live so far away.

"One of the hazards of mission work," as Roger would say. Juliette never bought into that argument but didn't bother correcting her husband. After all, Kennedy would still be six thousand miles from home if the Sterns were in China simply to

run their printing business as their visas claimed. Juliette sighed and turned off her computer. She would respond to Kennedy's email later when she felt a little more upbeat. She adjusted her glasses and reached for the last piece of fudge.

***

"We found the spy, Levi. He was right at Hoeryong where you told us."

Agent Ko let out a sigh at the director's report. His words were about the closest thing to a compliment any special agent could hope for. The director was ancient, having fought off Japanese imperialists as a young boy. He had worked his way up the Party ranks even though his ancestors before him had all been uneducated peasants. Ko, like most special agents, had two main goals in life: to help the Party achieve its glorious goals of reuniting the entire Korean Peninsula, and to keep from getting hauled off to prison camp for upsetting the director.

"Our initial interrogation with Levi led us to another one of the Yanji spies, the girl called Hannah," the director reported. "What can you tell us about her?"

Ko laughed and then stopped, remembering the director's distaste for humor. "She'll be the easiest of the lot to break."

The director was silent for a moment. "Actually ..." he let the word draw out, and Ko's hands began to sweat. "She's proving to be more difficult than we expected. She's been trained."

This time, the guffaw escaped automatically. "Trained? Only if you call sitting in a den listening to a fat American 'training.'"

"What do we need to do to break her?" the director demanded.

Ko thought about the petite little Secret Seminary disciple and knew just how to get to her. "Find the one I mentioned to you earlier. The one called Simon."

CHAPTER 16

"What are you doing?" Roger hadn't expected to see his wife awake. It was past midnight. He had spent another long day at the office. His back ached from hunching over the pile of paperwork on his desk. If he was lucky, Juliette would come with him one day to help him organize since she had more free time now. Roger put on his pajamas and sat down on the bed next to his wife. "How was your day?" He leaned over and kissed her on the forehead.

She put her glasses on the nightstand. "Not much to report. I taught Eve how to make fudge."

He grinned. "Then it must have been lovely." He reached over and fingered the knots in his wife's shoulder. When she sighed, Roger tilted his head to the side. "You doing okay?"

She nodded. "Yeah. Just having a hard time falling asleep, that's all."

"You sure?" Roger reached under her pillow. "Tell me the truth. How many Godiva bars have you had tonight?"

Juliette shoved his hand away playfully. "None." He stared down at her with furrowed eyebrows. She held her hands up high. "I mean it!"

"Wow. I guess you really are doing okay." He tousled his wife's hair.

"That's what I told you. You just wouldn't believe me." She smiled and lowered her voice. "Besides, we're out of Godiva."

Roger grinned. "That makes more sense." He stretched his arms and sighed. Tonight, he could rest. The shipment to New York finally made it out. The Secret Seminary graduates had moved on. Juliette was still by his side, and their daughter was adjusting to college life back in the States with grace and charm. Roger leaned his cheek on Juliette's dirty-blond hair. "Are you happy, Baby Cakes?"

"Mmm."

Roger studied his wife. "I can't tell if that's a yes or a no."

Juliette rubbed her temples. "Yes."

"Doesn't sound too convincing."

She shrugged. "What do you want me to say?"

Roger made his voice rise to a falsetto. "Yes, dear. In fact, I'm so happy to be married to such a sexy hunk like you that sometimes I feel like my heart is just going to beat its way right out of my chest."

That at least brought a soft laugh. "What you said, then."

Roger buried his face into Juliette's mess of curls and breathed in the sweet scent from her shampoo. "That's more like it."

She drifted off to sleep, and he drank her in with his eyes. What had he done to deserve someone so caring and selfless? She was an intelligent partner, devoted mother, passionate lover. She was always putting others' needs above her own. He dozed off, thanking God for such a perfect gift.

Several hours after midnight, Juliette's piercing cry woke up him. "What's the matter?" He jolted upright in bed and turned on the light. "What is it? What's wrong?" He shook his wife's shoulder, but she continued to sob even once her eyes were wide open.

Juliette took a choppy breath. "They got her." A desperate howl gurgled out from her throat. She had wailed like that at her mother's funeral. It was a sound Roger hoped to never hear again.

He clutched her arm and shook her gently. "Got who? What are you talking about?"

She grabbed her hair in both fists and clenched her eyes shut again. "Hannah. They got her. They have her now."

Roger wrapped both arms around his wife to stop her from

rocking back and forth. "Everything's fine. You were just having a bad dream."

She shook her head and tugged on her hair. "It's real."

For a moment, Roger wondered if his wife was still asleep. He remembered a few times when Kennedy was a toddler and had cried — no, sobbed — in her sleep as if tormented by the devil himself. Was Juliette having the adult equivalent of night terrors? The New York pediatrician had suggested they place Kennedy in a cool bath tub to snap her out of her fits. Roger could hardly do that to his wife, but he had to find a way to stop her. He put his face close to hers. "Juliette!" He barked out the word. "Juliette, look at me."

Her eyes fluttered open. "What? What's wrong?" Her crying stopped, and her words were coherent.

Roger was too surprised at first to say anything, but Juliette kept staring at him expectantly. "You were having a nightmare," he explained. "Sounded like a pretty bad one."

She wiped her cheeks. "Was I?"

"You were crying."

"I can hardly remember it." She smoothed out her hair. "Did I wake you up?"

He shrugged. "Don't worry about that. What were you dreaming about?"

Juliette paused for a moment and pouted. "You know, I think it had something to do with Kennedy. Something about her missing her flight and not being able to visit us next summer. An empty-nest nightmare, I guess."

"Yeah." Roger rolled over. "I guess."

***

"Did you have a hard time sleeping last night?" The voice startled Juliette. She looked up from her novel as Eve glided into the den with two cups of tea, the morning sun streaming in and lighting her up from the side.

Juliette motioned for her to sit down. "Just for a little bit. How could you tell?"

"I found some of the hot chocolate mix you left on the counter."

Juliette grinned. "You caught me."

"You know, I only had chocolate once before meeting you," Eve commented after taking a cautious sip of tea.

"Was that back in North Korea?" Juliette tried to imagine life without her Godiva bars.

Eve nibbled on her pinky. "No, it was after I got to Yanji." She lowered her eyes. "It was a gift from a customer."

Juliette tried to mask her curiosity. Eve never talked about her life before the Sterns rescued her from the hotel district. Back before they got so involved with the Secret Seminary, Roger would sometimes pose as one of the hundreds of nightly callers, seeking out the younger girls. If they passed his initial screening, he would return for further visits and eventually give them advice on how to escape. Sometimes the girls told their friends, which is how Eve arrived at their home.

"I'm glad I found you," Eve remarked, "because now I can have all the chocolate I want just about every day."

"How long did you say you lived at the hotel before you came here?" Juliette often wondered where Eve would be if the Sterns hadn't taken her in. Eventually, Roger got in enough trouble with the inn managers he had to stop his work. By then, they had already conceived the idea for the Secret Seminary and didn't have the time to give the hotel district a second thought.

"Too long," Eve answered.

Juliette sipped slowly. She didn't want to run out of tea too soon for fear that Eve would jump up to make more and never finish her story. Juliette never forced the refugees to talk about their pasts, but she was dying to know more of her housekeeper's history. "How exactly did you hear about us?"

"The girl from the room next door to me. Mr. Stern visited her one night, and she told me about it the next day. I memorized the directions he gave her and got out about a week later."

"I remember the night you came." Juliette smiled.

"Me, too." Eve returned her grin. "I had never met an American before. I was surprised when you spoke to me in perfect Korean. I couldn't believe it."

"I'm so glad you made it here." Juliette wondered how much emptier her life would be if Eve had never come to them, especially now that Kennedy and the Secret Seminary students had moved on. "Whatever became of the other girl? The one who gave you directions here?"

"I never saw her again." Eve bit her fingernail and frowned into her empty cup. "I left a lot of friends back at that hotel, you know."

"Maybe God will show us a way to help some of them."

Eve giggled behind her hand. "Maybe Mr. Stern should visit there again."

CHAPTER 17

"No, I'm not setting a single foot back in the hotel district." Why couldn't his wife understand? Juliette had arrived at Roger's office that morning under the pretense of helping him clean off his desk, but she obviously had ulterior motives for visiting him today.

"It was just an idea I had." Juliette threw a granola bar wrapper into the trash can.

Roger couldn't remember how many times Juliette said, *"It was just an idea I had,"* and he ended up risking his life or reputation. He took the unopened envelope she passed him. "We burned all those bridges already." Didn't she remember the threats? Didn't she remember crying, hugging her husband, and pleading with him to stop going into the brothels once the managers found out what he was doing?

Juliette stuck some old invoices in the filing cabinet. "I guess I just thought it might be a good time to get back into it, now that we've sent all the students out."

Roger moved a box off his desk and sat down. "I know it hasn't been easy for you, Baby Cakes." Juliette had been so wrapped up in motherhood for the past eighteen years that the empty nest would have been hard on her no matter what. Losing the Secret Seminary students at the same time only worsened the blow. "Do you think that maybe God just wants you to relax a little? Do we have to jump right into another round of ministry right away?"

Juliette labeled a new filing folder. "I like to stay busy."

He smiled. "I know. But sometimes all that does is leave the rest of us exhausted. Why don't you spend some extra time with Eve or something? She enjoys your attention."

Juliette stopped working long enough to brush some curls behind her ear and out of her face. "It was actually talking to Eve that gave me the idea."

"Eve talked with you? About the brothel?"

She nodded. "I know. I was surprised, too. But it just made me start thinking about doing something there again."

Roger sighed. "Why don't you go visit the hotel district yourself?" he asked.

She didn't respond to his joke. Roger couldn't remember the last time his wife laughed heartily. Probably sometime before Kennedy went off to college.

"I'm about done with this pile over here," Juliette announced abruptly. "Do you want me to start on the human resource file now or save it for later?"

"Let's forget it until tomorrow," Roger answered. "It's a pretty big one." He patted her bottom as she walked by. "You've been working hard. Why don't you go get a candy bar from the vending machine as an early payment?"

She turned the corners of her mouth up. "Just let me sort through this junk mail first." Roger wondered when the smile would return to his wife's eyes.

***

Eve sat in the den, staring down at the scene below. A fine layer of frost covered Mrs. Stern's bushes and herbs. She spread a blanket across her lap. In the garden, Benjamin dug holes to fit posts for a new gate around the garden. She studied him through the slats in the blinds, her eyes tracing the outline of his bare arm muscles. She counted back the months on her fingers. How long had it been?

Eve glanced at the tall grandfather clock, its ticking frustratingly out of sync with Benjamin's shoveling. Mrs. Stern had gone to help her husband at the office. Besides Benjamin, there was nobody else home, and nobody was expected back for several more hours. She pouted and brought a finger to her lip. She nibbled on her nail in rhythm with Benjamin's labor. He looked up once. She pulled back, startled. Could he see her even through the blinds? She let the blanket fall to the ground. They might be the only two at home, but Eve may as well have been completely alone.

CHAPTER 18

Juliette held up a sheet of paper. "Does this order from Liberty Press go in this month's file or last's?"

Roger glanced at the letterhead. "This month's." He bent down over the shredder.

"What about this one?" She held up an unopened envelope.

"That's just trash. Pass it here." After feeding the junk mail through the shredder, Roger straightened up and stretched his back. He ran his hand over his head, fingering his small bald spot. Last year it was the size of a penny. Now it was at least as large as a quarter. "Think you'll be ready for some lunch soon?"

Juliette straightened a stack of papers on his desk. "Whatever."

"Well, don't sound so excited."

She shrugged one shoulder but didn't look up. "I'm not really hungry."

Roger was about to joke about how rare it was for his wife to turn down food of any kind, but his twenty-two years of experience suggested it wouldn't go over very well. He walked over to Juliette and placed his hand over hers. "You've been working all morning. Why don't we at least take a break? We can go for a walk or something."

"Actually, I should get home before too long. Eve might have made lunch already." She shifted some papers around on the desk. It wasn't nearly as cluttered as it had been this morning, but there were still foot-tall stacks waiting to be sorted.

Roger frowned. "Baby Cakes, what's wrong?"

"Nothing. I just thought that once I was done here I'd go home and have lunch with Eve. She's been all by herself all morning, and she's probably gotten lonely."

"You know Eve's old enough to take care of herself, don't you? She did just fine when you spent eight hours a day in the den with the Secret Seminary students."

Juliette glared up at Roger. "It was less than a week ago. Did you think I'd forgotten?"

Roger threw his hands to his side. "Of course not. I was only trying to say that Eve's a big girl. She can be on her own for a few hours. That's all."

Juliette dropped a file of papers onto the table and spun around without looking at the strewn contents. "I think I know more about my housekeeper than you."

Roger rolled his eyes. Juliette flung the door wide open and huffed out. Roger reached for his coat to follow after her, changed his mind, and went back to the shredder.

***

In Pyongyang's Office 341, Special Agent Chun-Hee leaned back and stared at the director. "So the information from Yanji was solid?

The director took a sip of his coffee. "Rock solid."

Chun-Hee raised an eyebrow.

"You don't need to act so startled," the director commented. "You know Agent Ko is top quality."

Chun-Hee let out a huff of air.

The director scowled. "The two of you will have to put your differences behind you. Once Ko's out of Yanji, you'll be working together on your next assignment."

Chun-Hee's thoughts trailed back to the Academy. "Can't wait."

***

"I've been thinking about trying to rescue a few more girls like you." Juliette watched Eve closely to gauge her reaction. The girl betrayed no emotion as she cracked the egg into the mixing bowl.

"Has Mr. Stern decided to go back to the hotel district?"

Juliette took a deep breath. "Not exactly." She grabbed the spoon from Eve and stirred the batter. Roger had not only flat-out refused, but at one point he mentioned something about cleansing the house from all trace of chocolate and sweets if Juliette happened to broach the subject again.

Eve dumped the oil into the bowl. "How do you plan to help the girls there, then?"

Juliette stuck her finger in and tasted the batter. "I haven't figured that part out yet." She thought about the refugee they hired as their security guard. "I guess we could see if Benjamin wanted to."

Eve's head shot up. "Not Benjamin."

Juliette peered down at Eve from over the top of her glasses. "Why not?"

Eve glanced out the window to the garden. "No girl's going to trust a man who's using her."

"What's that got to do with Benjamin?"

Eve stared into the dark batter. "Just because someone says he's a Christian, that doesn't mean they always act like it." Her face was so low her nose almost touched the mix.

Juliette smoothed out the back of her hair. "So you don't think Benjamin is sincere?" Eve fidgeted with the mixing spoon, and her face turned red. Juliette sighed. "Never mind. You don't have to answer that. I guess we'll just have to find someone else who can go in for us."

Later that afternoon, Juliette sat alone in the den in front of a half-filled Scrabble board. She had been trying all afternoon to think about something besides the hotel district. She rested her chin on her knuckles and stared absently at the wall. If she was quiet enough, beneath the ticking of the grandfather clock she could almost hear the hymns of the Secret Seminary students echoing against the bookshelves. There was Hannah with her quivering little bird-like voice, and Simon with his out-of-tune confidence. Juliette closed her eyes and let out a deep breath.

With a frown, she moved a few tiles around with her finger. "Well you're really racking up the points," she muttered into the loneliness. She hadn't laid a new word down in ten minutes or more. She never bothered keeping score when playing by herself, but the sum of her three- and four-letter words probably wouldn't even break a hundred.

Besides one granola bar and the brownies she and Eve baked, Juliette hadn't eaten all day, which would worry Roger if he found out. Juliette hadn't completely lost her appetite like this since her mom died, and back then it had taken almost a month until she could even consider the taste of chocolate. She took a sip of unsweetened tea. The herbal concoction was bitter and already tepid.

"Do you need anything?" Eve's voice from the doorway drowned out the sacred echoes in Juliette's memory.

She didn't turn around. "No, I'm fine." The housekeeper left without saying anything.

Juliette still hadn't played another word by the time Roger walked in. She straightened her back and smoothed her hair as her husband sat down on the opposite side of the game table and eyed her board. "This all you got?"

She shrugged and tried to smile. The last thing she needed was for Roger to pester her about her mood. "Yeah, it is pretty pathetic, isn't it?"

"Not if you were Eve and didn't know how to read English."

Her laugh sounded forced, even to her own ears. "Let's just pretend this was an English lesson for Eve, then."

"So, you want to play a game for real?"

Juliette considered for a minute. "I'm actually getting pretty tired. I spent all morning slaving in some American executive's office."

"I hope he paid you well."

Juliette adjusted her glasses. "He keeps a running tab."

Roger chuckled and sat down. "So did you have a good afternoon with Eve?"

Juliette played with her hair. "Mmm-hmm."

"What'd you make this time? Chocolate fondue? Grandma Sherry's no-bakes?"

"Ordinary brownies." She noted Roger's slight grin.

"Tell me the truth. How many did you eat?"

"Just two."

"Uh-huh." Roger sounded unconvinced, but Juliette didn't have the energy to defend herself. "So, are you going to clear the board so I can beat you or what?"

She yawned. "Actually, I wasn't joking about being tired. I don't know why that kind of office work always feels so draining. I think I might just take a bath and go to bed."

"Have you had dinner yet?"

She laughed. "Oh, yeah. Bath, dinner, and then bed."

Roger watched Juliette. With his head cocked to the side like that, he reminded her of the parakeet they bought their daughter when they first arrived in Yanji. "Don't tell me you've lost your appetite."

"Never," Juliette lied. "You know me."

"Of course I know you. That's why I got you this." Beaming like a schoolboy, Roger reached into his coat and pulled out a candy bar. "It's not Godiva, but it's a step up from plain generic, right?"

She took the gift. "Two steps up."

"So now I figure you owe me at least one chance to beat you at Scrabble. A real game this time."

Juliette didn't even glance at the chocolate in her hand. "If that's what you want."

"Don't look so excited, Baby Cakes."

She forced herself to look at him. "I guess I'm a whole lot hungrier than I thought. Sorry. Being hungry makes me forget my manners."

Roger gave her playful pat on her backside when she stood up. He always claimed to love her shape and size, but considering the extra sixty pounds she carried, she was pretty sure he was either lying or delusional. Her husband winked. "I won't tell Eve if you eat it all up before dinner."

She made a show of opening the wrapper. "You know me too well."

"Go take your bath." He eyed her flirtatiously. "I'll ask Eve to serve us dinner in here, and I'll play you a proper game of Scrabble while we eat. Deal?"

"Deal." After she locked herself in the master bathroom and started the water running in the hot tub, Juliette looked for a place to hide Roger's gift.

CHAPTER 19

"I thought we were through talking about this."

Juliette crossed her arms. This conversation was going about as well as the others had. She scowled at her husband and snatched up two more Scrabble tiles. "I just wondered why Eve would say Benjamin isn't trustworthy."

Roger put down a five-letter word and added up his score. "I've had doubts about Benjamin myself."

"Really? Why didn't you say something?"

He didn't look up from the board, even when his turn was over. "Because you thought it'd be a great idea to have a security guard."

"Well, I do. All the other expats in Yanji have one." Juliette frowned. That hadn't come out quite right. "If everyone else thinks security is important, we shouldn't take it lightly," she tried again.

"I never said we should take it lightly. But now I'm starting to wonder why we hired an illegal alien in the first place."

"What's wrong with him being a refugee? It gives Benjamin a job, and it keeps us protected."

Roger took out more letters. "It also gives him the perfect reason to betray us."

Juliette hadn't even looked at her tiles since her husband played his last word. "Why would Benjamin ever consider going against us? We've done nothing but help him since the day he came here."

"Think about it." Roger put his elbows on the game table and leaned toward his wife. "Benjamin's position in Yanji isn't exactly above board."

Juliette narrowed her eyes. "So?"

"So all it takes is one person to find out he's an illegal alien, and then they can hold it over him for as long as he's here."

"You think someone would blackmail him to get at us?"

Roger indicated the Scrabble board, which was waiting for Juliette's move. "The thought has crossed my mind, yes. And did you ever wonder how he got to be so big? I mean, have you ever seen anybody from North Korea with that kind of muscle? Or that tall?"

Juliette shrugged. "So, he's got good genes. And besides, if you were concerned about this for so long, why didn't you think to tell me before now?"

Roger moved a few tiles around on his letter board. "Because whenever you get ideas in your head about rescuing somebody, it's a waste of energy trying to stop you."

Juliette laid down the word *rams*. It only gave her six points, but at least Roger couldn't blame her for holding up the game. "I was just trying to help him. He needed a job, and we needed a security guard."

Roger was ready with *modern*, which he laid down for twenty-four points. "Not everyone who needs rescuing is our responsibility. I guess that's all I wanted to say."

"So what do we do about Benjamin?" Juliette stared at her tiles, but without any vowels open on the board, she couldn't play a single word.

He took out a few more letters. "Nothing, at least not until I have a chance to think things through more. The last thing we need is to give him a reason to get back at us. He knows all about what we do now. It's your move," Roger added.

Juliette sighed. Game night was turning out just about as badly as she expected.

***

102

Roger stood behind his wife. Even while doing the simplest things like brushing her teeth, Juliette was stunning. He brought his nose close to her blond curls. "So tell me honestly. Was that chocolate bar as good as a Godiva?"

Juliette spat in the sink. "Good as a Godiva? Watch your tongue."

Roger wrapped his arms around his wife. "But it was an okay present? Okay enough, at least?"

"Of course."

Roger studied her in the bathroom mirror as she rinsed her mouth one more time. "You sure?"

"I already told you. It was great."

"You didn't eat much at dinner."

She dried her face. "Guess your little present spoiled my appetite after all."

Roger kept staring at her reflection as she headed toward the closet. "You sure nothing's wrong?"

"Mmm-hmm."

Roger plopped onto the mattress and watched Juliette prepare for bed. He couldn't really blame her for her recent mood swings. It was hard enough for him not knowing what was going on with the Secret Seminary students, but at least he had work to focus on. Juliette spent all day here alone, with nothing to do but teach her housekeeper new recipes and worry about those she loved. What else could he do to help her stay encouraged and engaged? A nice dinner out? Maybe even a weekend at one of the fancy tourist resorts? They didn't have any obligations right now besides the business. There weren't any new refugees to think of. Maybe it was time to plan a little get-away.

Roger rubbed the back of his head before stretching out on the bed. He would take the next few weeks to plan something really special.

PART 3

CHAPTER 20

"Get up. Now." The proprietor barely managed to fit his girth through the width of Sun's door. Mee-Kyong felt a chill on the base of her neck as he summoned the girl.

Sun glanced up tentatively toward Mee-Kyong, who gave her hand a pat. "Go on, little cousin. I'll be here waiting for you." Sun followed Mr. Lee out into the hallway, looking back once at Mee-Kyong. For the next thirty minutes, Mee-Kyong paced back and forth, her eyes continually darting toward the closed door. Why had Mr. Lee called her? Was he upset with her performance? Were her customers unhappy?

Mee-Kyong kneaded her abdomen. Two weeks after the delivery, she was now able to stand up tall without hunching over from the pain. Her breasts felt a little heavier than normal but didn't ache like they had with her initial engorgement. She was tired, but that had as much to do with her schedule at the Round Robin as it did with the delivery. She should rest before her shift started, but that would be impossible while she waited for Sun to return. Besides, the scant sleep she could find these days was muddled with dreams of Pang. The method of the murder in her nightmares varied considerably, from drowning to strangulation to shooting. What stayed the same was that he always woke up right before she killed him. She was lucky if she got two hours of sleep at a time. It didn't matter. Conditions had been worse in the gulag. Much worse.

She eventually stopped her pacing and sat on the bed, fidgeting with her sash and staring at the door. Would things be much different if Pang were still alive? Probably not. Her setting would change; she could go from place to place, but her work at the Round Robin was a lot like her life with the former National Security officer.

She jumped off the bed at the sound of the door's soft creak and was halfway to Sun before the girl even entered the room. "What is it? What did Mr. Lee want?"

Sun's lip quivered. Mee-Kyong shut the door behind her. When she brushed Sun's shoulder, she felt the small shudder from the girl's fragile figure.

Sun didn't raise her eyes. "Mr. Lee says I'm to be married."

Married. The word sat in Mee-Kyong's gut like a rock. "What happened?" She took the girl by the shoulders and scanned her for signs of bruises or tears or trauma. Sun smelled of cheap perfume too liberally applied. Her hair had been done up already, and she had on more make-up than usual. "What did Mr. Lee say to you?"

Sun's right eye twitched. "There's a rich businessman with a grown son. He came here tonight and made Mr. Lee an offer."

"It must have been a pretty good offer." Mee-Kyong hadn't meant to speak the words out loud, but for a proprietor like Mr. Lee to even consider selling one of his star attractions would require an inconceivable amount of money. Sun had only been working in the Round Robin for two weeks, but she had already become the most sought-after of all the girls.

Sun bit her lip, but Mee-Kyong saw that it was still trembling. "I'm supposed to get myself ready."

"You're leaving tonight?" Mee-Kyong wanted to sweep aside the clump of overgrown black bangs that hung in front of Sun's face, but she kept her hands on the girl's shoulders as if she might hold her down indefinitely.

"Not yet. The father wants to make sure … He wants proof that I'll be … adequate."

Mee-Kyong bit the inside of her cheek to make sure her sense of repulsion didn't creep into her expression. After a moment,

Sun's shoulders relaxed just a little. Mee-Kyong took a deep breath. "He must be very rich."

Sun didn't reply.

Mee-Kyong spoke slowly, examining the girl out of the corner of her eye to gauge her reaction. "And with all that money, he could probably do a better job than Mr. Lee taking care of you." She waited for the girl's muscles to ease up again before she continued. "A husband like that usually likes to buy his wife lots of pretty things. New clothes. Jewelry."

"The son is already married," Sun whined. "I would just be the *little wife*."

Mee-Kyong made her voice sound as soothing as possible, the same tone she once used to assure Pang that she forgave him for his numerous outbursts. "Even so, it might be kind of nice to only have one man to entertain every night."

Sun lowered her head. Cautiously, Mee-Kyong reached out and patted her back. She didn't pull away. "I'm too young to marry." Sun's voice was choppy. "I'm too young to have a husband."

You're also too young to be working in the Round Robin. This time, Mee-Kyong kept the thought to herself. "What's so bad about marrying, as long as he's rich and can take care of you?" She crossed her arms. "It couldn't be worse than it is here, could it?"

Sun's shoulders shook. She didn't look up. Mee-Kyong couldn't understand what the girl was whispering. Sun had to repeat herself several times until finally Mee-Kyong made out the word *baby*.

"You don't want to have a baby?" Mee-Kyong balked. "But you could already ..." She shut her mouth. Now it made sense. The poor girl didn't even know. "You don't want to get married, because you don't want to end up pregnant, is that it?"

Sun nodded. Mee-Kyong took a deep breath. "Listen, there's something about what we're doing here, about the work Mr. Lee has us do, that you should know." Sun wiped her tears with her tiny hand and blinked up at Mee-Kyong. "You say you don't want to end up pregnant. But what you need to realize is that ..." She stopped herself once more. What could her words do besides pile yet another burden on Sun's petite shoulders? Mee-Kyong stared past the girl's ear. "You need to realize that marriage isn't all that bad. Even if you end up having kids. When you're with child, you know, your husband might not want you as often."

"They say it hurts."

Mee-Kyong shrugged. "What? Having babies? Old women just tell young girls that to scare them. It's not actually true, you know."

"Really?"

Mee-Kyong pretended to laugh. "Of course! Think about it. If delivering babies hurts so bad, why do so many women have more than one child?"

"But they say it's worse than your introduction. And messier."

"Who says that?" Mee-Kyong tossed her hair over her shoulder with the flick of her hand.

Sun hung her head. "Some of the other girls here."

"Pffft." Mee-Kyong forced a chuckle. "What do these silly inn workers know? They've probably lived in this hotel for years, most of them. They've never been married, have they? Have they ever had babies themselves?"

"No." Sun looked up slowly, raising her eyes until they met Mee-Kyong's. "Have you?"

Mee-Kyong tilted up her chin. When she noted how carefully Sun was studying her features, she made herself grin again and relaxed her posture. "I know enough to understand marriage isn't all that bad. Especially if your husband is wealthy."

"Mr. Lee said the father is very particular. He wants me to make sure he enjoys himself, no matter what he asks." Mee-Kyong reached out to wipe a stray tear from Sun's red-tinged cheek. "If I don't do it right, Mr. Lee will take away all my pay, the money I was saving to send home to my family."

Mee-Kyong took a deep breath. "If you do what Mr. Lee tells you, then you wouldn't ever have to work at a place like this again."

Sun hugged her arms around herself. "I'm not old enough to have children. I want to go home. I want my mother."

Mee-Kyong tried to recall her own mother's face, but it blended in her memory with all the other resigned and miserable middle-aged ghosts from Camp 22. She kept her hands on Sun's shoulders until the girl met her gaze again. "Your life might be a lot better there than it is here, little cousin. You're sure you don't want to leave with this man? Get out of this place?"

"I saw him. He's old. And fat. Almost as fat as Mr. Lee."

Mee-Kyong tried one last time. "That probably means you'd be well fed."

Sun tilted her chin up. The gesture reminded Mee-Kyong of herself. "I want to stay here. And when I've earned enough money to make Mr. Lee happy, I'm going back home to my family."

"So you're positive you don't want to escape with him?"

"Yes." Sun's voice was so low, Mee-Kyong hardly heard her. "Besides, I wouldn't want to leave you here by yourself."

Mee-Kyong knew she should throw Sun out the door. She should tie her up and force her to marry the wealthy heir. But she looked at Sun trembling on the bed. The silly girl didn't know what a good chance she was missing out on. She was probably so scared she'd mess things up with the potential father-in-law anyway. Mee-Kyong fingered Sun's red dress, the same one she wore on the first night they arrived at the Round Robin. *Only one man a night, and a rich man at that* … She held the dress up by one strap.

"If you really don't want to go with him, I may be able to help you."

***

Sun buttoned the top of her nightgown, her fingers trembling. "Are you sure this will work? What if someone sees me?" She turned to Mee-Kyong, who struggled to squeeze herself into the tiny red dress.

"If you want to get married, hurry up and get ready," Mee-Kyong hissed as she zipped herself up in the back. Sun lowered her eyes. "If not, you'll do as I say and sneak over to my room. Then wait there. No matter what happens. Just wait there."

Sun looked at Mee-Kyong. Her broad shoulders barely squeezed into the dress. She looked beautiful, so grown-up and mature, just the kind of girl Sun imagined her brother Jae would fall in love with. "Thank you for doing this for me."

Mee-Kyong narrowed her eyes. "Get out of here."

Sun tried to convince herself that Mee-Kyong was just feeling rushed; she wasn't really angry. A knock sounded on the door. Sun froze and turned to Mee-Kyong. What should they do now? Without warning, Mee-Kyong shoved her down and pushed her under the bed. "Stay there. And don't come out." Sun had never seen anyone else when they were with a customer. She covered her face with her arms and wrapped her body into as small of a ball as she could.

She heard the door swing open and felt the small vibrations as the knob hit the adjoining wall. "And this must be the illustrious Sun. I've heard so much about you." The voice came out in a strong baritone and reverberated against the walls. The rich inspector's heavy footsteps caused the floor to tremble ominously. "My son is going to be so pleased to make your acquaintance, I have no doubt."

CHAPTER 21

Mr. Lee bit into his bean-filled donut and then brought his napkin to his lips. Thanks to a very rich businessman looking for a young and delectable daughter-in-law, he could gorge himself on donuts every night for a year if he wanted to. He took a large swig of soju and laughed out loud.

That acne-faced broker from over the border had no idea how much his little find was worth. Mr. Lee got nearly tenfold his purchase price from Sun's introduction alone. He knew by the increase in traffic to the Round Robin news of his humble inn's little starlet had spread around Jilin Province. A dozen men or more came in every night requesting Sun by name. New customers Mr. Lee had never dreamed of attracting found their way to his establishment, asking for the new girl with bangs. If they had money and she wasn't too busy, he sent them over to Sun's room at the end of the hall. Otherwise, he just hustled them over to one of the other workers. He had one of the older girls give several of them the same hair style as Sun's. Money flowed in, but he had no idea Sun's fame had reached as far as Dashitou until Inspector Wong stopped by the Round Robin earlier that night.

Until then, he only knew of Inspector Wong by reputation. The government-official turned money-lender was the wealthiest man in the entire province, if rumors were to be trusted. The Round Robin usually catered to a much humbler clientele. Mr. Lee had worked himself into a cold sweat bustling around to make Inspector Wong as comfortable as possible. He ordered soju and fresh red-bean donuts, even though the bakeries were long since closed. He called two of his girls to massage the inspector's shoulders and legs as the men negotiated.

"My son's first wife is with child, which leaves him in search of a *little bride*. He heard of the girl Sun here and asked me to visit you." As soon as the inspector mentioned how much he was offering — even before any real bidding got started — the inn proprietor swallowed down his curiosity. The son could be some drooling, immobile imbecile, but why should Mr. Lee care as long as the father was willing to pay such a large sum?

He haggled, enjoying the process immensely, and then the inspector stated his closing cost and stipulation. "I will spend half an hour with her before I go." Mr. Lee nodded, as if his request was already anticipated. The inspector grunted. "I want to make sure she is appropriate for my son. If I find her satisfactory, you will have your pay."

It was here that Mr. Lee had wavered. The inspector was welcome to spend half an hour with Sun, of course, but it was customary to pay first. The inspector, however, demonstrated little sympathy for Mr. Lee's concerns. "The money will be yours, I assure you. *If* the girl is adequate."

Mr. Lee hadn't asked what kind of payment he might receive if the inspector didn't find the girl "adequate." Instead, he had begged for Inspector Wong's patience and then bustled down the hall to tell Sun what was expected of her. Now, Mr. Lee looked at his watch. The half an hour was almost up. And Mr. Lee was about to double his fortune.

The door swung open without warning. Surprised, Mr. Lee fixed a smile onto his face, but it vanished as soon as the inspector stormed in swearing. Mr. Lee jumped up and rushed to his guest. "Is something wrong?" he asked and felt his chest squeeze in on his palpitating heart.

"Wrong? I should make you pay my travel expenses. If I wanted a common whore, I would have stayed in Dashitou."

"Common …?" Mr. Lee began. The blood in his face burned hot enough to boil, the effects of the soju and also of his fear. "I'm telling you, she is my best worker. You must have heard the reports or you wouldn't have traveled all this way to see her for yourself." He wiped his brow, but the sweat immediately beaded on it again.

"A complete waste of time, I assure you, and an insult." The inspector's nose was only a few centimeters from Mr. Lee's. Neither man was about to back up. Mr. Lee looked past the angry customer at his two bodyguards who stood in the doorway. One put his hand to his pocket and raised an eyebrow. Mr. Lee gave him a slight shake of his head.

"I just don't understand how this could have happened," he whined. "She's still a little modest, but surely that's not a detrimental quality in a daughter-in-law. Believe me when I tell you that I have never had a customer complain about Sun."

"Allow me to be the first."

Mr. Lee clasped his hands together in supplication. "Tell me what happened. Please. If one of my girls has done something to anger you, I guarantee that I will personally address the problem. That's my job as the proprietor here." Mr. Lee lowered his voice. "She didn't refuse you, did she?"

The inspector snorted. "If she had, I would have paid you double my offer for the sake of her modesty."

Mr. Lee wiped more sweat off his forehead. "So she didn't deny you?"

"Quite the opposite." Inspector Wong's voice lowered to a quiet growl. "I was told that your girls here were discreet and tasteful. I was certainly misinformed. My son will be most displeased when I return home alone."

Mr. Lee resisted the urge to drop to his knees, but his legs threatened to buckle under his weight at any moment. "Please, let me talk to her. This must all be some sort of misunderstanding. Perhaps she thought you would like …"

The inspector snarled from the back of his throat and held up his hand. "Enough. I've already wasted two hours traveling. Now I've got to go back home without a wife for my son." The inspector glared at Mr. Lee through narrow slits. "If you're lucky, Mr. Proprietor, I might forget tonight ever happened. You'd be fortunate if I did."

The inspector brushed past the two guards unhindered, leaving Mr. Lee alone with a platter of half-eaten pastries. Inspector Wong hadn't even paid for his thirty minutes.

CHAPTER 22

"Get out of here fast." Mee-Kyong reached under the bed and pulled Sun out, ignoring her shocked expression and scooting her up onto the mattress. The rich man wasn't happy. Mee-Kyong had tried her best, but she had failed. She needed to get Sun out of the room, but the child was frozen in place, her unblinking eyes as wide as the nozzle on a National Security agent's revolver.

Mee-Kyong gripped the girl by the shoulders and pushed her to the door. "Go to my room and get in bed. If anyone comes in, just pretend to be asleep. I'll take care of everything." Mee-Kyong swore under her breath. She hadn't planned on making the inspector that angry. Mr. Lee would find out what happened right away, if he hadn't already. He would be furious. Mee-Kyong braced herself, preparing to absorb as much of Mr. Lee's rage as she could.

She went to open the door for Sun but heard heavy footsteps sounding down the hall. There was no time. She pushed the girl back toward the bed and shoved her down. "You're asleep," she hissed. The door flung open.

"Where is she?" Mr. Lee barged into the room and shoved Mee-Kyong aside. By the time she caught up with him, he was already at Sun's bed. Mee-Kyong lunged for him as he grabbed a handful of Sun's hair and yanked her on to her feet. The child didn't even cry out. Mee-Kyong threw her arms around Mr. Lee, grasping at his clammy neck and cheeks, and tried to tackle him from behind. The fat man didn't lose his footing. While one hand still clutched Sun's hair, he slapped the girl across the cheek with his other. "Do you know how much yuan you just lost me?" Sun brought her arms to her face but couldn't block Mr. Lee's fist in time. Blood spurted out from her nose.

Mee-Kyong grabbed as much of Mr. Lee's wide frame as she could and scratched at his fleshy neck. "She's only a child! Let her go!"

The proprietor ignored her. "Do you have any idea how long it will take you to work off that kind of a debt?" The sweat from Mr. Lee's armpits leaked all the way through his collared shirt as well as his suit coat. Mee-Kyong felt his weight shift. His next punch came from below, collided with Sun's chin, and snapped her head back. She dropped onto the bed. Why didn't the child try to protect herself? If they were in Mee-Kyong's room, it would only take a few seconds to yank the knife out of the nightstand drawer and end Mr. Lee's brutality for good.

"I was the one who met with the inspector." Mee-Kyong grabbed Mr. Lee by the hair and shouted in his ear. "I was with Inspector Wong this evening."

A drop of sweat splashed onto Mee-Kyong's forearm. She cringed involuntarily when Mr. Lee snarled, "This was never your business to sniff around in."

"Sun told me about the inspector coming. I wanted out of here, so I made her give me her dress, and I pretended to be her." Mee-Kyong backed up toward the door. She wanted to be as far away from Sun as she could when Mr. Lee grasped the severity of her transgression. "It was my idea. Sun went along with it because I roughed her up a little bit. You know she's too scared to go against any of us. She'd never come up with something like this on her own."

Mee-Kyong's one goal was to get Mr. Lee next door to her own room. Then Sun wouldn't witness whatever it was that Mr. Lee chose to do to her for costing him the richest customer in the province. And if she was lucky, she might have a chance to reach for that knife. As soon as he let her go for just a moment, she slipped free and was to the door before she heard his lumbering steps behind her. He was panting by the time she reached her room. He overtook her in the entryway.

"You filthy pig," Mr. Lee roared in her face. She covered her head, clenching her teeth and trying not to make any sounds. She didn't want Sun to hear from the other room. At least for now, the girl was safe. "You'll regret this. You'll regret this for the rest of your short, miserable life." He punched her so she fell back on the bed and was against her in a second. Mee-Kyong could smell the soju on Mr. Lee's breath and on his clothes. A wet crumb dropped from his mouth onto her cheek. She tried to push his heavy torso off. He leaned so hard into her that her lungs only worked in shallow bursts. "Nobody disrespects me or my customers." He maneuvered his weight just enough to punch her in the ribs, blasting a splintering pain up her side.

Mee-Kyong's body ached for air. *Just tell him what he needs to hear. Make him think you really mean it. Get out of this alive, for Sun's sake if nothing else.* "I'm sorry for making you angry." The words came automatically, the same apology she doled out to Pang dozens of times. She had freed herself from Pang. If she could just reach the nightstand, she could free herself from Mr. Lee as well. She lowered her eyes. "It won't ever happen again."

"I know it won't." His grin sent waves of panic shooting out from her throbbing side. He bent his elbow and pressed his forearm against her neck. "In fact, I guarantee it."

She thrashed. With Mr. Lee's full weight on top of her, his arm planted against her throat, Mee-Kyong stretched her arm out as far as it would go. Her fingers just barely brushed the handle of the nightstand drawer.

***

Sun buried her head in her pillow and tried folding it around her ears. She didn't know what was happening to Mee-Kyong in the room next door but couldn't bear hearing Mr. Lee's angry shouts. This was all Sun's fault. Mee-Kyong had only been trying to help. If Sun had agreed to go with the ugly Inspector Wong and marry his wealthy son, if she hadn't been so stubborn and scared, her friend wouldn't be in danger right now.

She heard a crash next door and bit down on her blanket to keep from screaming out loud. Suddenly chilled, she hugged herself tight and shivered under the covers. Why had she ever left Chongsong? How could she have been so foolish to trust a complete stranger? Had she been so blinded by a new dress and a promise of an easier life for her family? Her ignorance had cost her freedom. Now Mee-Kyong was paying the price as well.

Sun wished she could change into a man, someone strong and courageous like her brother Jae. She would rush into Mee-Kyong's room and free her from Mr. Lee's anger. If she were brave enough, she would kill Mr. Lee if that meant she could save her friend. But she was just a little girl, nothing more than a child. A child who could never dream of fighting off a man as big and heavy and angry as Mr. Lee. She slowly rocked beneath the blankets, begging the night to end, begging Mee-Kyong to return safe. She wished there was a way to make herself black out. She would give just about anything to forget.

When all was silent, she lifted her head off the pillow and strained her ears. Nothing. Did that mean Mr. Lee was finished? Was he going to come into her room next? For a moment, she thought about jumping underneath the bed again. She was working up the courage to force her legs over the side when her door flung open. Sun sucked in her breath and envisioned herself pulling the blanket over her face, but her body didn't respond. She sat staring, her paralyzed muscles not even bothering to tremble.

It was Mee-Kyong. From behind her back she pulled out a blood-stained knife. Panting, she grasped her side with one hand, staggered into the room, and shut the door. "Mr. Lee won't bother us anymore, little cousin."

CHAPTER 23

Roger wrinkled up his brow. Juliette hadn't acted normally since their first conversation about the hotel district two weeks earlier. He studied the way she picked at her greens. He thought back as far as he could and finally decided the last time she ordered a salad at a restaurant was right after she delivered Kennedy and wanted to get back to her pre-pregnancy weight, which still remained elusive almost two decades later. "Is that really all you're going to eat?" he asked.

Juliette frowned into her plate. "I'm going on a diet. If I work at it, I figure I can drop ten pounds by New Year's."

Roger put down his rib and wiped barbecue sauce off his chin. "You know you don't need to do that. You're gorgeous just the way you are."

Juliette took a sip of water. "I've decided it's time to take better care of my health. Live to see our grandkids grow up. That kind of thing."

Roger smiled. "Kennedy's just starting undergrad, Baby Cakes. She's got eight years ahead of her and then residency. I wouldn't say you're quite to grandma stage yet."

Juliette shrugged. "I just want to be around when it does finally happen."

Roger couldn't argue with her logic, but somewhere in the back of his mind ran the truth he had discovered twenty-two years ago: *A happy wife is better than a skinny wife*. He reached for another rib. "What's Eve doing this evening?"

Juliette poked at a cherry tomato. "It's Benjamin's night off, so she's home alone."

Roger was glad she could keep track of these things. There was no way he could remember all the schedules of their hired help. Roger was so busy at the office, it had taken him two weeks just to find time to take his wife out to a nice dinner. He hoped some time alone together would help Juliette out of her empty-nest funk. "What did you do today?" he asked, his mouth full of barbecue sauce and pork.

"Little of this, little of that." She picked at a limp spinach leaf with her fork.

He rubbed his bald spot. "Well, that's enlightening."

From behind her glasses, a single eyebrow shot up. "You want me to spell it out? All right. I helped Eve with the laundry, we cleaned the kitchen, scrubbed the bathrooms, uprooted some of the bulbs to bring them in for winter, wiped the windows, and then after that I read a little bit from my new novel and wrote Kennedy an email. Is that specific enough for you?"

Roger gulped down his Coke. If this is what he had to look forward to with Juliette on a diet, he'd take her a hundred pounds heavier. "How's your salad?" he asked after a minute.

"Wilted."

"I suppose that's the point." Roger forced a little laugh, but Juliette's expression remained unchanged. "You did order the wilted spinach salad, didn't you?"

She shrugged. "I guess that's what they called it."

He finished his rib and mounted a calculated assault on his coleslaw. The American-style diner had only been in Yanji for the past two years. It wasn't anything like the cuisine they were used to back in New York, but it was nice to get a taste of home, however fabricated it turned out to be. From a 50's-style jukebox, Elvis crooned about his baby leaving while Roger devoured his side dish. "So, you going to tell me what's been bothering you?"

The denial he expected didn't come. Juliette put her fork down by her full plate. "Life sucks right about now."

He was so taken aback by her abrupt reply, the best response he could manage was, "What's the matter?"

Juliette tossed her crumpled napkin on the table. "I'm bored. There's nothing for me to do. All I've got is a housekeeper who won't leave me alone and a security guard who hardly says a word."

"Maybe you could teach Eve to play the piano." It was meant to be a joke. Back in New York, Juliette had spent three years trying to turn her pyromaniac, NASA-astronaut-wannabe daughter into a classical pianist by the time she started first grade. Roger realized as soon as the words escaped his mouth his response was ill-timed, to say the least. "I'm sorry," he whispered, not even waiting to hear Juliette's objections.

"Forget it."

"No, I shouldn't have said that. I'm sorry."

"I know." It wasn't quite *"I forgive you,"* but it would have to be close enough.

Roger took another swig of Coke. "Is there anything I can do to help you get through this hard time?" *There. That was better.* "You want me to go to the hotel district and buy you another housekeeper? One who likes to garden?"

Juliette's face dropped. Her throat constricted visibly. Roger wiped his mouth with his napkin and closed his eyes. *Nice one.* Juliette still hadn't stopped talking about getting back into brothel-rescue work. And Roger had to agree with part of her reasoning. If Juliette had some other girls around, young women she could teach and pour into day after day, she would feel sense of purpose she had been missing since the graduates left. The problem with the plan — besides the fact his life had been threatened the last time he went into the hotel district — was he was the one who had to actually go and get the girls out. And frankly, business at the office had picked up so much he couldn't spare the time even if he wanted to.

Which he didn't. Still, it had been callous of him to make that kind of a comment. Roger looked at his wife, her hair about as wilted as her veggies, and sighed. "Tell you what. I'm going to make you a promise, okay?" He leaned toward her. "I'll start praying about the hotel district. I'll ask God to give us a really clear, really definite sign if he wants us to do that kind of work again. How's that sound?"

Juliette took a sip of water, crossed her arms, and stared out the window.

***

Eve was glad to have the house totally to herself. The Sterns hadn't been getting along with each other lately, so Mrs. Stern hadn't been helping her husband out at his office as much. There was only so much baking and snacking Eve could put up with in a given two-week period. Job or no job, she had certainly maxed out on sweets and tea with her fat mistress.

She would have never thought she'd regret seeing all the Secret Seminary students shipped off over the border. Ironically, when the house was full, Eve had been able to enjoy more time alone. None of this brownie-making every single day. Now she consumed these beloved treats as part of her job, but she wondered how anyone could actually enjoy the grainy texture or bittersweet aftertaste. In some ways, Eve felt sorry for Mrs. Stern. The poor woman was clueless about so many things. Eve wondered if it would be pleasant to exist in such mind-numbing ignorance.

Eve picked up the Sterns' phone — another perk of having the house to herself. She was sick of sneaking calls in secret. "It's me," she whispered once he answered. "Everyone's out. Want to come over?"

***

"You're awfully quiet." Roger commented as they walked out of the restaurant. It had been the slowest dining experience in Juliette's recent memory. "You doing okay?"

Juliette had already decided if her husband asked her that question one more time before the evening was over, she would buy herself a plane ticket and spend the next eight years in Cambridge with Kennedy. Instead, she quickened her pace as they left the restaurant. "I'm fine." Roger's promise to at least pray about resuming brothel work was reassuring. It was the first step in getting her way, at least.

"Got some change, lady?"

Juliette frowned. She was used to pan-handlers soliciting her when she was out by herself, but she found it even more insulting to be addressed directly when she was with her husband. She lifted her chin and walked on without glancing down.

"You gots a pretty skirt. What's it made of?" The old man reached out and grabbed the hem of her dress. When she couldn't free herself right away, she nudged him with the heel of her shoe.

Once they were a few paces ahead, Roger chuckled. "Did you have to kick him?"

"I didn't kick him. I just didn't want him touching me."

"Baby Cakes, you kicked him."

Juliette scowled. "I wouldn't have had to if you did it for me." She felt her husband tense and for a moment regretted her words. "Maybe I should go apologize."

Roger took Juliette's arm in his. "Just forget it. I would have probably done the same thing if I were you." Juliette would like very much to see that, but she didn't say anything. If Roger were more proactive, if he were willing to go back to the hotel district, for instance, she wouldn't be in such a slump. He was just too much of a pacifist, always worried about making a loving Christian impression. Some people respond to justice and the fear of God a lot more than love and wishy-washy kindness.

Juliette thought about the ragged old man, thought about turning around to make sure he wasn't hurt, and then sped up her pace. It was getting late.

CHAPTER 24

She giggled and pushed him back down onto the pillow. "You know I'm not supposed to talk about that."

Tiger dropped a candy wrapper on the floor, stretched his arms behind his head, and stared at the ceiling. He wondered what it would be like to live in a mansion where the roof never leaked. "Come on. You said you trusted me."

"I do." She smiled flirtatiously.

He never could stand how pointy her chin was. It made her look like some big-nosed Western teenager. Oh, well. He wasn't with her for her looks. "Come on. Tell me. I just want to know where they all went. I mean, did they all get fired? Did your mistress turn them over to the police? What happened?"

Eve hadn't stopped that ridiculous giggling. "I already told you, I can't tell. I'd get in big trouble."

"Aw, relax a little." He flashed a smile. She was wearing far too much perfume. "I just want to know where everybody went."

She lowered her eyes and tried a little too hard to make her eyelids flutter. "You really want to know?" she asked in a low, husky voice.

If he wasn't so interested in pilfering whatever intelligence she carried around in that airy brain of hers, he might have laughed right in her face. "Yeah." He lowered his tone to make it as exaggeratedly serious as hers. "I really want to know."

***

Benjamin stumbled out of the bar, holding on to the doorframe for support. He staggered a few more feet and steadied himself on the pole of a street lamp. He wondered what the Sterns would do if they saw him. Probably send him away for good.

A young girl in a miniskirt flitted her way toward him, swinging her hips and puckering her red painted lips. An unwelcome sense of desire stirred up in Benjamin, and he craned his neck to get a better view as she departed. She turned around once with a questioning look on her face. Benjamin smiled shyly and glanced away. He thought about the Secret Seminary students who left the Sterns' house two weeks ago. They certainly wouldn't give in to such base temptations. And what about his employer? Mr. Stern would never let a young tart in a short skirt turn his head, and Mrs. Stern certainly wouldn't allow for it either. But the Americans weren't Benjamin. Did they know what it was like having a Party official show up at your school and whisk you away to a prestigious training program? Did they know how it felt to receive an honor so high you weren't even allowed to let your parents know where you were going or say good-bye to your brothers and sisters? Did they know what it was like being fed meat every day so you could grow to be the biggest and strongest elite agent, knowing your family — upper class by North Korean standards — was struggling to scrounge two meals a day?

Benjamin held onto his spinning head. Maybe if the Sterns understood a little better, they wouldn't begrudge him a night or two out when all he wanted to do was forget. Forget what it felt like to have a family you couldn't care for. Forget what it felt like to act as the Party's war machine. Unfortunately, living with the Sterns in their nice little mansion, fattening himself up in their nice little kitchen, sitting around listening to everyone sing their nice little hymns didn't do anything to help Benjamin forget.

He tried their Western religion. He let Mr. Stern go so far as to baptize him in the oversized hot tub. It was the only time Benjamin had set foot in the master bathroom. He even tried to act like a Christian. But the promised peace never came. The platitudes and Bible verses the Sterns doled out didn't ease the pain, and they certainly didn't erase the memories.

Benjamin didn't have a watch, but he knew it was getting late. He just needed to sit down and steady himself before going home. He'd sober up by morning and do his usual work around the house and yard. Sometimes he felt like the Sterns were no different than his superiors from the Party; they only wanted a strong body to show off and keep potential enemies at bay.

He shook his head. In a nearby alley, a young man rummaged through a trash pile. When he glanced up, Benjamin turned his face and stumbled away.

***

In the alley outside the American restaurant, the aroma wasn't quite as nauseating as in the main thoroughfare. It looked like Jae would be feasting on old vegetables and stale dinner rolls tonight. It was no worse than the way he was used to eating back in Chongsong.

The money he stole from the captain had lasted long enough to bring him to Yanji. It had taken Jae two weeks to make the journey, but sources he met on his search for the broker all eventually pointed here. Jae still didn't know which brothel to visit first, and he couldn't exactly afford soliciting door to door. Even now, he just barely had the bribe money he'd need to cross the border and return to North Korea, but that didn't matter. All he cared about was finding Sun. His hunt had brought him as far as Yanji. He only hoped his luck would last long enough to reach his sister before he went completely broke.

Jae gnawed on a discarded bone. The sauce was sweet and made his throat even more parched. Yanji was a filthy city, with its outdoor garbage heaps stinking up the air, bright lights polluting the night sky, and half-clad women parading like gaggles of geese. It was getting late, and with each passing hour, the costumes of the girls passing back and forth grew more and more ridiculous. Jae clenched his jaw and resolved to find Sun even if he had to eat trash in the alleyway for a year.

He didn't look up when an old man squatted down next to him and poked through the garbage with a stick. Jae almost gagged at the scent of human waste mixed with cheap beer. "Gimme your bone, boy." The man pointed to the leftovers in Jae's lap.

Jae found no reason to hide his disdain. "If you had teeth enough in your mouth to chew, granddad, I'd consider it."

The old man chortled, revealing two yellowing incisors. "Where I comes from, boy, a kid gots respect for his elders." The man's words were slurred, from drink or from his toothless gums, or maybe both.

Where I come from, old men like you are the first to starve. Jae left the thought unsaid and tossed the ancient beggar one of the bones.

"The others, too."

Jae ignored him. The man reached out, but Jae slapped his hand away. "Watch it, granddad." Jae turned his back and picked more at his dinner.

The old man sniggered again. "You gots to watch yourself, river hopper."

Jae set his jaw. He wouldn't be baited. Koreans swarmed all over Yanji, outnumbering even the ethnic Chinese. There was no way a half-blind hobo could prove Jae was from across the border. The old man poked at the trash pile one last time. "Something I say upset you, then, did it?" he wheezed. "Just hold on to that temper of yours, or it might gets you in trouble, river boy."

The old man's gummy smile took away all that remained of Jae's appetite.

***

Old Joo sniffed the night air, a pungent mix of restaurant compost and stagnant water, and sauntered down the sidewalk. Even his encounter with the fat foreign woman didn't upset him like it might have some other night. That boy in the alley was an alien, all right. And the police paid handsomely for help catching the illegal immigrants. If only he were young again, Old Joo wouldn't have to split profits with anyone else.

He shook his head. These river hoppers thought they'd blend in with the rest of the Korean-Chinese population in Yanji. Didn't they know Old Joo could single them out from half a kilometer away? Shabbily dressed and bone-thin, they stood out based on their stunted height alone but were even more recognizable by their eyes, their haunted, vacant, famished expressions. It didn't matter if they were twelve-year-old boys or fifty-year-old grandmothers. Old Joo could sniff them out. And the police were always happy to reward him for his particular set of skills.

Of course, he couldn't just tell the police he found an illegal alien. He had to bring him in. That's why he needed help. Fortunately, there were always strong young men willing to come to his aid, especially this time of night as they passed Old Joo's little corner on their way to the hotel district, their anticipation heavy but their pockets light.

He had learned from experience how to pick his brutes. He had been cheated more times than he cared to recount. The ideal candidate had to be strong, obviously, and calloused enough to turn in another human being, but also dumb enough to still share profits with Old Joo once the mission was complete.

He kept his eye on the river hopper in the alley while scanning the passing crowds for the right business partner. The man who stumbled by was tall, broad across the shoulders but not too bright in the eyes. He was drunk, too. Old Joo slid up to him and flashed his most winsome grin.

"I don't have any money," he grumbled.

"No, but you could." Old Joo sniffed loudly. The stranger's sweaty odor overshadowed the scent of beer. His nails were incrusted with dirt, and his body reeked of soil. A manual laborer with a weakness for drink. Yes, he would do the trick. "I gots a little business proposition for you. What's your name?"

***

Even drunk, Benjamin found the old man repulsive. Age and squalor masked the true color of his hair, and his stench was so strong Benjamin was surprised there were only two flies circling his head instead of a whole swarm.

"It's like this." The old man leaned in toward Benjamin, assaulting his nostrils. "There's a young man I've gots my eye on. One of them river hoppers." Benjamin nodded. The only reason he himself wasn't instantly mistaken for a refugee was that the Party had given him international food aid packets and forced him to eat double allotments every day.

"You look like a man who knows how to watch out for hisself." He scratched his beard, and Benjamin winced, wondering what kind of critters might have found a home in that mess of mange. "He'll be worth about eight hundred yuan to the police. How about we splits it halfway?"

Benjamin frowned. "Halfway?" He raised himself up to his full height and glared down at the bearded vagrant.

The old man shrugged. "I could always hire another brute."

"You paying up front?"

Old Joo lifted up his hands. "Can't give you what I ain't gots. But you catch him and bring him to me, and I tell you what. We'll go and see the police together and split the money right then and there. Fair-like. Old Joo's good for his word, I promises that."

Benjamin looked down the alley at the refugee hovering over

the trash pile. He didn't look like much of a threat. Benjamin turned back to the old, toothless hobo. "Deal."

Old Joo cackled and rubbed his grubby hands together. "So you goes and gets him out of the alley. You bring him here to me at this bench, and we take him together to the police. Then we split the money."

Benjamin scrunched his forehead up. "Might run."

A dribble of drool ran down from the side of Old Joo's mouth and trickled into his beard. "He won't be nothing for a big strong man like you. You coulds probably wrestle him to the ground in your sleep." He cackled once more.

Benjamin didn't deny it. "Shame if he ran away." He scratched his jaw. "Better take him out aways. Knock the fight out."

Old Joo squinted. "And how's do I know you ain't gonna take him and lug him off to the police yourself and keep that reward money?"

Benjamin shrugged. "Meet me at the police. I won't sneak by."

Old Joo reached out a gnarled finger and scratched his beard. "You sure you ain't gonna try to run off with him?"

Benjamin nodded. "Just making it easier."

Old Joo squeezed one eye shut. "Positive?"

"Yup."

CHAPTER 25

Jae's limbs ached from exhaustion, but he couldn't sleep yet. Sun was somewhere in this city, at least if his sources were reliable. There might be dozens of brothels, but he hadn't traveled this far to give up. If he ran out of money, he'd beg or cheat or steal. It didn't matter how long it took. He was here for his sister, which was all that mattered.

He stretched his back, ready to set out, when the streetlight was blocked by a looming shadow. He reached for his stick, but the massive stranger gripped one end and jerked it out of his hands. He leaned down and growled in Jae's ear. "Walk with me. Now."

Jae sized up his attacker. What did he want? Money? Jae would kill with his bare hands before he gave that up. His sister was only kilometers away. He darted his eyes back and forth, looking for a route of escape. The brute clenched down on Jae's wrist almost hard enough to crush the bones. It looked like he could outrun Jae, even if he outweighed him two kilos to one. His best defense was the rope in his back pocket. He needed to be ready to grab it as soon as he got the chance. He didn't know what the stranger planned to do to him, but by the way things were going, one of them was about to die.

Still, Jae refused to show his fear. He was quick, and he was experienced. He had worked for the Chongsong police for three years, and before that had held his own in numerous village scrapes. What he lacked in body mass, he could make up for in dexterity. And he still carried the rope that had come in so handy at the captain's house.

Jae was completely lost after countless twists and turns down unexpected side streets. Instead of leading him to some remote alley, the brute dragged him through the heart and into the outskirts of the city, into the neighborhoods where the houses grew increasingly larger and more impressive. When they reached a row of mansions with wrought-iron fences and massive gates, the man stopped. "I won't hurt you." He kept his voice low, its bass coming out in a surprisingly melodic tone. Jae tensed and let his free hand crawl closer to the rope in his pocket. The man grabbed Jae's arm in an instant and twisted his wrist backward. "You deaf?" Jae stared up into the hard-set face. He could smell the liquor on the man's breath. "I work there." The man gestured with his head to the largest of the houses on the block. "They help refugees."

Jae twisted in an attempt to run. *Refugee?* How could he have known?

The giant hardened his grip. "I said they help."

Jae wasn't going anywhere, at least not until the stranger released him. "I don't need charity," he finally muttered.

"Suit yourself." He shrugged. "But you need new clothes. Police'll have you by morning."

Jae eyed the mansion and wondered what was inside. His stomach growled.

"I'm not sticking around," the man stated. "Do what you like." With that, he turned away. Jae stood staring long after the figure disappeared into the shadows. The entire scenario reeked of a setup. Jae wasn't gullible enough to believe the man would have led him here if there wasn't something insidious going on. What it could be, he could only guess.

He thought of all the questions he should have asked. He was stupid for letting the man get away. Jae hadn't known of anybody back in Chongsong who would risk their safety to help someone else like that, not without expecting something pretty substantial in return. What game was this man playing? And what would happen now Jae found himself a pawn in it?

He studied the estate. What was the worst that could happen? He could get deported. But not if he was able to wield his rope and escape first. He glanced down at his rags, the only clothes he brought with him across the border. Maybe the stranger was right. Maybe it was time for a wardrobe change. And if the people there were wealthy, maybe he'd find a solution to his financial problems, too.

He inched up the walkway, never taking his hand off the rope in his back pocket.

CHAPTER 26

With the chance the Chinese government was censoring her emails, it was hard for Juliette to tell Kennedy what was really going on. She slouched behind her keyboard at her writing table and plunked one key at a time. She was a slow typist, but that was mostly because it took her a while to think of what she wanted to say.

We haven't heard from our guests since they went back home, so we're assuming they're doing just fine. We hope so, anyway. Juliette spent the next several minutes staring out the window at her garden before continuing.

Dad's busy as ever with the printing. Benjamin's working on that gate in the back yard. It's hard to know what to do with myself. She stopped again and rested her head in her hands.

"Are you all right?" It was Eve. She was so light-footed, Juliette hadn't even heard her come into the room.

"Just tired, that's all."

"It's getting late."

Sometimes Juliette wondered if Eve thought the Sterns hired her so she could take care of them, instead of it being the other way around. "You're right. I'll be getting to bed soon." Juliette clicked off her monitor. She'd finish the email in the morning.

"How's Kennedy doing?"

Since Eve never really got along with Kennedy, Juliette wondered if she was hoping to hear good news or bad. "She's doing quite well, thanks." When Eve first came to live with the Sterns, she and Kennedy had quarreled, some dispute over a boy Roger took in or something like that. Their relationship had been strained ever since.

"Will you be going to Mr. Stern's office again tomorrow?" Eve asked.

Juliette frowned. "Maybe." When Eve still didn't leave, Juliette sighed and turned around in her chair to face her. It wasn't the girl's fault that there was no one else to talk to anymore. "There's still a lot of work left to do there. You know how Mr. Stern is when it comes to keeping track of things."

Eve smiled but didn't laugh at Juliette's attempt at humor. It was just as well, Juliette figured. It probably wouldn't be appropriate for Eve to giggle at her boss's tendency for clutter. Figuring the conversation probably wasn't going to get any better from there, Juliette pushed her chair back and stood up from her writing table. "Good-night, then. Thanks for your hard work today." She wondered if Eve would follow her upstairs like an imprinted duckling when someone pounded on the front door.

Eve reached out and took Juliette's arm. "Who's that?"

Juliette couldn't blame the girl for being nervous. "I'll see. Why don't you go get Benjamin?"

Eve dug her fingers into Juliette's fleshy arm. "He's out."

"That's right. Well, go get Mr. Stern. I think he's in the den." Juliette lowered her voice. "And then stay there. I'll call you if I need anything."

Eve nodded and went toward the stairs. Juliette took calm, stately steps to the door. She should wait for Roger, but the pounding persisted. The inside latch was locked, so she straightened her spine and opened the door an inch or two, just as far as the metal chain allowed. Her husband would come down any minute. "Can I help you?"

The man was short, his hair disheveled and his clothes filthy. His torn shirt would have screamed *refugee* if his hollow cheekbones hadn't already given him away. "I met a man who told me to come here." He kept his eyes on the ground and mumbled into his stomach. "He said you might have some better clothes I could change into."

Juliette nodded and unlatched the inside chain just as Roger appeared behind her. He shoved one hand out to the frame and placed the other firmly on the door. Before she even looked behind her, Juliette sensed Roger's fury boring into her back. She ducked under his arm as he stood physically barring the entrance. "I'll take care of this," he snarled at her in English.

Juliette lowered her head. She should have waited, but the refugee on the other side looked so weak, even Eve could probably have tackled him single-handedly if she needed to.

Roger glared down at the young man. "What do you want?" he growled.

Juliette watched her husband until his expression softened just a touch. Once she was certain Roger wasn't going to just throw the poor boy back out in the street, she went upstairs.

"Never slows down around here, does it?"

"Did you say something, ma'am?"

She looked up at Eve, who was standing in the open doorway of her bedroom. "Oh, never mind. I was just talking to myself."

Eve put her hand on the doorframe, leaning inside Juliette's room but keeping her feet outside the threshold. "Who was at the door?" she asked in a timid voice.

Juliette plodded out of the closet, wiping her hands on her pants legs. She still hadn't changed for bed yet. "Another refugee by the looks of it. You should probably go ask Mr. Stern if he wants some refreshments. The boy looked half starved."

"It was a young man, then? Was he traveling by himself?"

Juliette looked down over her glasses at her housekeeper. "Why does it matter?"

Eve bowed her head. "I just wondered how much food I should prepare. That's all." She turned to go.

Juliette reached her hand out toward the Eve. "Just a minute."

Eve stopped. Juliette had never let anyone see her hidden supply of cash. Roger would be furious if he knew about it, but

136

then again, he was annoyed at just about everything she did these days. She thrust her hand into one of the smaller closet drawers and pulled out a small wad of bills. "If Mr. Stern sends him away tonight," Juliette whispered as she held out the money, "try to find a way to give this to him."

Eve hesitated for several seconds before reaching out to take the cash.

"Oh, one more thing," Juliette added, adjusting her glasses and studying the housekeeper.

"Yes, ma'am?"

"Don't mention the money to Mr. Stern. Ever."

***

Jae glanced up at the Westerner and took a step back. The woman had been about to let him in, but her husband didn't seem so easily persuaded. His light hair made him look just like the American soldiers in those paintings from the Peninsula War. Jae kept his gaze downward. "I'm looking for my sister."

The Westerner set his face and kept his arm across the doorway. He was over a head taller than Jae. "It's late."

Jae bowed his chin to his chest, trying to forget the pale-skinned villains from the propaganda posters. "It's my sister, sir. I'm told she made it to Yanji. I only want to bring her home."

"At this hour? Most folks are getting ready for bed by now, if they're not asleep already." The man's Korean was heavily accented, but his meaning was clear.

"I apologize, sir." Jae lowered his voice. "I met a man downtown, a big guy. He told me to come here." Jae kept his eyes to the floor. "He said you might be willing to help."

The Westerner paused before he stepped out of the doorway and nodded. "Come in." He took Jae lightly by the arm and shut the door behind him. "You've traveled a long way, I imagine."

There was a hint of a question in the remark, but Jae didn't respond to him. The man crossed his arms. "And your sister? You followed her here?"

Jae unclenched his fists deliberately, but he kept his body alert and ready to run at a moment's notice. "My sister is very young." A muscle near the veins in his neck spasmed. Jae swallowed and tried to breathe evenly.

The Westerner nodded, and a slight look of sympathy passed quickly over his brow. A petite wisp of a Korean girl tiptoed up behind him without a sound and announced, "I can find something for you to eat."

Jae followed her with his eyes as she glided out of the room but stopped when he caught a glimpse of the Westerner scrutinizing him with a severe frown.

***

Old Joo sat outside the police office, smacking his gums with satisfaction. Everything about the business deal had worked out smoothly so far. He regretted offering fifty percent up front, but if this transaction went over well, maybe he and the big guy could form a little partnership. It looked like Benjamin could use some new clothes, and he obviously shared Old Joo's predilection for drink. With physical strength like that at his disposal, Old Joo could retire from digging through trash piles for good.

He let his jaw hang open and scratched his stubbly cheek. The restaurant across the street tantalized him with the smell of ginger and roasted garlic. It wouldn't be much longer. And then he would be rich again. He chuckled to himself and picked his gums with a small stick, a habit vestigial to the days when he still had a full set of teeth and could enjoy the taste of meat every day. His mouth salivated. He'd be having soju tonight. And lots of it. There was no way the scrawny river hopper could outrun Benjamin, and

Benjamin wasn't stupid enough to kill an eight-hundred-yuan investment. Old Joo tapped his fingers against his knees. He'd just wait a little longer. His leg bounced up and down. He wiped his brow and imagined the taste of the first sip of soju he'd enjoy with all the cash their little river-hopping friend would bring in.

He looked over his shoulder, got up from the bench, and walked around. He just needed to stretch. How long could Benjamin take, unless he had to carry the body all the way to the police station? Old Joo should have insisted on going with him. At least that way he'd have something to do besides breathe in the scent of day-old vomit from the drunks on the sidewalk. He sat down once more and drummed his fingers on the back of the street bench, his feet keeping time with the beat. A few minutes later he stood up and walked around again. If that Benjamin didn't get here with his catch soon, Old Joo was going to dock some of his pay, no matter how strong or intimidating the giant was.

CHAPTER 27

Jae kept his fists clenched as he left the Westerners' house. He had accepted a new pair of clothes and quick bite to eat but declined the invitation to spend the night. He was only halfway down the street when soft footsteps padded on the pavement behind him. He threw a glance over his shoulder. It was just the housekeeper. She ran up beside him and laid a hand on his bicep. "Please," she panted. "I ... I have something for you."

Jae didn't stop. "There's nothing you can do to help."

She crossed her arms and stood with her weight on one leg, her hip jutting out to the side in a stance that contradicted her demure behavior at the Westerners' home. She showed him what she was holding, her eyebrows forming two defiant peaks. "I'd say this might help. Wouldn't you?"

Jae balked at the bills. "Where'd that come from?"

The light of the single street lamp illuminated her face as she grinned. "I'm not supposed to say anything else." He reached for the money, but she evaded his grasp. "Don't I deserve a thank you?" She pouted her lips, and the evening breeze carried a whiff of the same perfume he had detected on the Western woman.

A wave of revulsion overpowered the baser sense of desire welling up in him. "Thanks," he grumbled, plucking the bills out of her hand.

"There's better ways to show your gratitude, you know." The girl's voice held something of an invitation, almost a plea. Jae scowled at her angular face, her sharp jaw. He pocketed the money, balled his hands into fists, and turned away without looking back.

An hour later, he still wasn't any closer to finding Sun. He had already checked out four other hotels, and the one he now entered was significantly cheaper and dirtier than the last.

"You say you're looking for someone?" The girl crossed her legs on the plush loveseat and fingered the top of her robe. The pointy heel of her shoe made a small dent in the upholstery where she reclined, and she smiled at Jae from behind a wine glass. "You sure I'm not the one you want?"

Jae didn't sit down. He was wasting his time here. Even more disgusting, he was wasting his money. The inn proprietor refused to let him see the girl before he paid, and now he was stuck waiting. "I thought she might be here, but maybe not."

"What's so special about her?" The woman took a drink of wine and lifted a glass to Jae with an upturned eyebrow.

"That's my business, as I see it." Jae glared at the closed door. Ten more minutes. Ten more minutes until he could go try another inn.

The woman shrugged. Without a word, she took another swig of wine, this time right from the bottle. He waited most of his time out so he wouldn't arouse anyone's suspicions and hurried to the hotel on the corner.

"Is there a new girl here?" Jae clenched the pile of bills in his pocket and willed his heart to beat a little lower in his chest as he strode up to the counter.

The fat proprietor put down his red-bean donut and leaned forward, his jowls jiggling as he talked. "You got money?" Jae took out some of the cash the Westerners' housekeeper had thrown at him. The corner of the proprietor's lips curled upward. Fat rolls wrinkled around his face, almost hiding his eyes completely. "Oh, yes. We have a new girl who started only two weeks ago. Very popular with the young men."

"What does she look like?" Jae clenched his jaw and leaned so close to the proprietor he could smell his sweaty odor.

"Short hair. Bangs like this." The man motioned with his hands. "Rosy cheeks."

Jae did what he could to keep his voice down. "How old is she?"

The proprietor frowned. "Old enough for you, I'll wager. But she's busy tonight."

"I'll wait." Jae took out a few more bills. "How much?"

The fat man eyed Jae's wad and named his price. Jae flinched and sniffed the dank, mildewy air. To judge by the surroundings, this brothel was no more upscale than the others he had already visited, but the man was demanding over three times the regular amount.

Jae counted out half the money. "Could I see her for only a few minutes?"

The proprietor grunted and didn't touch the bills. Jae slammed the rest of the fee on the counter. The fat man beckoned to a door. "Go up those stairs. First on the left."

Once he got to the right level, it took every ounce of Jae's willpower to keep from rushing down the hall and barging into the room. *A new arrival. Long bangs and rosy cheeks. Two weeks ago ... Who else could it be?* Jae held his breath and knocked, and then he let it out in a disappointed, "Oh," when he saw the woman who opened the door.

Her entire countenance fell. One eye was bruised like a spotted banana left out in the cold. "Is something wrong?" She looked a year or two older than his sister. She hugged her robe around her skeletal frame, and Jae wondered if the workers here were fed any better than his neighbors back in Chongsong. She held the door open, and he entered.

"I was looking for someone." Jae slunk down on the side of the bed and rested his chin on his hand. "I thought she might be here."

"The new one?" The girl sat down about an arm's length from him.

"Yeah. How'd you know?"

She hung her head. "A lot of them come looking for her. Sometimes Mr. Lee sends them to me."

Jae spun toward the girl. She took a startled jump backward on the bed. "Sun's here?"

"Never asked her name."

Jae leaned forward. "What does she look like? Short hair and bangs over to the side? And big cheeks when she smiles?"

The girl shrugged. "I don't see her smile."

He clutched her arm. "How can I get to her? Which room is hers?"

"What?"

"Which room is Sun's? Can you tell me?"

She shook her head and recoiled slightly. Jae jumped up to leave, but she grabbed his wrist. "You can't go yet. Please."

"Look, I came here to find Sun. If you're telling me she's here somewhere…"

"There are guards." She didn't let go of his arm. Her grip was stronger than Jae anticipated.

"I know how to take care of myself."

The girl jumped off the bed without letting go of Jae. "Mr. Lee will be angry with me." The tremor in her voice made him tarry. "Please. You have to stay here with me. At least until your time's up. I'll tell you whatever you want to know, I promise. Just don't tell Mr. Lee I didn't … I wasn't …"

Jae sat on the bed.

The girl sighed heavily. "Thank you, sir."

Jae crossed his arms. "Well, I'm listening."

CHAPTER 28

Mee-Kyong grimaced and yanked off Sun's bed sheet with one hand. She pressed her other hand into her ribs, where a stabbing pain seared her side with each breath she took. She limped over to Sun's closet and managed to pile the girl's clothes in a heap.

Her lungs cried out for more oxygen, but each inhale sent a fiery twinge through her ribcage that radiated all the way to her tailbone. She kept her hand on her side and pressed down as hard as she could. With her free arm, she gathered what they would need. She had to hurry. Mr. Lee's guards would figure out what happened before long. She and Sun had to be out of the Round Robin and as far away as possible by then.

"Put this on." Mee-Kyong flung an extra dress to Sun. The girl obeyed without saying a word. Mee-Kyong yanked away the bathrobe the girl had been wearing and put it in the bundle with the rest of their things, and then she stared at the window and gritted her teeth. *Get ready, you coward. You can't wimp out now.* The pain of that simple breath made Mee-Kyong want to cry out, but she saved her energy for the impact. She threw her shoulder against the glass, the pain instantly dropping her to her knees.

Harder than that, you lazy sloth, if you want to stay alive another day. She positioned her hand on the window sill to try to raise herself, but the agony in her side barraged her senses until she was sure she would vomit. Mee-Kyong collapsed again on the floor. *To die and never have to breathe again ...*

Sun's voice was surprisingly calm. "Watch out." She had picked up a pottery jar, letting three fake flowers drop to the ground. Mee-Kyong only had time to cover her head before Sun smashed the vase against the window. Shards of glass and broken pottery scattered around them. Tiptoeing gingerly around the debris, Sun lifted Mee-Kyong up by the arm.

Mee-Kyong leaned on the window sill and looked out. Getting down to the pavement in her condition wouldn't be easy, but she would do it if she wanted to live, and she would bring Sun with her. She steadied herself on the sill, swallowing down her nausea. Hearing a ripping sound, she turned slowly, keeping her hand on her ribcage. Sun was cutting the bed sheet into strips with the stained knife. Understanding her plan, Mee-Kyong staggered to the bedside and tied the strips together, testing each knot with the small amount of strength she had.

"Here." Sun held out a long piece of cut fabric. She wrapped it several times across Mee-Kyong's ribs, pulling it in tight before tucking it in at the end.

Mee-Kyong winced once, but her breath came a little easier after she was bound. "Thank you."

Sun tied one end of their makeshift rope onto the bed stand and whispered, "I should say the same to you."

***

It didn't take Jae long to incapacitate the two guards. He tucked his rope into the back of his pants and covered it with his shirt, ready to pull it out again in an instant if he needed to.

According to the girl with the cut bangs, Sun's door was the last at the end of the long hallway. Jae frowned at the moldy ceiling and stained walls. How could Sun survive in a place like this? She deserved a mansion, a palace in the heart of Pyongyang, where performers entertained every night and rice was served three times a day. He felt no remorse for attacking the guards. Anyone who held his sister captive deserved even worse.

His hands remained steady as he cracked open the door. Even though her back was facing him, he recognized Sun immediately. She was thinner, though he wouldn't have thought it possible, and he noted several bruises on her arms. He fought the urge to run to her and stood transfixed. *What's happened to you?* The question didn't escape his lips. He shut his eyes once, clenched his fists, and took in the wounds on his sister's flesh. Until now, he had held on to hope, some kind of irrational possibility that everything was a mistake — the broker, the baby, the brothel. But here she was, with the make-up and nightclothes of a cheap prostitute and the injuries to prove her new position.

It was no less than the wench deserved. In fact, bruises were too good for the likes of her.

Sun turned around and gasped when she saw him. Her face lit up. "Brother Jae!" Sun ran to him, flung her arms around his neck, and kissed him on the cheeks, the familiar embrace scalding his skin, warming his heart. "How did you find me?"

Jae cleared his throat. With both hands on her shoulders, he held her an arm's length away. She moved as if to embrace him again. "I didn't hope you'd ever find me. I'm so sorry, Brother. I must have made you and Mother sick with worry." She put her hands on top of his and gazed into his eyes. She was radiant. Radiant and beautiful. Jae's blood pressure rose. Sun was charming, deviously charming and clever with her lies. After what she had put her family through, how could she act so relieved? Had she no shame? Jae shook his head, blinking to try to break free of his sister's spell, trying to fight the instinct to pick her up in his arms like he had that day the river swept her away.

"You found us just in time." Sun prattled on, clutching Jae's hands, examining them from every angle. Repulsion threaded its way up his veins. "You probably have it all planned out, right? We don't even need to keep making this rope anymore, do we?"

Jae narrowed his eyes. "Have what planned out?"

"Our escape. How you'll help us get back home. We need to take my friend, too. Mee-Kyong's in trouble."

Jae looked at the woman in the gaudy red dress, which clung several sizes too small for her body in spite of her emaciated appearance. How could his sister consort with such a creature? He crinkled his face in disgust and swallowed down the lump in his throat. "That's not why I'm here."

***

Sun grasped Jae's hands and wished he would just look at her. "What's the matter, Brother?" Behind him, Mee-Kyong edged closer, her beady eyes fixed on Jae like a hungry cat's. Why was he so angry? What could make him act this way, unless ...? She gasped. "Is it Mother? Is something wrong?" A heavy rock sank to the bottom of Sun's stomach. Had Mother died of grief or anxiety? How could she ever forgive herself?

Jae shook his head and said nothing. She clutched his hands and brought them together in front of her chest. "Please, Brother, I know I should have talked with you before I left. I made a terrible mistake." His muscles tensed, but Sun continued. If she could only make him understand, everything would be all right. "I was wrong. I should have known better. I should never have trusted that man ..."

Jae raised his fist. "Don't you dare mention him to me." Sun stared at the floor while Jae continued, his voice rising. "You brought shame on all of us, sleeping around behind Mother's back. After she worked so hard for you just to keep you from starving."

Sun forced herself not to cry. Not here. Not now, when they were so close to freedom. She bit down on her lip. "I didn't mean to dishonor Mother."

"Don't you think you should have thought of that before killing off her grandbaby?"

"What?"

"I know about the child," Jae snarled.

Sun sank down on the bed, trying pitifully to blink away her tears. "I don't know what you're talking about." Her sob was cut short by a slap across the face.

Bringing her hand to her stunned cheek, Sun looked once to Mee-Kyong, whose eyes were locked on Jae, and then back to her brother. He was trembling. He set his jaw and spoke in a shaky voice, pausing after each syllable. "You are a whore."

Sun had never heard the word before but knew exactly what it meant. She lowered her head as hot tears streamed unchecked down her cheeks. "I'm sorry, Brother. I didn't mean ..." One glance at Jae's scowl silenced her protests.

"You have disgraced your family. You have disgraced me." He spat on her bowed head. She covered her ears. This couldn't be happening. Not now. Not when she was so close to getting away. All she wanted was to go home. To go home and forget she had ever stepped foot across the border or heard of the Round Robin Inn.

"You are no sister of mine." His voice was low and controlled, like a wild dog warning off a rival. "You think I came here to bring you back? I would never allow a promiscuous pig like you from the hotel district to take a single step into my mother's home."

Sun sank her fingers deep into her hair and tugged at the clumps while silent sobs wracked her entire body. "Please, forgive me!"

Mee-Kyong stepped forward. "I'm not sure you understand." Sun sniffed once and then froze. Mee-Kyong's words were logical. Calm. Maybe she could help.

"You stay out of this, wench." Jae pulled a rope out of the back of his pants with one hand and made a fist with his other.

Mee-Kyong took another step between him and Sun. "Your sister hasn't done anything wrong."

"Shut up." Sun hid her face but heard the crunch of Jae's fist on her friend's cheek. Mee-Kyong stumbled into the side of the bed and grasped her bound ribcage.

Sun reached for her brother's arm. "She's only trying to help," she shrieked. They had all been so loud, Sun wondered why the security guards weren't already there.

Jae glared at her. "One more word out of you, and I'll ..." Sun jumped when Mee-Kyong brought the lamp down on Jae's back. He turned and raised his rope toward her throat. Sun had to stop them. She flung herself onto her brother's back, flailing her arms wildly to try to snatch the weapon away. She froze when Mee-Kyong picked up the knife from the bed.

For one horrible second, nobody moved. Sun's only thought was to keep her brother away from her friend. Mee-Kyong was protective. Too protective. Jae wasn't really about to hurt her. Sun wanted to tell her to put the knife down, but she couldn't find her voice.

She felt Jae's muscles tense a split second before he lunged for the blade. It happened so quickly, she didn't even have the chance to cry out. She held on tight to Jae's shoulders as Mee-Kyong whizzed the knife through the air. Where were the guards? Why weren't they here yet? Sun gasped as she fell off Jae's back. She knew she should scream. She should make them both stop fighting before someone got hurt. Maybe if she could seize the knife herself ...

Mee-Kyong repositioned the weapon, and Sun bolted towards it. Jae reached it first, knocking Sun onto the mattress. Mee-Kyong cried out as Jae yanked the weapon out of her hand and slashed it toward the bed. Everything was so chaotic Sun didn't know she was cut until both Mee-Kyong and Jae froze. Mee-Kyong gawked down at her with a ghastly pale face. Her jaw hung open in an inaudible gasp.

Sun put her hand to her neck. Sticky blood soaked her fingers with the first sputtering pulse. She opened her mouth to speak, but found that she had no breath. Jae took one step closer, his entire body trembling. Sweat beaded on his forehead where a bluish vein popped up beneath the skin. His face was contorted, and Sun saw the torture she had caused him etched on each wrinkle. "Forgive me," she wanted to whisper, but she couldn't find the air.

***

Mee-Kyong gawked down at the bed as the dirty white sheets turned a familiar shade of deep red. With a wail that sounded more like a shriek than a sob, she sprang onto Sun's brother, ignoring the pain in her side. "What did you do?"

They fell to the ground. Mee-Kyong made a grab for the knife, barely escaping the blade as it sliced through the air toward her. She punched Sun's brother in the gut then grasped her bandaged side. Jae lunged, ripping the low-cut red dress she was wearing. He stood up, and she cried out in pain as she sprang at one of his legs.

"I'll kill you for this!" she shouted. Jae gave one final kick to free his leg and leaped out the door. Mee-Kyong stumbled into the hallway in time to see him disappear down the stairwell. One of the other worker girls dressed in a fake silk robe opened her door and peeked out. Mee-Kyong growled at her, and the door quickly shut.

Crawling back to the room, Mee-Kyong fumbled to Sun's bed, tossed aside the discarded rope, and hoisted herself up. Panting, she leaned over the child. Sun lay sprawled on her back, her mouth open. Mee-Kyong picked up her limp wrist and waited for a silent eternity. She gawked at the puddle of blood beneath the child's neck and swept the unruly bangs out of her eyes.

"I'm sorry, little cousin."

A minute later, Mee-Kyong let go of the makeshift rope and stumbled to the sidewalk. The wind stung her face, whipping strands of hair against her skin. Tears nipped the corners of her eyes, but she blinked them away. Crying had never helped anyone.

It wouldn't help her now. Mee-Kyong tilted her face toward the wind. The red dress was torn. The knife had grazed her skin without causing any real damage. She was exhausted, and her injuries kept her traveling at an impossibly slow speed. She continued on, stopping every minute or so, wincing as she caught her breath. Several times she adjusted the wrapping Sun made for her, but she could never get it as tight as she needed.

How could things have gone so wrong? Mr. Lee was dead. She and Sun could have escaped. Mee-Kyong didn't know where they would have gone, but she would have found a place. She would have kept them both alive. Why had Sun's brother come? Her stomach churned. She had to get herself away, but she longed for rest. Rest and something hot to drink. There wasn't much she wouldn't give in exchange for a blanket to wrap up in.

Shut up, spoiled brat. Did you have extra blankets and tea in the gulag? Mee-Kyong kept moving. She had to survive. She owed that much to Sun.

CHAPTER 29

Roger had better things to do tonight than fight with his wife. Like sleep. "All I said was I don't trust him," he said, frowning as he put on his pajamas.

Juliette studied her husband from over the top of her lenses. "Think he's undercover?"

Roger tugged on the drawstring of his silk pants. "Probably not. But he was hiding something."

Juliette took off her glasses. "Benjamin sent him. That's got to count for something."

"You already know how I feel about Benjamin."

"If you can't trust your own security guard, then why don't you fire him?" she retorted.

Roger shrugged. "He's yet another one of your pets. Far be it from me to get in the way of you and your mission to win the Nobel Peace Prize one starving refugee at a time."

Juliette turned her head sharply, and her curls whipped across her cheek. "It's more meaningful than printing baby board books all day, isn't it?" Roger waved his hand like he was trying to rid himself of a pesky mosquito. Juliette crossed her arms. "So what are we going to do about Mr. Lost Sister?"

"What do you mean, '*What are we going to do?*'"

"Well, if Benjamin thought to send him to us, he obviously needs something."

"Then why didn't Benjamin help him out? I'm sure a vigorous young man like him knows the way to the hotel district."

Juliette sucked in her breath. "Benjamin is a hard-working, big loveable teddy bear. And he's a Christian."

152

"What's that got to do with it?" Roger muttered.

"You have no reason to doubt that boy."

He pressed his temples. "I don't know. I'm tired, it's been a long night. Let's just get some sleep."

He rolled onto his side, but Juliette remained sitting up in bed and tugged on his shoulder. "So you're just going to forget this guy ever came to our door, is that it?"

Roger turned toward his wife but didn't sit up again. "Look, if he needs more help, he's welcome to come back to us. We can assess his needs just like any other refugee and figure out what we can do for him. Does that make you happy? Can we go to sleep now, please?"

She yanked her brush through her hair. "And you don't think it's slightly strange that a mere few hours after you promise to pray about resuming our rescue ministry in the hotel district, a young man comes to our door, asking us to help him find his lost sister?"

Roger squeezed his eyes shut. His head was throbbing. "He didn't ask us to help him find her. He just asked for some clothes so he wouldn't get arrested the moment the police laid eyes on him." He turned off the lamp on his side of the bed and waited for his wife to do the same. He needed to be up early to take care of his paperwork for the month. He didn't have time or energy to waste arguing all night long.

Juliette, however, didn't seem to care. "I still think if you were more open-minded to this whole thing then you'd at least consider that this guy's visit might be Providence. I mean, you were asking God to give you a sign, weren't you?"

Roger huffed. "Baby Cakes, can we just talk about this more in the morning?" He tried to soften his words. "I'm tired. We're both grumpy. I already told you I'd pray about this, but I can't even do that if we spend the whole night bickering. Think about Eve. She's probably heard every word we've said."

"That's nothing new." Juliette was going at it so hard with her brush, Roger wondered if she'd have any hair left by the time their argument was over. "I just think we should have gone with that boy. Followed him. Helped him look around."

"When you say 'we,' I assume you mean *me*. That's what bugs me the most about this whole brothel-rescue business. You're welcome to fill your free time with any type of ministry you set your heart on, but you've been fixating on brothel ministry since you and Eve started talking about it, and that kind of work eats up a whole chunk of my time, time I don't have if I'm to keep running this printing business to put our daughter through eight full years at Harvard."

"I just have this nagging feeling about it." Juliette finally put down her brush and collapsed on the bed. Roger knew what it was like to have a nagging feeling, but he kept his mouth shut. The sooner they finished talking, the sooner he could get some sleep. He scooted down on his pillow and wrapped the comforter around his body. When his eyes were closed, he heard the creaking of springs. Juliette swung her legs over the side of the bed.

"What are you doing now?"

"I'm going downstairs."

Roger rolled his eyes. "What do you think you're going to do?"

"I'll figure something out." Juliette slammed the door behind her. Roger pulled the comforter up to his chin and sighed.

***

Juliette spent twenty minutes opening cupboards and then closing them again. Whenever she reached the end of the row, she went back to the beginning and repeated the entire mindless procedure. Roger wouldn't recognize a sign from God if it fell down from heaven and split open his thick skull. It was bad enough her husband just stood by while she was accosted by a homeless bum. Now he was sitting back, doing absolutely nothing when there was a poor girl who needed rescuing just a few kilometers away. Roger had said he would ask God for confirmation. What did he think tonight's visitor was — just some pickled cabbage?

Juliette slammed the pantry door a little harder than she meant to. "Nothing to eat?" Roger's voice was sharp. She turned around, but her retort was surprised out of her when she saw him zip up his coat.

"What are you doing?" Juliette demanded.

"I thought God already told you. There's a girl out there in trouble. Who better to risk his reputation to find her than me? If you're lucky, I'll have a new brothel babe for you to adopt by morning. Wouldn't that be sweet of me?"

Juliette glanced down at him over her glasses. "Are you really serious?"

"You said you wanted me to rescue a girl. Well, here I go. I'm off to rescue a girl." Roger strode past, swaying his arms in exaggerated arches.

"You're not worried about the managers recognizing you?" Juliette wondered if she should go after him.

"Oh, I'm plenty worried." He paused and flung his hands out to his sides. "Last time I was there, they threatened to castrate me if I remember right. But you know, my wife can be a very persuasive woman. And it seems like God has it out for me, too, because he sent a messenger tonight to tell me how right you were. We're supposed to jump back into brothel rescues only two weeks after sending out the Secret Seminary graduates. You were absolutely correct. I just wish I had realized it as soon as you did." Roger doffed an imaginary hat and feigned a bow.

"You're really going to the hotel district? Now?" Juliette leaned against the counter. Should she take him up to bed?

"That's absolutely right. Because far be it from me to ignore the call of God himself, who was so considerate to pass his marching orders on to you first. Don't worry. I'll be home in time to get ready for work first thing in the morning, if the hotel managers don't call the police to arrest me on sight, that is."

Roger marched himself out the door into the dark night. Juliette gawked after him, her hand still on one of the open cupboard doors.

***

Agent Ko made sure nobody could overhear before dialing the number for headquarters. "It's me. I'm scheduled to check in with the director."

"Hi there, Ko. The director said you might call in today."

"Chun-Hee?" Ko thought about ending the call right then.

"You recognized my voice. How touching."

"How could I forget? It's got that squealing-pig quality that's so endearing."

"Nice one. Well, how are things? I'm just dying to hear how that little security guard from Yanji is doing." Chun-Hee's voice dripped with sarcasm, but Ko wouldn't be baited.

"Digging fences. Not much else."

"You must get terribly bored," Chun-Hee sang out in a nasally tone. "How long do you think the director plans to keep you there?"

"As long as my country needs me."

"That's right," Chun-Hee taunted melodically. "Serving the Party one tray of tea at a time. Not quite what we expected when we were at the Academy together, I'd dare wager."

Training with Chun-Hee was the last thing Ko wanted to think about. "Does the director have any messages for me?"

"Just one. He says to tell you they found the spy named Simon. I take it you knew him?"

Ko smiled inwardly but wouldn't gloat. Not now. There would be time for that later. "Yeah. Anything else?"

"Not officially. You can go back to caring for your little American family. And call me if you ever get in trouble, all right? For old time's sake. It'll be just like the Academy."

Ko punched the button to end the call before Chun-Hee could say anything else.

CHAPTER 30

Roger rubbed his thinning hair. Why had he let his wife talk him into this? What had he been thinking? With the house empty now, he had encouraged Juliette to spend some time on herself, to pursue some of the hobbies she had always put off when their daughter was little. She had often expressed interest in creating her own line of children's picture books, and Roger even offered to turn the den into an artist's studio. But she wanted something more. She needed people. People she could teach. People she could talk to. People she could nurture and watch grow. Roger couldn't offer that, not out of thin air. And so here he was, on the outskirts of the hotel district. And what was he supposed to do — ask around to see if someone's nameless sister was working behind any of the curtained windows?

Another reason he had been so reluctant to go along with Juliette's plan was because he knew what it would do to their relationship. He was sure Juliette would deny it if he ever found the guts to bring it up, but her temperament changed each and every time he got back from the brothel, whether his visit had been a success or not. She held herself a little higher around him, resisted his advances with an abnormal coolness. And even though he'd never admit it out loud, Roger always needed a few days after his visits before he could just fall back into his regular marital routine.

With his hands in his pockets, he glowered at the puddles on the ground. What did Juliette expect would happen? A trapped girl would lean out of the window, waving a flag and shouting, "Rescue me! Rescue me!"? He had no business being out this late. He had work to do in the morning. Work he couldn't complete if he spent his evenings prancing up and down the hotel district, hoping for some needy damsel to fall from the sky.

Roger glared at his watch. He had waited long enough. He turned toward home, hoping Juliette's mid-life crisis wouldn't translate into more sleepless nights in the hotel district. She really needed to find some other sort of diversion: yoga, Sudoku, anything. In the chilly autumn air, Roger toyed with the idea of buying her a puppy. Maybe that would satisfy her need to be useful and loved, at least for a little while. He blew on his hands to keep them warm. Would it even be worth trying to sleep once he got home? The orders at the office kept pouring in, and Roger was behind on paperwork. He wished Juliette tackled secretarial duties with the same zeal she bestowed on the desperate and downtrodden.

He thought about her behavior when the young man came to their home earlier that night. It was a perfect example of how Juliette's passion was a nuisance at best and a danger at worst. If that refugee hadn't come around with his sob story of his lost sister, she would have fallen asleep, her tummy full of hot chocolate, her conscience easy. And then Roger could have nabbed some sleep, too.

Sleep. He'd be lucky if he got three hours by morning. He wrapped his coat tight around his chest and strained against the wind. He was out of the main district now, where the street lights weren't as close together. He turned once to glance over his shoulder and for a moment wished he wasn't out here alone. A vague form stumbled across the street. He stopped beneath a street lamp and strained his eyes.

She dragged herself along in slow motion, a shadow in a short-fitting dress. She stumbled toward an alleyway. Roger studied his surroundings. The streets were deserted. If she had looked behind, if she had made any indication she noticed him, Roger would know it was a setup — a trap meant to lure compassionate foreigners. He would be wary, but he would at least check to make sure she was all right. A young girl alone on the streets on a night like this … Roger thought about his daughter back in the States and shivered from the chill. He quickened his pace as he crossed the street.

***

Mee-Kyong collapsed in the dark passageway. She didn't know how far she had walked, but she must be at least a kilometer or more away from the Round Robin by now. She slid herself to the ground, sucking in cold air through her teeth.

She had nothing, just Sun's old torn dress. She had rushed so fast out of the building, she left the bundle of clothes behind. For the hundredth time or more, she recalled each feature of the murderer's face. *Jae.* Sun called him Jae. Mee-Kyong wouldn't forget. But now, she just needed rest. With goose bumps dancing up and down her arms, she hugged herself. She wouldn't even try to lie down. Not tonight. The injury to her ribs was no worse than what she had experienced with Pang. In two or three days, the searing pain would turn to soreness. A week or so after that, and she would feel almost back to normal. At least she would be able to breathe again without feeling like she would pass out.

Her entire body begged for sleep, but whenever she closed her eyes, she saw those blood-stained sheets. She wished she could stop shivering — it only made the pain in her rib that much worse.

"Can I help you?"

Mee-Kyong jerked at the sound. The movement sent another wave of anguish racing up her side. She grimaced and did what she could to scoot away from the stranger. The man spoke with an accent. He was tall. Tall and well-dressed.

He reached a hand down to her. "Looks like you could use a more comfortable place to sleep."

160

Mee-Kyong didn't say anything. From a distant streetlamp, she made out the man's Western features.

He bent down, frowning into her face. "You're injured." It wasn't a question. "Come with me." He wrapped one arm around her and placed his hand under her elbow before raising her to her feet. The pain stole her sight away for a second, and she felt her head droop forward with dizziness. Nearly unconscious from exhaustion, she was powerless to resist.

***

Juliette leaned back against her pillow and nibbled on some dark chocolate. She thought about what she might tell her more uppity church friends back home about the night she sent Roger off to the brothel. Imagining their painted, upturned eyebrows, she let out a soft laugh, although she doubted her husband would recognize the humor in the situation right now.

She hadn't spent much time that day in prayer, so to make up for her neglect she went through all the names on her usual list. She didn't want to focus on the Secret Seminary students, not this late at night. She would pray for them in the morning. First, she thought about Eve. The housekeeper had been much more subdued ever since the Sterns started talking in earnest about resuming work in the brothels. Was she thinking about the friends she left behind? After their initial conversation, Juliette tried every once in a while to ask again about her experiences in the hotel district, but Eve never answered more than a few words. Finally, Juliette gave up. Some things were too painful to relive through conversation. Juliette understood that much, at least.

She sighed and wondered what to say to Roger when he returned. He would be angry, no doubt. What had she been thinking, letting him go out alone? She shook her head. With enough luck and some extra prayer, maybe one day they would both remember tonight and laugh.

Juliette heard footsteps and only had a few seconds to tuck her chocolate bar behind her pillow before Roger came in. She put on a duly repentant pout and turned toward the door. She forgot all about her rehearsed apology when she saw his grin.

"Honey, put your chocolate away. I brought you a present."

***

Her stomach warmed with the American's tea, Mee-Kyong stretched out on the bed. The pink cotton sheets caressed her skin like a hot, velvety bath. She loosened her bandage a little and let out a small sigh.

She still wasn't sure what she had gotten herself into. The well-dressed American had said very little to her as he led her, or sometimes even carried her, back to his house. A mansion, really. Inside, everything smelled of lemons and pine. At first, she assumed it was just an upscale version of the Round Robin, and she couldn't understand why the proprietor would choose someone battered and torn, her youth already dried up. When she saw the American's wife, Mee-Kyong knew this wasn't like any brothel she had ever heard of. There were plenty of bedrooms, but most of them were empty from what she could tell. The woman hadn't said much, but she kept looking at Mee-Kyong with a strange, self-satisfied smile. Mee-Kyong didn't know what to expect when she woke up the next day. For now, she was content with a pillow, a blanket, and a bed. Everything else could sort itself out later.

PART 4

CHAPTER 31

As soon as she woke up, Mee-Kyong's fingers worked their way over to her belly and began their meticulous scratching. She wasn't nearly as swollen as she had been right after the delivery — Mr. Lee's rations at the Round Robin had made sure of that. She pried her eyelids open. The walls of the bedroom were painted a clean, soft shade of pink. A window curtain with frilly white laces did nothing to block out the late-morning sun that cast horizontal shadows across the bed. She winced as she sat up, convincing herself the wetness in the corners of her eyes came from the bright light, not the pain. She pressed her hand over her side and looked down. The long flannel nightgown bore no resemblance to her uniform in the prison camp or her usual attire at the Round Robin. A warm, soapy smell wafted up from its cotton creases. Across from her stood an open closet where Sun's red dress hung up like a monument.

Sun.

You heartless fool. Did your soft pillow and warm tea make you forget? Her fingers dug into the skin of her abdomen, tugging, poking, prodding, peeling. She didn't stop until she drew blood. Then she curled up her fingers and studied the red mess beneath her nails. *Red puddle on a dirty white sheet.* She inhaled deeply, welcoming the torment in her side, daring it to knock her senseless.

Sun.

Mee-Kyong's shoulders heaved. The fire from her injured rib raced through her veins all the way down to her filthy, blood-crusted fingernails. She slapped away a tear that threatened to streak down her cheek. *You didn't have the courage to save her while she was alive. You're not worthy to cry for her now.*

She assaulted her belly, etching scars across her skin in rhythm with her convulsing shoulders. She hated that girl. She hated the delicate frailty that begged for protection, the vulnerability that made those around her feel so powerless. Mee-Kyong had never felt so weak before, not even in the gulag. She hated Sun for dying, for having a brother who loved her enough to work out his twisted vengeance on her delicate, wispy body.

The brother. Mee-Kyong stopped scratching and forced herself to remember that face. She gritted her teeth. *Don't ever forget.* Ignoring her wet cheeks now, Mee-Kyong recalled his angular profile, his eyebrows that sloped down spitefully. She clenched her fingers into two trembling fists and vowed if she ever met him, if she ever came across that merciless beast again, he would die for what he did.

***

Juliette wouldn't entrust this morning's cooking to anyone else. She ordered Eve to take the day off and forced the girl outside to take a walk. Sometimes Juliette forgot Eve could go days — maybe even weeks — without leaving the house if nobody was paying attention. Juliette liked to do her own shopping in the marketplace where all the Korean-Chinese vendors congregated. It kept her language skills sharp when her ears were bombarded with dozens of conversations going on at once, and frankly, she hated being cooped up in that huge empty house all the time. She didn't always remember her housekeeper had the same needs for fresh air and time alone, and she couldn't even guess the last time Eve went out.

Juliette thought about the way her husband would tease her if he knew how high in her chest her heart was fluttering this morning. At least, she hoped he would tease her. When he came back from the hotel district, Roger seemed jovial enough, but for weeks Juliette had acted like a spoiled, pampered toddler, throwing fits until everyone around her caved in to her wishes. Could she blame him if he was still perturbed?

At least God had answered her prayers, though. If God really wanted them to get back into hotel district rescues, then that refugee who came to their door last night really was a sign from heaven. Which meant the girl in Kennedy's old room upstairs was sent directly from the Almighty himself. So why was Juliette in such a panic?

"What have you gotten into now?" she muttered to herself, cracking an egg into a pan along with half the shell. She didn't know if she should smile or cry. What had she been thinking? She and Roger weren't young anymore. They were middle-aged by every definition of the term. Their friends back in the States were going on vacation cruises and golfing five times a week. Some were just a year or two away from retirement. Why couldn't Juliette have picked some other charitable passion — like donating collections to local libraries or something?

The front door opened. Juliette wondered if Roger had decided to stop by the house. It would certainly help her know where things stood between them. Last night, they had both fallen asleep almost immediately after getting the rescued girl settled in her room, but Juliette wasn't sure if it was because they were both so tired or if they were avoiding each other. He left before she woke up in the morning, which didn't bode well. She strained her ears. "That you, honey?"

"It's just me." Eve peered around the kitchen corner, and Juliette forced her lips upward.

"I'm glad you're back. Did you have a nice walk?"

Eve nodded and looked around. "Everything smells good."

"Well, I hope our guest likes it." Juliette stopped and studied her housekeeper. "You know, I never really asked you how you feel about … well, I mean … last night, we were just so overwhelmed that we kind of forgot … I guess I'm just wondering …"

"How I feel with a former brothel girl living here?" Eve finished. Juliette nodded, flustered. Eve shrugged. "I guess I'll know once I meet her."

***

Mee-Kyong lay on her side, her face dry, her ribcage bound up even tighter with the linen strips Sun had cut for her. For the first time in weeks, she thought about the baby she had delivered a lifetime ago in Onsong, his wrinkled gray skin, his perfectly-formed fingers. She forced out small, shallow breaths and scratched tiny circles on her abdomen with her nail. She became vaguely conscious of a tapping outside her room but didn't acknowledge it. A moment later, the door teetered open. Mee-Kyong didn't move.

"I think she's still asleep." Mee-Kyong recognized the distinctive voice of the American woman. It wasn't quite an accent, but a certain peculiarity she had picked up on last night while her hostess bustled about making tea.

Someone else spoke. "No, her eyes are open." Mee-Kyong didn't recognize the voice and tensed her shoulders. "See," the girl said, "she's awake."

Mee-Kyong made herself sit up and nodded at the American who stood in the doorway holding a dainty little tray. In her periphery, she sized up the young woman standing next to her. "I'm awake." She addressed the American but focused on the other, keenly aware she was being assessed with the same degree of scrutiny.

The American sauntered in, and the floor creaked slightly under her weight. "We thought you might like some breakfast."

Her voice was far too chipper for so early in the morning.

Mee-Kyong reached out for the tray. "Thank you." After an awkward silence, the younger woman retreated, and the older one lowered herself onto the side of the bed, her sublime smile complementing the glossy look in her eyes. Mee-Kyong took a sip of tea, wondering what kind of house these people ran and what price they would charge her for her stay. The woman watched her eat.

"My husband would probably make me leave you alone and give you some privacy, but I just can't tell you enough how glad I am you came here. My name's Mrs. Stern, by the way. I don't know if my husband mentioned that last night when you …"

She stopped. Mee-Kyong was too hungry to pay much attention to what she said.

"Anyway, you're here now, and that's what matters." The American woman prattled on while Mee-Kyong ate her breakfast. Mrs. Stern acted like Mee-Kyong had done her household some magnificent service by showing up on their doorstep, battered and exhausted. In reality, Mee-Kyong couldn't even remember if the man last night had asked her to come with him or just carried her to his home. It was the events leading up to her escape she remembered so clearly.

"You don't need to tell me a thing about what you did." Mrs. Stern's voice quivered with sugary concern, setting Mee-Kyong's teeth on edge nearly as much as the sweetened tea. "I just want you to know that's all behind you now. It's not part of who you are today, and it doesn't have to play any part in who you become. The past is a closed book here."

Mee-Kyong didn't recognize the foreign phrase but sensed the woman's altruistic intentions. Were Americans really so ignorant that they reached adulthood with such a nauseating display of optimism still intact?

"I know you've been through a lot." Mrs. Stern reached her bejeweled fingers out to caress the back of Mee-Kyong's hand, hesitating only a moment as they hovered over her blood-encrusted nails. "You were so worn out last night I was sure you just needed sleep, but now that you're rested, we have a nice hot tub down the hall, and you can take as long as you'd like."

Mee-Kyong nodded, her mind screaming for solitude. She had spent the entire conversation with Mrs. Stern absorbing as much nonverbal information about her hostess as she could, and now she was exhausted. "A bath would be nice." Mee-Kyong set her teacup on the flowered tray as gracefully as possible, while visions flashed in her memory of Sun's hair billowing up in the tub around her.

***

Benjamin splashed water on his face, hoping the cold spray would clear his mind. He rinsed his mouth and stared into the porcelain as the drops splattered into the sink. He wiped the top of his brow, his body swaying slightly from the weight of his throbbing head.

He thought about the young man he brought to the Sterns' the night before. Had they taken him in? He listened but only heard a slight shuffling upstairs, probably Eve or Mrs. Stern getting ready for the day. He dried his face on the towel, letting the coarse fuzz scrape against his skin. He shut his eyes once, and the sound of metal clanking against metal echoed in his mind. *Not now. No, please, not now.* He leaned forward and held onto both sides of the sink, sucking in a deep, desperate breath.

A scream. A man's pitiful plea for mercy. Benjamin felt his innards descend and sit heavy on the base of his spine. He reached out his hand to splash more water on his face. He felt the wetness and remembered the blood. *So much blood ... dripping off his hands, staining his chest, splattering on the cement walls. "It's not my fault,"* Benjamin whispered to himself. *"I was just following orders."* The agony continued to drag him down the haunted corridors of his memory. Benjamin would have never guessed a grown man could squeal so loudly. His stomach churned. He forced his eyes open, gasping like a fish abandoned on the shore. He cupped his hands under the faucet and drank heavily.

"Jesus is my Redeemer." He repeated the phrase Mr. Stern taught him to ward off his attacks. "Jesus is my Redeemer." The shrieking stopped, its sound replaced by the impatient water flow from the sink. The dingy cement walls dissolved, and again he was surrounded by the Sterns' familiar off-white wallpaper.

If Jesus could bring about such great deliverance, as his employers always claimed, why was Benjamin still a slave to these waking nightmares?

CHAPTER 32

"I'm telling you, she's positively delightful."

Delightful wasn't the word Roger would have chosen for their new guest, but he grunted at the appropriate times as Juliette flitted around the kitchen, taking down at least twice as many ingredients from the cupboards as she actually put into the pan. A dash of this, a pinch of that. Chocolate powder smudged one of her cheeks right below her glasses frames.

"So things went well?" Roger leaned against the countertop, thankful for the chance to stretch his legs after a ten-hour day behind his desk.

For the past several weeks, Juliette had answered Roger's questions in monosyllables. Now, she wouldn't stop jabbering. "Well, she slept in pretty late, but I finally brought her breakfast around eleven. We had a little — just a minute, really — chat over tea, and then she must have taken an hour in that bath tub. She spent the rest of the afternoon in her room, but she said she'd join us for dinner, and I just can't wait for you to see her. She actually fits fairly well in some of Kennedy's old things. You've got to cinch up the belt quite a bit, but I think she's cleaned up nicely since you found her last night."

Roger studied his wife. Her face was lit up with a radiant glow and glistened with tiny drops of sweat as she labored over the stove. He couldn't remember the last time she had made such a mess in the kitchen. "Where's Eve?" He hadn't seen their housekeeper all evening.

"Oh, I told her to take the day off. She's been working so hard keeping me company lately, you know. I started to feel really

171

guilty for hogging up all her time. I think she's in her room. At least, I haven't seen her since I started cooking."

"Strange." Roger couldn't remember the last time Eve had stayed away from his wife. Even on Sundays, which were supposed to be her day to relax, she waited on the Sterns with the exact same puppy-dog dedication as on any other day of the week.

Juliette chopped up a garlic clove and uncovered some meat on a platter. "Everyone needs time off every once in a while."

Roger inhaled deeply. It was kind of pleasant coming home to his own wife in their own kitchen, just the two of them. He smiled. "Remember that vacation in Mexico when we tried to save money by eating-in every night?" Roger waited for his wife to smile at the memory. He put his arms around her from behind and breathed in the fresh scent of her curls.

"I hope Mee-Kyong likes chicken." Juliette reached up for one of the carving knives, and Roger let go.

"I'm going to wash up before we eat." He glanced back once while his wife hacked at the raw meat on the cutting board and doubted she'd even realize he was gone.

***

While she ate, Mee-Kyong glanced at the Americans' security guard seated across from her. His palms alone were probably larger than Mee-Kyong's face, and his demeanor reminded her of the officers she had encountered back at Camp 22. He hadn't said a word all meal. Gauging from the way he kept his eyes to his plate and fidgeted with those massive hands, she guessed he was hired more for his body size than intellect.

The Sterns' housekeeper looked just as out of place as she slouched in her chair next to Mee-Kyong, prompting Mrs. Stern to ask after her health every few minutes. Eve mumbled into her plate, "It's just a headache. Nothing to worry over."

In an exhausting display of verbosity, Mrs. Stern managed the conversation even with such a mismatched, sullen group. Unfortunately, she spent most of dinner talking directly to Mee-Kyong. "If you had arrived just a few weeks earlier, you would have had the chance to meet our daughter."

Several times during their morning meeting over tea, Mrs. Stern had assured Mee-Kyong there was no need to talk about her history. *"Your past is a closed book, and I'm not going to browse through the pages without invitation."* Mee-Kyong suspected behind the catchphrase was the expectation that in time she *would* invite Mrs. Stern to "browse the pages" of her short, pathetic life story, but for now, she intended to enjoy her well-earned right to privacy.

Mrs. Stern, by contrast, had no problem divulging more information about her own family than anyone would care to digest in a single sitting. Mee-Kyong's temples throbbed. The food was far richer than what she was accustomed to, and she had to fight the urge to devour every morsel in sight. Even the slightest swelling in her belly put extra pressure on her ribcage. As hard as she tried, she still couldn't figure out exactly what type of home this was. Who were these do-gooders, and what would they demand in return for room and board?

When Mrs. Stern was halfway through the story of their only daughter's seventh birthday party, her husband put his hand over hers. "Perhaps our guest would like some more water." He gestured subtly to Mee-Kyong's empty cup.

"Of course." Mrs. Stern stood up, nearly taking the cloth covering the table with her due to her wide girth. Before she made her way to the kitchen, the housekeeper overtook her.

"I'll get it, ma'am."

"It's really no problem," insisted the American. "Thank you anyway, but I don't mind."

Eve put her hand on Mrs. Stern's shoulder — a bold gesture

for a servant, in Mee-Kyong's opinion. "Please." There wasn't a trace of humility or questioning in the housekeeper's voice. "Allow me."

***

"So you had a good day, then?" Roger stretched his legs out on the bed and unbuttoned the top of his pants. He sighed and let his stuffed belly expand to a more comfortable diameter.

Juliette swung her head to the side as she brushed her hair, and Roger noticed how long it had grown lately. "Yeah. It was fun to have the kitchen to myself for a change."

"You know you'll be having even less time to yourself now that the new girl's here."

"Mee-Kyong," Juliette inserted.

Roger already knew her name but didn't want to spoil Juliette's mood by saying so. He hadn't seen his wife this chipper in months. If it would keep Juliette this content, he was willing to forget all about their late-night spats, their frequent arguing, their accident-prone floundering through the waters of empty-nesting. "She seems like a very nice girl." Roger didn't know if he believed the words himself yet, but as he finished dressing for bed, he decided to capitalize on Juliette's good humor as much as he could.

"She will be." Juliette put her brush down and joined Roger in bed.

"What's that supposed to mean?" Roger asked.

She snuggled herself up against him. "It means she's been through a lot, but with the right kind of love and direction, I think she'll end up just fine." Juliette made their new guest sound like some kind of meringue pie that had to be treated just a certain way in order to turn out right in the end, but Roger didn't say so. It didn't matter. Juliette was herself again. She had eaten more than flimsy greens for dinner, she had a new project to invest her time and energy into, and she wasn't constantly badgering Roger about going back to the hotel district. He breathed in deeply and shut his eyes.

Yes, life was good.

CHAPTER 33

"So your little protégé's lessons are coming along nicely, I assume?" Roger yanked the blanket off the bed. If he couldn't find his watch soon, he'd have to leave for work without it.

Juliette groped underneath the pillow. "Yeah. This week more than last. She seems to be picking things up pretty well."

"I sense there's a *but* there." Roger got down on his hands and knees and rummaged through a small pile of dirty clothes.

"No, she's doing really well. She can answer back just about anything I ask her now. And she's even coming up with questions on her own, like she's really engaging with the material."

"That must be because she has such a good teacher." Roger glanced at the clock on his bedside table. He should have been out the door at least fifteen minutes ago.

Juliette fumbled through the dresser drawers, scattering socks and underwear across the carpet. "I'm just excited. She seems like she's really getting it."

"Have you talked to her about being baptized yet?" *Where was that watch?* It's not like Roger couldn't make it through his work day without it; he just wanted to know what could have happened to it. He placed it on his end table every single night before bed.

"I mentioned baptism once. She didn't respond right away, and I didn't want to rush anything."

Roger stood up and ran his hands over the top of his head. "You, not rushing anything? What's happened here? It's been a few weeks since you took her under your wings. Are you going through chocolate withdrawals from all that dieting?"

Juliette's reflection in the dresser mirror smiled at him. *Man, was she gorgeous.* "I just don't want to push anything on her too fast," she confessed.

"Too fast? You guys are in there, what? Four, five hours each and every day?"

"It's not like that. I just want to be careful, you know?"

"Baby Cakes, last time we had a batch of refugees come through our doors, you practically had them baptized before they finished their first meal, and you signed them all up for underground mission work before breakfast the next day. What's going on?"

Juliette steadied herself on the dresser with both arms and frowned at his reflected image. Suddenly, he noticed the gray in her hair, the wrinkle in her brow, the telling signs of her age. "I don't want to see her ..." Juliette's throat constricted once. "I don't want to worry about her. Like I do with the others."

It took Roger only three paces to close the distance between him and his wife, but she was trembling by the time he arrived. Roger had been so busy at work, he hadn't thought much about the Secret Seminary students. Sure, he hoped they were doing all right, but other than at his regular prayer times, he tried not to give them much thought. It was the best way he had found to deal with the uncertainties, the nagging doubts, the guilt that threatened to creep in if left unchecked. He had, after all, sent some of the finest young believers he knew to what could very well be their deaths.

Roger had learned to tune out his emotions. He prayed for the students and knew their destinies were in God's hands, and God's alone. Of course, he should have realized his wife could never reach that same degree of detachment. This was Juliette, the woman who choked up at sappy black-and-white romances. He patted her back, feeling pitifully inadequate to address the anxiety, the fear he knew his wife was shouldering alone.

"This isn't the Secret Seminary anymore." His whispered assurances sounded weak and formulaic, even to his own ears. "No one's asking us to send Mee-Kyong anywhere."

***

Eve could hear her employers rummaging in their room, but she didn't make any move to get out of bed. It was too warm under the heavy quilt. She stretched her legs out and yawned. It had been another late night with Tiger, and she wasn't looking forward to a full day of cooking, cleaning, and pretending to care about her mistress's constant prattle. After eating two candy bars, Tiger had whined and moaned about not seeing her enough. Maybe now that Mrs. Stern was so caught up with her new brothel rescue, their visits could pick up again. She knew her relationship with Tiger wasn't perfect, but their time together helped her forget certain other things.

"You should find a new job," he suggested when she complained about how boring housekeeping was. He quizzed her again about the Americans, about the "students" who had lived with them until recently, about any cash or valuables her bosses kept around the house. "If you could only find out where all their money's stored, we could run away and get married."

They had both laughed at the absurdity of the idea.

***

"I just can't believe Mee-Kyong would do something like steal a watch." Juliette pulled out the end table by Roger's side of the bed and peered behind it again. He was wrong. The watch was around here somewhere. She was certain of it.

Roger rummaged through the shelves in the closet. "You can't judge what somebody is or isn't capable of after just a few weeks."

178

Juliette banged her head when she straightened up. "I'm telling you, I've been spending hours with her every day, and she's not the kind of person to steal something. That's all I'm saying."

"Then who else was it?" Roger dumped a pile of shirts on the bed. He probably wanted them ironed by evening, too. Juliette was glad his back was to her so he couldn't see her roll her eyes. He continued assaulting the clothes in the closet. "Eve and Benjamin have both been here over a year. If they were the kind to steal, we would have figured it out by now."

Juliette frowned. Everything had been going so perfectly. Mee-Kyong was learning every day, answering all of Juliette's questions. She hadn't complained once about the Scripture copying, a valuable but time-consuming spiritual discipline. She was a model houseguest and eager student. Roger was petty and prejudiced to accuse her of stealing. Juliette only had to make him realize that. "Just because she's a whore, that doesn't make her a thief, does it?"

Roger hung up a shirt he was holding, taking time to straighten it out impeccably. "I'm not the one calling Mee-Kyong a whore, am I?"

***

Mee-Kyong kept her eyes on the open book in front of her without focusing on any of the characters in particular. She had lost track of how much time over the past weeks she had already wasted stuck in the den with Mrs. Stern, her overzealous benefactress who was committed to saving her soul in three-hour installments.

"Look here, where it says he's the light of the world." Mrs. Stern tapped a line on the page. As she continued to prattle and extol the Western Savior she and her husband were so devoted to, Mee-Kyong shut off her mind and just nodded every once in a while. Mee-Kyong knew all about devotion. Pang had been a disciple of the Party at one point, back when he worked in the same factory where Mee-Kyong's unit slaved. She knew what it was to follow someone with a zeal that blinded you to reason and sense. She knew what it was to submit so fiercely, so foolishly. Mrs. Stern droned on about sacrifice and commitment, and all Mee-Kyong could think about was the crunching sound the cartilage made the first time Pang broke her nose.

At least she had no self-delusions. Her life as a prostitute began years before she set foot in the Round Robin Inn, back when she was nothing more than a child trying to survive in Camp 22. To get food, you gave a little bit of yourself. It didn't matter if you liked it or not, if you were terrified, if it was even more painful and humiliating than a teacher's lash with the whip. All that mattered was at the end of the day, your body didn't shut down and die. You had enough rations to ward off starvation for another twenty-four hours. If you worked the scenario out right, you ended up with more than just food — clothing, shelter, a warm bath instead of a biannual hose-down in freezing-cold water.

Life at the Sterns', Mee-Kyong had quickly learned, wasn't all that different. It wasn't her body she was selling, but her mind, her time, her feigned adoration. All she had to do was sit through Mrs. Stern's ritualistic lectures in the den, and she was paid with a soft pillow, a warm blanket, and three hot meals a day. The Sterns never asked Mee-Kyong where she was from or how she arrived in the hotel district. *"Your past is a closed book."* Mrs. Stern insisted Mee-Kyong could start a whole new life, as if her time in the gulag and the Round Robin didn't even matter. What a simpleton. Did this obese American truly believe that a cozy bedroom and full cafeteria service could erase Mee-Kyong's history and wipe away her past?

Still, there was no physical debasement. There were no nightly callers, no wheezing proprietors telling her who to entertain. She wasn't locked in a hotel room. At the Round Robin, she had been forced to work six to ten hours at a time, depending on the influx of lazy, middle-aged callers who frequented Mr. Lee's cheap establishment. Here, all that was required was a few sessions a day, a few hours pretending she cared about Mrs. Stern's Western deity, a few hours pretending she craved the kind of forgiveness their American Savior offered.

Secretly, Mee-Kyong didn't care all that much for the idea of free forgiveness. What about Mr. Lee, and those like him — men who sold innocent girls like Sun to be stripped and possessed and violated by the highest bidder? Or the smooth-skinned, angry-eyed brother who cut Sun's pathetic life so short? What about him? Did he deserve forgiveness? If there was a God of love and grace, as the Sterns always insisted, and if he was willing to overlook the offenses of men such as these, Mee-Kyong would despise him to her dying day.

Mrs. Stern interrupted her thoughts by pointing to a verse on the thin, fragile page. "Here, where it talks about the light of life, it means that we can live in joy. Freedom." There she went again. *Freedom*? What freedom was there in this mansion, where food and shelter were earned by accepting their fanatic propaganda? Mee-Kyong couldn't go out. She had no identity papers, none of the forms she would need to legally move around the city without being troubled by the police. Where was her freedom now? Where was her freedom at the Round Robin, where she was too weak to fight back or protect Sun from being used so mercilessly and murdered so senselessly?

Maybe freedom existed for wealthy, fat Americans, but not for gulag whores like her.

CHAPTER 34

"So I got your last report," the director stated.

"Agent Chun-Hee is the epitome of thoroughness, I'm sure." Ko knew the director could detect the bitterness behind the words. He knew better than anyone about Ko's history with Chun-Hee.

He took a deep breath and ignored the remark. "Ko, I think it's about time we pulled you out of there."

Ko froze, and it took several seconds to stammer the expected reply. "I'm ready to go wherever the Dear Leader and the Party lead me next."

"Of course you are." The director didn't sound convinced. "I assume if there's any more information you glean, you will pass it on to us."

Ko could almost taste the foreign cigarettes they gave to agents who returned home from successful stints over the border. "Naturally."

On the other end of the line, the director cleared his throat. "Well, we'll send word when we're ready to bring you home."

"Home?" The word sounded foreign on Ko's tongue.

"That's right. You're coming back to Pyongyang," he stated. "We'll need you here soon."

"It is an honor to serve," Ko whispered and stared at the cell phone long after the director disconnected the call.

***

Juliette hadn't entered Eve's room in at least six months. She tapped gently. "It's just me," she called out.

182

The door creaked open an inch. One of Eve's eyes peered through the crack. "Do you need something?"

Juliette fingered her eyeglasses back into place. "I'm really sorry to bother you right now, but do you mind if I come in for just a minute?"

Eve opened the door slowly and slid out of the way. Juliette bit her lip to hide her shock. Clothes were strewn across the floor and bed. Several dishes that had been missing from downstairs lay discarded in corners of the room. One blanket hung bunched up over some dirty laundry; the other dangled off the bed in a wrinkled mess. "I'm sorry about the clutter." Eve gestured to the single chair covered in food wrappers. "I didn't know you'd be coming."

"This is your room." The words were much more dignified than Juliette felt. She sat down carefully once Eve cleaned the junk off the seat. "You can do whatever you want with it." As much as she tried to act naturally, Juliette found her head turning from side to side as she let her eyes sweep across the room like a panorama camera. Eve didn't seem to know whether to sit or stand, so eventually Juliette motioned to the corner of the bed. "I'm actually here because Mr. Stern lost his watch. I was wondering if you happened to see it when you were cleaning up yesterday or today."

"No, ma'am. Is there anywhere in particular you'd like me to go over and look?"

Juliette shook her head. "It's probably in our room somewhere. He takes it off every night and puts it on his end table."

"How long has it been missing?"

"Just since this morning." Juliette continued to study Eve out of the corner of her eye. "I don't think you've been in there since then, have you?"

"No, ma'am. I usually only clean your room on Mondays and Thursdays."

"That's what I thought." Something in the far corner grabbed Juliette's attention, and she had her answer. She knew exactly where the watch was, but she kept her face expressionless and forced herself to continue chatting for the sake of etiquette. "So, how are you and Mee-Kyong getting along?"

Juliette could tell by Eve's face that the conversation would be short-lived.

***

Mee-Kyong bent over the table, her shoulders aching from the awkward angle. The kink in her neck made it feel like she was back in the fabric-cutting line at Camp 22. She slammed her pen down and let out an exasperated huff at the sound of approaching footsteps. Did Mrs. Stern seriously expect her to be done by now? She glared at the door.

"She got you copying?" It was Benjamin.

Mee-Kyong didn't look up. "I've had a cramp in my wrist for the past hour."

Benjamin went to the bookshelf, drawing his pointer finger across each title. "That's normal. Most students complained."

"Students?" Mee-Kyong leaned back in her chair and flexed her tired wrists.

"You know. Secret Seminary students ... The missionaries?" Benjamin turned away from the bookshelf for a moment. "You don't know?"

"Guess not." Mee-Kyong had always considered Benjamin either too quiet or too stupid to offer much by way of conversation, but she'd take just about any excuse right now for a break from her transcription work. "What's so secret about them?"

Benjamin leaned forward slightly in her direction but remained planted by Mr. Stern's theological library. "Last year, the Sterns took in other people like us."

"Us?" Until then, Mee-Kyong had assumed Benjamin was one of Yanji's countless Korean-Chinese citizens.

"Refugees." Benjamin held her gaze, and for a moment, Mee-Kyong recognized something in his eyes, something she might have noticed sooner if she looked for it. *Emptiness. Fear.* She tucked her hair behind her ear. He folded his arms across his massive chest and leaned against the bookshelf. "Kept them here for almost a year. Gave them lessons. Then sent them across the border."

"They did what?" Mee-Kyong knew her hosts were fanatics, but she didn't think they were actually insane.

"Over the border. Smuggle Scripture, things like that."

"So that's what I'm doing here?" Mee-Kyong gestured toward her Bible and half-empty paper. "Do they really expect me to agree …?"

Benjamin held up both palms. "Don't worry. They were volunteers. All of them."

"Who would actually want to go?" Mee-Kyong understood trading Bible-study sessions for room and board, but she couldn't fathom stealing over the border like an undercover spy, armed with nothing but Western propaganda.

Benjamin fingered his chin as if tugging an imaginary beard and sat down across from her. "Because they believe."

She narrowed her eyes at the security man, trying to read whatever mysteries were hidden in his expression. "You're still here. Don't you believe?"

Benjamin shrugged. "I believe."

"But you didn't cross the border?"

He put his elbow on the desk and leaned his cheek against his fist. Mee-Kyong gawked, wondering how much more difficult her life would have been if Pang had hands like that. Benjamin blinked once. "No."

"Well, it sounds like you were the only one in your right mind, then," she declared. He grimaced slightly, the corners of his eyes drawing into themselves. "I still can't believe the Sterns just let them go," Mee-Kyong continued. "Do they have any idea what happens to ...?"

"They know," Benjamin mumbled.

"So they send them out without any guidance, any defense, any provisions ..."

"Gave them three months' wages."

"Three months' wages?" Mee-Kyong fiddled with the pen in her hand, forcing her face to remain neutral. "And how long did you say their training lasted?"

"About a year. Don't remember exactly."

She pouted. A year of training. She had been doing that for the past several weeks at the Sterns' anyway. What was wrong with more of the same? The work was tedious, but it paid well. She had never eaten so much before. She had a closet filled with clothes from the Sterns' daughter and could take hot baths several times a day if she wanted to. For a year's worth of food and shelter, plus a nice cash bonus at the end, she could put up with the Americans' extremism. And then she'd be gone. She didn't know where, but twelve months would give her plenty of time to come up with a fool-proof plan.

She pictured Pang's expression right before he died. *You didn't think I could make it on my own, did you? You didn't think I could survive if you weren't there to watch out for me.* She smiled to herself. If she could just stomach twelve months locked up in this house, sitting in this den and pretending to care about Mrs. Stern's benign deity, she could leave here with enough money to start a new life. No more selling her body or her soul. No more living by someone else's agenda or schedule. The next year would prove horrifically dull, but if Mee-Kyong could endure labor camps and the hotel district, she could put up with a little boredom.

She picked up the pen and glanced back at the Sterns' Bible. The pen danced on the page.

***

Roger hated coming home so late, but his schedule probably wouldn't change any time soon. Sales had increased steadily for the past eighteen months, but the number of employees and machinery remained constant. He hadn't told Juliette yet, but he was toying with the idea of taking an entire month off in the spring so they could go back to the States and see Kennedy and some of their extended family on the East Coast. It would take a decent amount of planning, and Juliette would probably complain about leaving Mee-Kyong and their house staff, but their marriage could use some serious time away from Yanji.

He half expected Juliette to be asleep by the time he came in, but she was sitting up in bed reading when he swung their bedroom door open. She put her bookmark in place and looked up. "Hey, there."

"Hey, yourself." Roger loosened his tie and sat on the side of the bed to kick off his shoes. "You're up late."

"I was solving a little mystery." Juliette's smile hinted mischief as she laid her novel on the end table.

"And what mystery might that be?"

Juliette dangled Roger's watch like a prize from one finger. He unbuttoned his shirt and grinned. He hated thinking their new guest was a thief, but until he had evidence otherwise, he couldn't just dismiss his suspicions. "And where exactly did you find it, then, Mrs. Holmes? No, let me guess. In the kitchen with the butcher knife. Am I right?"

She chuckled. "No, it was in the trash downstairs." Juliette told him about going to Eve's room. "Her place was such a ridiculous mess — junk and candy wrappers all over."

Roger couldn't hide his amused smile and wondered how tidy their own room would be if Eve didn't clean it up twice a week for them.

"I saw a Hershey's wrapper over by her bed, and I remembered I had been eating a chocolate bar last night when you got up to take that phone call."

Roger sat on the bed and let his mouth drop open in mock surprise. "A chocolate bar?" he gasped. "I thought you were on a diet!"

Juliette looked aside but continued to smile. "Well, I wanted you to keep thinking that, so when I heard you coming back in, I swept the wrapper off the nightstand into a little bag. I carried it out first thing in the morning and dumped it in the kitchen trash. And that's where I found your watch."

Roger let his fingers play up and down Juliette's back. He loved the silky feel of her nightgown. "Sounds like it's a closed case, then." He wrapped his arms around his wife, but she tensed her muscles up and rolled over to face him. Roger sighed. "I'm sorry for thinking the worst about Mee-Kyong. You were right. She's no thief."

Juliette relaxed in Roger's embrace.

CHAPTER 35

"May I borrow a needle and thread?" Mee-Kyong hated asking Mrs. Stern for anything, but she forced herself to look into the American's eyes.

Mrs. Stern stood up from her computer desk. "Of course. Is there something you need help with? Do Kennedy's clothes need some more adjusting?"

Mee-Kyong wasn't worried about her wardrobe right now. "They still work fine. If you don't mind, I just need to fix something up."

"Of course." Mrs. Stern's expression was duly curious, but she adjusted her glasses and backed away from the computer. "Is there a certain color thread you'd like?"

"Red," Mee-Kyong answered. "If you have any."

Once she was alone again in her room, she took Sun's torn dress down from its hanger. She fingered the clingy nylon, toying with the lacy hem at the bottom. It wouldn't fit her anymore. Even on near-starvation rations at the Round Robin, she had barely managed to squeeze herself into it. The dress had been made for someone much smaller.

Mee-Kyong threaded the needle. She had only been trying to help Sun. She hadn't planned to make Mr. Lee so angry. The child didn't want to get married. What was wrong with manipulating the situation? Everyone could have had their way ... Everyone. She tied the thread in a knot at the bottom. *This is the perfect time to get sentimental. You're the one who stood by and let that man slaughter Sun right in front of your own eyes.* Mee-Kyong clutched at the torn section of fabric. She had tried. No one could accuse her of not trying.

Could they?

She stabbed the material and yanked the needle through the blood-red cloth. *Stupid dress.* She pulled the thread through until the end nearly snapped, and then she pierced the fabric once again. *Stupid hotel.* She closed up the knife tear with one tight jerk after another. The stitches were uneven, obvious, ugly. *Stupid, stupid girl.*

Half an hour later, Mee-Kyong sat hunched over the torn fabric, crying like a baby stolen from its mother.

***

"You're the one who keeps telling me what a great student she is." Roger had lost count of how often he and Juliette had rehashed this exact same conversation. He figured it could be another dozen times or so until anything really sank in.

With light from the setting sun pouring in through the window, Juliette sat across from her husband and eyed the Scrabble board. "I know, I'm just worried, that's all."

Roger put down a twenty-point word. "You're worried that she's going to leave like the other Secret Seminary students, and you're not going to know what happens to her, right?"

Juliette nodded and rearranged the tiles on her letter tray.

"I know, Baby Cakes. I know." Roger reached his arm across the table, his sleeve grazing one of the letters near the side of the board. The game was almost over. He had nearly twice as many points as his wife.

"I keep telling myself I'm going to bring it up to her," Juliette confessed, "but each time we come up here to study, I just fumble over the words. I guess I don't want anything to change. I don't want to think about sending her away. I want her to stay safe. She's been through enough already."

"Has she ever even talked to you about her past?"

Juliette shook her head. "No, but it's obvious. And I keep second-guessing myself. I don't want to push her too hard and have her agree and fly across the border, and I don't want to bring it up and scare her away so she never wants to spend another afternoon here with me."

Juliette's eight-point word did nothing to even the score. Roger was already prepared with his next move. "You can second-guess yourself until you're blue in the face, but Mee-Kyong needs to know if she's saved or not. It doesn't matter if she goes back to North Korea, if she heads off to South Korea or America or some other safe place, or if she stays here. All that matters is whether or not she'll be prepared to face her Creator if she were to die right now."

"She's doing so well in her studies …"

"You've said that before," Roger reminded her and looked up from his tiles. It wasn't like Juliette to stall this way. "I know the lessons are going smoothly. And I've seen her work. You've got her in this den doing Bible studies and copying Scripture for, what? Four hours a day? But no matter how well she does with it all, it's not going to matter if it hasn't changed what she believes."

"She believes." Juliette's voice was strained.

"Have you asked her?" Roger stared straight at his wife and clasped his hands in front of him. She shook her head. He laid down a six-letter word. "You might want to get on that, Baby Cakes."

***

Benjamin had worked his hands raw, but he refused to slow down. He grunted with each heave of the shovel before hefting the load off to the side. Mr. Stern didn't need the fence completed until springtime, but Benjamin welcomed the physical activity. He paused once to wipe his forehead and noticed Mee-Kyong coming out the back door. "I thought you might be thirsty." She passed him a glass of water. Benjamin drank the cup dry. "You've been out here all afternoon," she remarked.

"Just working." Benjamin set the glass down, suddenly forced to admit how tight his muscles were. He stretched from one side to the other and then arched his back until he was looking up at the bright sky. Self-conscious, he straightened up. "Need something?"

Mee-Kyong was still leaning against the side of the house, her arms crossed over her chest. She cocked her head to the side and eyed Benjamin's shovel. "Do you want an extra pair of hands?"

He squinted at her, not sure he had heard correctly. "You want to help?" He couldn't decide if he should decline her offer politely or laugh her away outright.

Her eyes were dead serious. "I'm tired of copying. I could use a distraction."

"Only one shovel." He shrugged.

"So we'll share." Mee-Kyong stretched out her hand. "You're not like other Christians, are you?" Mee-Kyong started to dig without even asking for directions.

"Meaning what?"

"The Sterns ... they're always talking about Jesus and heaven and prayer and salvation. But you, you don't really talk about anything."

"Not much to say."

"I don't think that's true." Mee-Kyong was huffing. She had only been at it for a few minutes, maybe five at most, before she passed the shovel back to Benjamin. Even as he worked, he felt her intense, curious stare. "Where do you come from?" she asked.

This time, Benjamin didn't slow down at all. "Does it matter?"

"Would I have asked if it didn't?"

Benjamin glanced once at Mee-Kyong before slicing the soil with the tip of the shovel. "Closed book. You know that."

"Maybe it's closed between us and the Sterns. That doesn't mean we can't talk about it with each other."

192

Benjamin looked back to his work. "Rather not."

Mee-Kyong shrugged. "Well, then, I have a different question for you. If you're a Christian, why do you go out drinking so often?"

Benjamin's back stiffened. He wiped a dirty hand through his sweaty hair. "What are you talking about?"

"I'm not stupid." Mee-Kyong crossed her arms. "Given what you know about me, don't you think I can smell booze from half a kilometer away?"

Benjamin shrugged. "Everyone's got secrets."

She turned her head to the side, the way girls do when they want to flirt. "What secrets do you think I'm carrying around?"

"Closed book." Benjamin resumed his work.

***

Eve dragged the vacuum down the hallway and into the guest bedroom. She knocked once but didn't pause before opening the door. Mee-Kyong had been in the den all afternoon, working on her Scripture assignment. Eve heaved the vacuum in and shut the door behind her. It wasn't fair that the new girl got the big bed, when Eve's mattress was no larger than a child's. Mee-Kyong was only a few centimeters taller than she, certainly not enough to merit double the sleeping area.

She skulked to the closet and fingered the clothes on the hangers. Some of them she remembered Kennedy wearing. Of course, at the time she never questioned why that spoiled American brat had dozens of spare outfits, some she only wore a few times a year. Kennedy was the Sterns' daughter. Obviously she would have a nice wardrobe. That didn't explain, however, why Mee-Kyong was wearing all the leftovers Kennedy didn't take with her back to America. Wouldn't they fit Eve just as well? When was the last time the Sterns had given her anything new?

Eve took a sheer blouse off the hanger and held it up to her shoulders. Turning from side to side in front of the ornate mirror, she imagined how she would look in it. Her figure would certainly fill it out better than Mee-Kyong's. She turned to put the blouse away, and something draped over the chair in the corner of the room caught her eye. She walked over and fingered the soft nylon fabric. She picked it up by one of the stringy shoulder straps. She had seen that kind of dress many times before.

Mrs. Stern thought she knew all about Eve and her past, but the fat American was completely clueless. Mrs. Stern had spent all her energy lately clucking over Mee-Kyong like an old mother hen, but whatever the new girl went through, it couldn't measure up to what Eve had suffered. Torn from her family, ripped from her old life, used up by men who didn't care about her and would never love her. She clutched the red dress so tightly her knuckles were white. It didn't matter where Mee-Kyong came from, or how sorry Mrs. Stern was for her. Whatever she thought she had suffered would pale next to the misery Eve had endured, and nobody would convince her otherwise.

Compliments paid in hushed whispers. "Your daughter has so much potential. It would be a shame to waste a talent like hers."

Tears ignored in the darkness of night. "Please don't send me away, Mama. I don't want to go with him."

Threats and coercion. "You'll go with him because your father and I told you to."

Eve needed to get to Benjamin. She flung the red dress back over the chair and retreated from Mee-Kyong's room. Benjamin would understand. It had been so long …

With old memories warming her fluttering stomach, she scurried down the stairs on tiptoes and rushed to the back door. Her hand was already on the handle when she saw them. For a moment, Eve froze, and then she flung the back door open. "What are you doing out here? Did you finish all your copy work?"

Mee-Kyong leaned back against the house and lifted her gaze just enough to give Eve a passing glance. "I decided to take a break."

Eve fixed her hands on her hips. "Did Mrs. Stern say you could?"

"You can mop a floor whether or not I'm out here, can't you?" Mee-Kyong turned toward Benjamin, who heaved shovelfuls of dirt over to the mound next to him.

"We'll see," Eve growled, but Mee-Kyong wasn't even looking at her. "We'll see," she repeated to herself. She stomped back into the house and up the stairs to the intruder's room.

***

Roger was right. Juliette had to stop comparing Mee-Kyong to the Secret Seminary students. She had spent hours each day worrying Mee-Kyong would slip over the border and never contact the Sterns again. But Mee-Kyong wasn't Hannah, or Simon, or any of the others. She was a battered woman who obviously had come to them from horrific circumstances, a rescued girl who deserved a new chance at life — a chance Juliette had been loath to mention.

She thought back over the past several weeks with Mee-Kyong. They had studied Scripture together, broken down the history of the Bible, outlined the life of Christ and a dozen other characters. But Juliette had never reached out to Mee-Kyong and asked her the most important question of all: *Do you know what it means to be saved?* And the more she thought about it, the more she realized her husband was right. She didn't want to lose Mee-Kyong. She wasn't ready to carry the girl through another year of training only to send her across the border to her death. She couldn't pour her tears and sweat and prayers into Mee-Kyong for twelve months just to turn her out and never hear from her again.

Of course, Juliette was getting ahead of herself. Mee-Kyong hadn't even accepted Christ yet. If any of their Bible studies on salvation and forgiveness had meant anything, she still hadn't made any official declaration of faith. Juliette just needed to take it one step at a time. She wasn't rushing into another round of Secret Seminary training. She was just sharing the gospel with someone who needed it. Juliette didn't know anything about Mee-Kyong's history, except that she was in the hotel district and dressed for the part when Roger found her. She hadn't said more than a few words those first days at the Sterns'. She just hovered around like a frail ghost. Over the next weeks, her body got stronger, her face filled out, her color improved, but the haunted expression never left her eyes.

Juliette's own past wasn't a feel-good, family-friendly sitcom, either. She hated the stress of growing up as an ambassador's daughter, and when she went back to the States for college, all that pent-up tension and resentment snapped out of her like a slingshot. Juliette shut her eyes. She couldn't think about her own college experience without growing even more anxious for her daughter. She hoped sending Kennedy off to Harvard was the right decision, but how could she be sure? Roger always teased her for worrying too much, but sometimes Juliette wondered if she really just cared too much. If she didn't love her daughter, it wouldn't matter if Kennedy rebelled against everything her parents had tried to teach her. If Juliette's heart didn't break for Mee-Kyong and her silent, secret trauma, it wouldn't matter if she ever returned to North Korea or not.

Juliette swept her hair off her shoulder. Sending Mee-Kyong back across the border wasn't the issue. Her salvation was. She took a last sip of tea and headed toward the den.

***

"It's time. Your travel plans are all arranged."

Agent Ko took a deep breath. "I'm ready."

"I'm sure you are. Agent Ryuk will give you the information you need when you meet him."

"How soon?" Ko wanted to sound prepared but not too eager. The director was a genius at picking up verbal nuances.

"When can you get out? Did you tie up all your loose ends?"

"All but one. It won't take long."

"Well, hurry. I'll make sure Ryuk's expecting you."

***

Religion that God our Father accepts as pure and faultless is this: to look after orphans and widows in their distress and to keep oneself from being polluted by the world. Mee-Kyong copied the characters and let her eyes linger on the page before she went to the next verse. Who had looked over her in her distress? Who had cared about her while prison guards raised her behind barbed wire?

Nobody.

Even into her adulthood, who cared for her? Who delivered her from Pang and his unpredictable violence? Who rescued her from Mr. Lee's attack in the Round Robin Inn? She took care of herself. Mee-Kyong had survived, but it wasn't because the Sterns' all-knowing deity had stepped down from heaven and condescended to come to her aid. It was because she was smart. Smart and determined. She didn't let a life of slavery destroy her spirit. That's why she was still alive. That's why she was here and not in the Round Robin or the prison camp or some makeshift gutter grave.

She had just moved on to the next verse when Mrs. Stern came in, balancing two cups of tea on her dainty tray. Mrs. Stern set the arrangement on the table beside the Bible and notebook. "You've been working hard. Another few days, and you might complete all the epistles."

Mee-Kyong responded with the expected smile and shook a cramp out of her wrist.

Mrs. Stern poured the tea. "I think it's fair to say you've earned yourself a snack. What do you think?"

Mee-Kyong accepted the mug and muttered her appreciation. The temperature outside had been dropping steadily with the promise of a fast-approaching winter, and she was chilled from her break outside with Benjamin. She lowered her face into the steam from her cup.

"You're awfully quiet." Mrs. Stern stirred a spoonful of honey into her tea.

"I guess I was just absorbed in my work, that's all." Mee-Kyong knew she had responded appropriately when Mrs. Stern beamed at her.

"And what particular passage in James are you working on right now?"

Mee-Kyong turned her notebook around to show her benefactress. "Orphans and widows."

Mrs. Stern adjusted her glasses and read the passage out loud. "So true," she breathed afterward.

"I thought you said it was all true."

"It is. You're absolutely right. Which, in a roundabout way, is why I've come to talk to you."

Mee-Kyong felt her eyebrows furrow before she had the chance to stop them. Something in Mrs. Stern's face reminded her of a cat preparing to pounce on its prey. "Talk about what?" She turned her head to the side and watched Mrs. Stern from the corner of her eye.

"Well, let's see." Mrs. Stern wiped her glasses, which had fogged over with her last sip of tea. "You've been here for a while now. You've been an excellent pupil, and I couldn't be happier with your studies." Why did it feel like Mee-Kyong was back in one of her nightly self-criticism sessions at Camp 22? Mrs. Stern kept her glasses in her hand and opened and shut one of its hinges methodically. "But there comes a point in your life when you need to make the shift from book-learning to actual personal experience."

Mee-Kyong kept her eyes on the desk. The cost of room and board had just increased.

"I certainly don't want to rush you." Mrs. Stern waved one hand as if she could flick away the very thought. "But I wanted to know where you stand right now. In your heart, I mean. What do you think about all this we've been studying, deep, deep down in your soul?"

Some moments in Mee-Kyong's life were determined in a flash, a single moment with no hesitation. When Pang told her he could help her escape Camp 22, she didn't lay awake for nights on end pondering her next course of action. She didn't waste time deliberating before stabbing Mr. Lee back at the Round Robin. Mee-Kyong forced her posture to match the conviction in her tone. "I believe." She watched Mrs. Stern's face wrinkle, frown, and eventually melt into a cautious smile.

"You're sure? I mean, you don't need more time to think about this?"

"I've already thought about it." *What else does she think I'd be doing while I'm cooped up here copying Scripture for hours every afternoon?*

Mrs. Stern put her glasses back on. "You know what you're saying? You're saying you agree that Jesus is everything he said he is, that he died for your sins and came back to life."

Mee-Kyong wanted to rush her answers and end the interrogation, but she forced herself to respond with stately calm. "I've been thinking about it quite a bit, and yes, I believe."

Mrs. Stern's smile found its way all the way up to her eyes. "That's wonderful news." She turned her face away for a moment and nudged her glasses a little higher on her nose. "Very, very wonderful."

Mee-Kyong tried to look duly pensive. "I guess I just don't know what's supposed to happen next."

"Happen?" Mrs. Stern poured another round of tea. "You get baptized, of course."

CHAPTER 36

Eve cringed with each cautious step she planted upon the stairs. The smallest creak in the woodwork made her skin tingle. She held her breath and waited. Had anyone heard? It had been an hour since everyone went to bed, but that didn't mean they were asleep.

In the dim light in the hallway, Eve paused in front of the mirror. Her figure was more developed than Mee-Kyong's, but her face was too angular, her features a little too harsh. She smoothed down her hair, tucked one strand behind her left ear, studied the effect, and then set it back how it was. She ran her hands over Kennedy's blouse. Good thing the little American princess was too far away to care if some of her clothes went missing tonight.

Eve was almost to the front door when she turned into the small secondary hallway. She padded silently down a set of two stairs and brushed the door with her fingertips. "Are you awake?" She pressed her cheek against the wooden frame and tapped it twice with one finger. "It's me."

Then he was there.

Benjamin still had on his work pants from the day but had taken his shirt off. As he opened the door, he pulled a sleeveless undershirt over his torso. He placed one arm on his doorframe and leaned against it. "What do you want?"

Eve positioned her body at a slight angle to his, willing him to notice her hair, her blouse, her skirt — which Eve knew for a fact Mr. Stern had forbidden his daughter to wear out of the house when she was still in high school. "I was having a hard time sleeping. Just thought I'd come down for a visit.'"

Benjamin continued to block the door with his bulky frame. "You know we can't do that anymore." She saw the way the lump in his throat worked when he swallowed. "It's different now."

Eve lifted one shoulder. "It doesn't have to be."

Benjamin grunted, but he didn't make any move to shut the door. His eyes wandered slowly, shyly. "We can't." He snapped his head back up. "I can't."

His flushed face gave Eve the courage to put one arm against his chest. Her palm was on the cloth of his undershirt, and her fingertips brushed the hard smoothness of his skin. "The Sterns never found out before," she purred. "They don't need to now."

Benjamin glanced quickly down the hall. "I'm trying to change."

"For what? Good-conduct badges in heaven?" Eve deliberately let her volume rise more than necessary. With another shush, Benjamin grabbed her by the arm and pulled her inside. He kept the door open and whispered in her ear, "You need to stop this. It's not right."

Eve let the corners of her lips curl up as she wrapped both arms around Benjamin's neck. One swift motion from her foot shut the door behind them. "I've got a whole lifetime to earn back my reward points from God."

***

Juliette couldn't even think of lying down yet. She paced from one bedpost to another, gesturing with her hands every now and then and almost panting from walking so fast. "I can't believe how quickly she's changed." She glanced at Roger every now and then to make sure he was still listening. "I've been so worried about her leaving, about going through another round of good-byes, you know. All that stuff." Roger nodded, so Juliette continued. "And then it just came together. I mean, you encouraged me to have the conversation and get it out of the way, and it was like she had just been waiting for that very moment, for that exact question. She wasn't flippant, but there wasn't any second guessing, either."

"Almost sounds like it was too easy."

At Roger's murmur, Juliette froze halfway between the mahogany bedposts. "What was that?"

She had already resumed her pacing before Roger replied, "I still don't know how to read that girl. That's all. She was so tough when she came here. She's got an iron will, that one, so it's hard for me to see her accepting the truth that readily."

Juliette was too excited, and her spirits were too high for her husband's words to discourage her. He wasn't there in that den. He didn't know. He wasn't the one who had studied with Mee-Kyong for weeks on end. He saw her as a hardened young woman from the brothel, but Juliette had seen glimpses into Mee-Kyong's heart, and it was beautiful. "I was thinking we could plan the baptism for Sunday afternoon."

"Fine with me."

Juliette placed her hands on her hips. "Maybe you could at least pretend to be enthusiastic."

Roger sighed. "I'm just tired, Baby Cakes." Juliette glanced at the clock. It had already been an hour since they got ready for bed. "In the morning, I'll have more energy to be ecstatic with you, all right? For now, I just want to rest."

Juliette threw on her slippers. "Well, there's no way I'm getting any sleep yet. I'm going downstairs to email Kennedy."

Roger muttered his consent.

***

As soon as his door slammed shut, Benjamin threw on his sweatshirt and wrapped his arms over his chest. The spot above his heart burned where Eve's fingers had brushed his skin. The heat seeped all the way down into his lungs. He wiped his chest as if he could erase his body's memory of that touch.

The base of his spine tingled with an icy chill, and small drops of sweat beaded on the back of his neck. He rubbed his clammy hands on his cheeks, while his body shivered once in protest against his morals. Maybe he shouldn't have sent her away. After all, it had been so long …

What right did she think she had, coming to him in the middle of the night? How many months had she regaled him with that cold, indifferent stare? How long had she spent ignoring him, only to throw herself at him now? What had changed? Benjamin slumped onto his bed but jumped back up just a minute later. He knew exactly what changed.

Mee-Kyong had arrived.

***

"What are you doing up?" Juliette put both hands on Eve's shoulders after nearly running into her on the dimly lit staircase.

Eve wiped her cheek where mascara dribbled down her face like an oil spill. "Nothing. I was just thirsty."

Juliette squinted. Something was wrong besides the smeared makeup. "Aren't those Kennedy's clothes?"

Eve shoved Juliette's hands away. Shouldering past, she vaulted up the steps. Juliette spun around and just barely caught her wrist. "I'm not angry, sweetie. I just want to know what's going on."

Eve yanked her hand free and mumbled something. The only word Juliette could make out was *alone.* Her experience raising one moody teenage daughter kept her from following Eve up the stairs. "It's always something," she muttered to herself. Brushing her hair with her hand, Juliette straightened her back and reminded herself of the good news she had to tell Kennedy. She would worry about Eve in the morning.

She made herself some hot chocolate while she waited for her computer to start up, wondering how to tell her daughter about Mee-Kyong's conversion. She'd have to be careful, just in case the Chinese government decided to sneak a peek into her outbox one day, but there were ways to get around the potential censoring. With a mug of steaming chocolate perched on the desk next to her, Juliette told her daughter about a new "friend" who had decided to join the family. *In fact, she'll be going for a little swim this coming Sunday!* The line reminded her Mee-Kyong would need something to wear at the baptism. *I hope you don't mind if she borrows one of your bathing suits.*

After getting the news out of the way, she turned her attention toward Kennedy. *Are you getting enough sleep? How many dates have you been asked on so far?* Juliette sighed. Sometimes living so far away from Kennedy felt like someone shoved a vacuum tube right in the center of her gut and turned it on. *I miss you. I hope we get to see you soon. I know you'll have a great time at your aunt's at Christmas. She's looking forward to spoiling you. Wish I could, too.*

Juliette thought about Kennedy thousands of miles away, across oceans and continents. It had been over a week since she had last heard her daughter's laugh. Sometimes she shut her eyes and forced herself to recall Kennedy's voice in her mind, just so she wouldn't one day forget it completely.

Send me some pictures of you and your friends when you get the chance.

Love, Mom

Juliette rested her chin on her hand. Was it really last year when Kennedy sent in her applications and got accepted into Harvard? Was it just last spring Juliette had dressed Kennedy up in her gown and watched her throw her cap in the air with the other graduates from the All Girls American School?

She took a sip of cocoa and reminded herself raising Kennedy wasn't always easy. The older her daughter grew, the more stubborn she became. She didn't want her mom breathing down her back about homework or curfews or chaperones. She took offense whenever her dad raised questions about her outfits or her boyfriends. They had a huge fight when Kennedy tried to wear that miniskirt to the school dance. Juliette shook her head and turned off the computer, nostalgic for the days when her family's only troubles were how far a hemline fell above the knee.

She pouted to herself, trying to remember. Was that the same skirt Eve had been wearing on the stairs? What had that girl been up to? Juliette got up and stretched, the stiffness in her joints and heaviness in her head reminding her it was way past bedtime. Tomorrow she would talk with Eve. Tonight she would at least try to relax.

***

Roger squeezed his eyes shut, his groggy mind trying to wish away the tapping sounds. "Who is it?" he muttered, surprised to find that Juliette's side of the bed was still empty. The knocking persisted.

He rolled over and swung his feet to the floor. "Coming." He cleared his throat in an attempt to make his voice sound less irritated and then opened the door. "Benjamin?"

Roger squinted in the light from the hall. Benjamin stood fidgeting with his fingers and tossing glances in nearly every direction. Roger held the door open and hoped his mind would clear soon. How long had it been since Juliette went downstairs? Roger hadn't even looked at the clock. "Do you want to come in?" He flipped on the switch, and Benjamin ducked his head when the lights came on. Roger gestured to a chair by the bureau.

Benjamin planted himself down, his bulk threatening to demolish the dainty cushion Juliette perched on to preen every morning. "I've come to make confession."

Roger raised his eyebrow. "You know it's the middle of the night, don't you?" He studied the way Benjamin's hands rubbed the tops of his thighs. "But if it's going to help you sleep better, then go ahead." He forced himself to keep his eyes open.

Benjamin gazed into his lap. "I slept with Eve."

Roger scratched at his bald spot with one hand and ran the other across his stubbly cheek. *Slept with Eve?* Roger's Korean was pretty good by now, but he still ran over the words in his mind just to make sure he had gotten them right. He cleared his throat, aware that he wasn't as awake as he should be for a conversation of this magnitude, especially one in a foreign language. "Slept with Eve? Just now?"

Benjamin's shook his head, reminding Roger of a massive horse swishing his tail from side to side. "Long time ago."

"So why are you telling me?" Roger knew it was the wrong thing to say as soon as the question left his mouth, but he couldn't take it back. What did Benjamin expect this late?

The security guard curled his shoulders even closer to his chest. "She came again. Tonight." Roger heard the catch in Benjamin's throat and wished to cough for him.

"So you were together in the past, and she thought it might be fun to spend some time together again. And you ..."

"Forced her out." Benjamin stopped rubbing his pants legs and started tapping his knee which bounced rhythmically.

Roger thought about his housekeeper. Beneath a sharp and somewhat angular exterior lay an obvious feminine allure, easy to catch the eye of a young man like Benjamin. "That must not have been easy."

Benjamin shook his head once more. His brow was sweaty. "I didn't want her to go."

"You didn't want her to go, but you knew she couldn't stay, so you did the right thing and sent her out."

Benjamin held his large palms open. "I hurt her."

Roger leaned forward. "Hurt her feelings, you mean?"

"No. I pushed her. Made her fall."

"Where is she now, then?"

Benjamin shrugged. "Her room, I guess. Didn't see her after that."

"Well, then, she's probably not injured too bad. Physically at least." Roger stared at Benjamin's reflection in the dresser mirror and noticed his back trembling.

"I'm awfully sorry," Benjamin remarked.

"Sorry for what?"

"For that. It was before I was baptized."

Roger shook his head once to get a little more oxygen flowing to his brain. "You weren't even saved. It makes sense you would have acted that way. I can see how that might make living and working in the same house together somewhat awkward, but you have nothing to apologize to me for. Now, if you caused our housekeeper to fall and break her ankle so she can't cook us Saturday brunch tomorrow, then I might be a little upset." Benjamin made no response to Roger's attempt at humor. Roger sighed. "Tell you what. It's late now. I'm not thinking clearly. We could talk about this all night long, but I probably wouldn't make very much sense. This sounds like something you need to deal with between yourself and God. Why don't you go back to your room, spend some time in the Word, and tomorrow after brunch, we can talk about it more."

Benjamin scrunched his face up. "I guess."

Roger thought back to when he was saved right out of college, the temptations that assaulted him as soon as he confessed his beliefs, the late nights alone in his room with only his memories, his thoughts, his fleshly desires. He put his hand on Benjamin's shoulder once more. "Here's another option. If you don't want to go back to your room just yet, head to the den. You can pray and study there, hopefully without as many distractions."

Benjamin nodded, his eyes almost rising to meet Roger's for the first time that night.

Roger held the door open. "Good luck, Brother."

CHAPTER 37

Even after several weeks living with the Sterns, the ticking from the stately grandfather clock made Mee-Kyong cringe each time she tried to fall asleep. The Round Robin had been noisy, customers coming and going at all hours of the night, and the pedestrians and taxi cabs polluting the days when Mee-Kyong tried to rest. Here at the Sterns', that incessant *tick* was the only sound to be heard at night, lying to its listeners that all was right in the world as it lulled the household to sleep with its deceptive consistency.

Mee-Kyong gritted her teeth and wrapped her arms over her head so they covered her ears. Why did everything at the Sterns' have to be so tidy? Life wasn't tidy. And no matter how serenely that old clock clicked away time's passage, she wouldn't let it fool her. She thought back to the night sounds from Camp 22 — girls shrieking in their sleep, harsh and angry whispers between rivals vying for the better spot on the cold concrete floor. It was only the newcomers who ever cried, though, keeping their neighbors awake with their pitiful mewing. She squirmed underneath the thick comforter. When she escaped with Pang, she never expected she would prefer the familiar sounds of the over-packed girls' dorm to the meticulous ticking of a fancy antique clock. She squeezed her eyes shut.

In the labor camp, she hadn't realized she was miserable. *You ignorant fool.* How could she miss those girls in the dorm, now that she was fed amply three times a day and given a whole closet full of fashionable clothes? How could she long for girls she never really knew, girls who might already be dead, when here at the Sterns' she was doted on and smothered with attention? She scowled. What kind of commitment had she given Mrs. Stern? Now that she had proclaimed faith in the American's deity, what would they ask of her next?

She dressed herself in the dark. It didn't matter what they demanded. She knew how to keep her patrons happy. Whether the currency was in flesh or scribbled verses, it made little difference as long as she got what she needed. She placed her hand on the door frame. Why did her bedroom always feel so stuffy, even as winter crept upon them all? The air was thick with poisonous doubts and fears. She tiptoed down the hall. She would copy that entire Bible of theirs ten times over if it meant keeping her position here.

Mee-Kyong had survived this far. And she certainly wasn't about to quit now.

***

Benjamin wasn't used to spending vast amounts of time with the Lord. His prayers were the kind conjured up in the moment of need or guiltily recited at the end of the day. Tonight he lowered his head to his lap and begged for forgiveness. Mr. Stern had acted like Benjamin hadn't done anything wrong. What did he know? Had Mr. Stern ever had a half-clad young woman come tapping on his door in bare feet in the middle of the night? How could a godly man like Mr. Stern experience such an overwhelming swell of desire that his blood pressure continued to rise even half an hour later? When he first committed himself to a life of purity, Benjamin expected the Lord to erase his body's memory. Where was the deliverance the Sterns were always talking about? Where was the freedom? Almost a year after his baptism, Benjamin was still here, his stomach nauseous with the intensity of his own longings.

"Oh." It was a timid sound, but it sent Benjamin flying up off the couch, blinded by the sudden brightness. Mee-Kyong stood in the doorway of the den, her hand raised to the light switch. "I didn't know anyone was in here." She looked around with a frown. "What are you doing?"

Benjamin glanced at his palms, which he held open like a culprit caught in the middle of a crime. "Just reading. That's all."

"In the dark?" Mee-Kyong's voice held the slightest trace of bemusement.

"What about you?" Benjamin shuffled his weight from one foot to the other. "It's late," he added lamely.

Mee-Kyong sat down at her desk. "I couldn't sleep. I decided to get some extra work done."

Benjamin watched her pull out her notebook and pen. "I'll go." He scratched the back of his neck but made no move to leave.

"No, stay." Mee-Kyong crossed her arms and looked up at him. Her smile was crooked, mischievous, mocking. She didn't open her notebook. "So you like to come here and read in the dark?"

"Tired of my room."

"I can understand that," she muttered. "Well, since you're here, maybe you can tell me what's expected of me now."

Benjamin looked up. "Now?"

Mee-Kyong tossed her hair over her shoulder. "Now that I'm a Christian, or whatever it is you guys call yourselves."

Benjamin laughed mirthlessly. "Ask Mrs. Stern."

"Oh, I'm sure I will. But I want to hear it from you. You've been here, what, at least a year?"

"Little over."

"And did you 'get saved' right away?"

Thinking about his arrival at the Sterns' opened the gateway for a flood of other unwelcome memories. "Something like that."

"Why?"

The pointedness of the question startled Benjamin. He snapped up his head. "Why what?"

"Why did you go along with it? I mean, did you genuinely believe, or was it just that you wanted a place to stay, or what?"

Benjamin's head drooped once more. "I believed," he muttered into his chest.

"And that's all?" Mee-Kyong folded her arms and leaned back in her chair.

Benjamin shrugged. "Got baptized later."

"That's when they put you under the water, right?"

Benjamin nodded. His cheek tickled.

"And did it work?" Mee-Kyong stared straight at him.

"What work?"

"Washing your guilt away. Did it do it?"

Benjamin pressed his lips together. "All Christians struggle."

"So it didn't work."

"Didn't say that."

Mee-Kyong turned her face away, twirling her hair with her pointer finger. "No, but it's what I figured."

***

Eve's only regret was that she couldn't get into Mee-Kyong's room again to grab more clothes. Oh, well. She stuffed her belongings into one of the small bags she used to carry groceries home from the market.

Home. Not anymore. She looked around her room. The Sterns' room, actually. She smiled once to herself when she thought of Mee-Kyong having to clean up after her for a change. She pressed her shoulder where Benjamin had pinched her when he spun her around and sent her away. Wouldn't it be nice if she were here tomorrow and could show him the bruise? But it was too late for him. Benjamin could have the mansion. He could have the Sterns and their religious fanaticism. He could even have Mee-Kyong.

Eve was done.

213

Her eyes scanned the clutter one last time. Was there anything else she would need? She paused in front of a leather-bound Bible, a gift from Mrs. Stern on some holiday or other. She thumbed through the pages. The book's spine was still stiff. With a small grunt, she hefted the bag over her shoulder and walked out the door, leaving the book in its place on the shelf.

CHAPTER 38

Juliette's nose reminded her it was Saturday even before she opened her eyes. Saturday brunch. The family tradition began before the Sterns moved to Yanji and continued after nearly everyone left. Eve usually spent an hour or more getting everything ready. Roger would join them before putting in a half day at the office. Juliette breathed in the scent of garlic and onions, imagined the warmth from the oven steaming all the way up the stairs, and thought she heard bacon sizzling.

She took her time getting dressed, enjoying the slow, lazy feel of the day. She couldn't remember the last time she slept in so late. She thought of her friends back in the States who held subscription boxes at the opera and pitied Juliette and her "backward" existence overseas. Did any of them wake up to homemade feasts like these? Juliette's smug smile reversed into a frown, and she remembered Eve. What had she been doing last night in Kennedy's clothes? Juliette suspected some of her housekeeper's erratic behavior lately was because of Mee-Kyong. Was Eve jealous she didn't have Juliette's full attention anymore? Or did having Mee-Kyong here remind Eve too much about working in the hotel district? Whatever it was, Juliette knew she'd have to bring it up.

Today.

After a quick make-up job, Juliette headed downstairs toward the yeasty smell of hot rolls and the fresh-roast coffee Roger loved. The house was surprisingly quiet for this late in the morning. Juliette walked into the kitchen and stopped. Roger stood over the stove, a spatula carefully poised over bubbling batter. "Good morning, Baby Cakes."

Juliette immediately noticed the way Roger focused on her forehead, not her eyes. "What are you doing?"

"Making breakfast." He turned back to the stovetop and flipped over a perfectly golden pancake.

She couldn't remember the last time she saw her husband cook. "Where's Eve?"

"Gone."

Juliette didn't say anything. Roger passed her a scribbled note. "She left this downstairs."

She reached out for the paper tentatively, skimming Eve's scrawled message before placing it on the counter. "Why would she do something so rash?" Juliette asked.

"I have a pretty good idea." He told her about his conversation with Benjamin.

"And so she just left?"

Roger shrugged. "Would you want to keep on living here after something like that?"

Juliette didn't say anything. She thought about her own past, the lengths she went to after she met Roger to erase all those reminders. "Does Benjamin know?"

Roger poured more batter onto the griddle. "I haven't seen him yet. He was up pretty late, I'm guessing."

"Sounds like we all were." Juliette took out a pitcher and mixed some lemonade. "Mee-Kyong hasn't come downstairs yet, either?"

Roger sampled a bit of bacon. "Nope. Looks like it's just the two of us."

Juliette laid her head on her husband's shoulder. "I can think of worse ways to start the weekend." She sensed her husband's body tense and looked to the hallway. Mee-Kyong was standing in the entryway, eyeing them both with a small smirk. "Good morning," Juliette squeaked. She and Roger bounced away from each other, like children caught with their hands in the cookie jar.

Mee-Kyong furrowed her brow. "What's going on?"

Juliette and Roger shared a quick glance. "We'll be doing the cooking for the next few days," Roger answered. Mee-Kyong raised an eyebrow but didn't ask any more questions.

"Would you like some lemonade?" Juliette reached to the cupboard to pull down a glass. "Breakfast is just about ready."

***

Benjamin woke up to a tight spasm in his back. He groaned to himself and reached for his pillow. Where was it? He sat up, hunched over to ease the tension in his lumbar region, and realized he wasn't in his own bed. What had happened?

Eve. He groaned once. How could he have been so stupid? How could he have let himself ... *No.* He shook his head. Nothing happened. He was tempted, but he remembered sending her away. He had sent her away, hadn't he? His heart caught somewhere near his throat. He looked around. No, this definitely wasn't Eve's room. Benjamin let out his breath.

Glancing around the den, he recalled his conversation with Mee-Kyong. How late had they stayed up? He was relieved to note she wasn't still in here. He got up to stretch his back some more. Judging by the amount of sunlight, he had overslept by several hours. He smelled bacon coming from the kitchen downstairs, and his mouth watered. Still, he hesitated. He didn't want to go down and face Eve. He couldn't be sure, but he had a pretty good feeling he had used more force than necessary when he sent her away. Was she injured? Bruised? He squeezed his eyes tight as an unwelcome heaviness seeped into the empty space in his stomach.

He squatted down on the ground and started his morning push-ups — a habit from his special military training he had never outgrown. He focused on his breathing and wondered what would have happened to him if he hadn't met the Sterns. Would he have tried to go back to see his family? He thought about the toothless old man who hired him to track down an illegal immigrant and wondered if he would have supported himself by turning in his own countrymen. Twenty minutes later, his muscles amply warmed up, Benjamin gave his body one final stretch and headed downstairs. He had hidden in the den long enough.

***

It was one of the quietest meals Mee-Kyong could remember having at the Sterns'. Benjamin kept his face to his plate and was so bent over he looked like he was impersonating a boulder. Mr. Stern munched one bacon strip after another, while Mrs. Stern poked her plate with her fork. She would look around every now and then to steal a glance at Benjamin, her eyes full of questions and compassion, and open her mouth only to fill it with another small bite of eggs.

"Well." Mrs. Stern punctuated the word as if it were a sentence in and of itself. "I guess we've had enough pancakes. I'll go see if the rolls are ready."

While she was out, Mee-Kyong glanced over at Benjamin. Their late-night conversation in the den was by far the longest they had shared together, but if that meant anything to him, he only showed it by shoveling more pancakes into his mouth.

Mrs. Stern returned and dumped a bun on each of their plates. "I'm sorry we don't have any extra butter. I'll go get some from the market later today." She sat and exchanged a quick glance with her husband. "So." Mrs. Stern wiped her mouth with a cloth napkin embroidered with tiny purple flowers and looked directly at Mee-Kyong. "Tomorrow's a big day."

Mee-Kyong smiled and took a sip of lemonade. She reminded herself that if she went through the initiation tomorrow, she could enjoy hot brunches like this every Saturday for at least the next year.

Mrs. Stern leaned forward in her chair. "Are you nervous?"

Benjamin coughed from his corner of the table, the first sound Mee-Kyong heard him make all morning. "Just a little," she answered and returned Benjamin's raised eyebrows with a defiant tilt of her chin.

Mrs. Stern cleared her throat. "Well, after we eat, we'll go upstairs together and make sure Kennedy's old bathing suit fits you. Sound all right?"

Mee-Kyong fabricated an enthusiastic nod.

Benjamin scooted his chair back noisily. "Thank you for breakfast," he mumbled, his mouth still stuffed with hot roll. All their gazes followed him as he sulked away from the table, turned down the hallway, and slammed the door to his room.

***

Eve thought she heard a woman's voice on the other side of the door. "Come on, Tiger," she yelled. "Open up." She heard a series of rustles, accompanied by a suppressed giggle. Eve had been out all night getting everything ready. She didn't have time for games. The door swung open just as she was about to throw her shoulder against it.

Tiger stood there in shorts and an undershirt, his hair disheveled and his cheeks flushed. Eve regained her balance. Had he been drinking already? She peeked around the corner. "Is someone else in here?"

He leaned against the doorframe and smirked. "What are you talking about, sugar?"

She walked in and looked around. "I thought I heard someone."

He grabbed her wrist and brushed her cheek with the back of one finger. "You might need to get your ears checked. Let me give you an examination."

"That's not why I'm here." She clutched her handbag, shoved him aside, and then strode to the small closet door.

He jumped in front of her and put both hands on her shoulders. "You look tense, baby. You tired? I wasn't expecting you today."

She glanced at the closet and crossed her arms. "Yeah, I can see that."

His face grew red, and his eyes widened imploringly. "Come on, sugar. Let me ..."

Eve kicked the door in. A woman shrieked and covered her face. "Just a friend?" Eve asked with one eyebrow raised. Before Tiger could answer, Eve pulled her revolver from her handbag and fired a single round into the woman's skull.

Tiger gawked, his arms frozen in front of his body. "You ... She was ... What ...?"

Eve didn't have time for his babbling. She raised the revolver to his chest and pulled the trigger. Then she grabbed her cell phone from her purse and punched in Ryuk's number.

"This is Agent Ko. I'm ready."

CHAPTER 39

The next morning, Mee-Kyong woke up with a gnawing emptiness in her gut that twisted up her insides into a tangled, knotted mess. Mrs. Stern rapped lightly on her door. "Are you awake, sweetheart?"

Mee-Kyong wondered if pet names and early-morning wake-up calls were blessings reserved just for the initiated. She pulled the quilt up to her shoulders. "Come in."

Her benefactress waddled through the door, her smile as wide as her girth. "It's your special day," she chirped in a sing-songy voice. Mee-Kyong hoped the early hour would excuse her from having to gush enthusiasm.

Mrs. Stern held up a hairbrush and a handbag. "I brought you some things. To get ready." Mee-Kyong sat up. Mrs. Stern lowered herself behind her on the bed and ran the brush through her hair. "I remember the day I was baptized," she sighed. Mee-Kyong felt ill. Almost an hour later, after yanking, braiding, combing, twisting, and eventually pinning Mee-Kyong's hair up in a simple braid, Mrs. Stern was satisfied. She then moved to the other side of the bed and dumped out the contents of her bag. Colorful tubes and jars of lipstick, skin cream, eye make-up, and facial powder spilled out on the mattress between them.

Mee-Kyong's jaw ached from being clenched so tightly. She shook her head. "No."

Mrs. Stern leaned back. "No?"

"I'm not wearing make-up."

Mrs. Stern gently rested two fingers on a tube of lipstick. "I just thought that … with it being such an important day …"

Mee-Kyong turned her face away so she didn't have to look at the rainbow of Mrs. Stern's vials. "No make-up."

Mrs. Stern took her hands off the lipstick and held them up in surrender. "Okay. No make-up. Do you want help getting dressed?"

Mee-Kyong crossed her arms. "I used to earn a living taking off my clothes. I think I can figure out how to put them back on."

***

"She's probably just nervous." Roger ran his fingers up and down his wife's spine. "Weren't you just a little bit nervous the day you got baptized?"

"Even if I was, I didn't bite anyone's head off."

Through her sweater, Roger felt Juliette tighten up all her muscles. He put both hands on her shoulders and started to knead the tension away. "She's young. You've said it before; she's been through a lot."

"That's still no reason to get crass with me."

"No, it's not." Roger locked his thumbs to get a deeper rub. "But what's done is done. Mee-Kyong's getting baptized. It's because of your hard work and compassion for her that she's come this far. So let's not ruin the day splitting hairs over who said what, okay? Let's make this a great day for Mee-Kyong, a day she'll never forget." He glanced toward the clock on the nightstand, but his wife's head blocked his view. "How much longer do we have?"

Juliette looked over. "Little less than an hour. Should we start getting the hot tub filled?"

"Not yet. We still have time." Roger paused. "There's one more thing I wanted to tell you, Baby Cakes." He swallowed once. "Benjamin's decided not to join us this afternoon."

"Not join us?" Juliette glared at him in the mirror. "What's going on? Has every single refugee living under our roof turned against us for some reason?"

Her pitch was rising, and Roger knew he needed to deescalate things quickly. "It's nothing like that, Baby Cakes. It's just … well, he didn't say it in so many words, but after what happened with Eve, I just don't think he wants to be around."

"Eve?" Juliette huffed, and Roger realized what a mistake it was to remind his wife of their ministry's most recent drop-out. "What's Eve got to do with this?"

Roger sighed. Did she really need him to spell this out for her? "It's a baptism," he stated. "It's in our bedroom, in a hot tub." Juliette's face still hadn't relaxed. "She'll be wearing a swimsuit."

Juliette's exasperated breath was hot on Roger's arm. "It's not like it's a bikini. Besides, she'll have a T-shirt on over it."

Roger sighed. "Baby Cakes, it's a guy thing. And probably a cultural one, too. Let's just not push it, okay? This can still be a great day for all of us if we just go into it with the right attitude."

"That's what I was trying to do all along," Juliette muttered.

***

Mee-Kyong glowered at herself in the mirror, scowling at the way Mrs. Stern had swept her bangs to the side of her face. She picked at the strands and tucked them into her braid. *Make-up?* Mrs. Stern had actually expected her to paint her face just for some aquatic ritual? The clinging bathing suit stretched across her belly. The material prickled against her skin but clung too tight for her to scratch the flea-bite tingles away. Her fingernails set to work methodically on her skin instead until her neck and shoulders glared red in the mirror.

She scowled at her reflection. If Sun had kept herself alive, they could be out of Yanji. Life might have been hard at first, but Mee-Kyong would have watched out for them both. She would have found a situation for them by the first snowfall, one that didn't involve entertaining hotel guests or copying Western literature until their finger muscles seized up.

Mee-Kyong wet her hands and tried to rub away the scratch marks on her neck. It wouldn't matter anyway. None of the Sterns could see them once she put the oversized cotton shirt on over the bathing suit. She let out a short, mirthless laugh. How ironic the Sterns were concerned about the modesty of their little brothel rescue.

She turned her head toward the door. "Almost ready, dear?" Mrs. Stern's voice was mouse-like, almost apologetic.

Mee-Kyong stood and yanked the big red shirt over her suit. It was the same shade as Sun's old dress. "I'm ready," she called out, throwing her shoulders back as she swung open the bedroom door.

***

"You did well, Agent Ko. I hear the director is already planning for your next assignment."

There was no reason for Eve to blush before Ryuk. She had known the old man even before she started training at the Academy. She also knew platitudes meant nothing to him, so she swallowed down her pre-programmed reply about honor and service to the Party. She would save the rhetoric for her meeting with the director.

"I'm curious," Ryuk continued as the two agents made their way to the train station. "What did you find out about the big one? The security guard."

Eve checked her lipstick in her compact mirror. She hated not getting enough sleep. It worked horrors on her skin. "I sent my write-up on to the bureau. They never told me they wanted anything else."

Ryuk took her arm. It was a paternal gesture, fitting for their assumed roles as father and daughter. "You wouldn't be covering up anything for him, would you?"

"Of course not." Eve puckered her lips, scowled at her reflection, and snapped the mirror shut. Ryuk scrutinized her out of the corners of his eyes, so she added, "He never meant anything to me."

A lopsided grin crept to one side of his face. "I've read your reports to the director," he reminded her. "I also know there was information you deliberately left out."

Eve buried her mirror in her handbag and flung her hair off her shoulder. "Have you been checking up on me, Ryuk? I didn't think you were the type to get jealous." She pressed her body a little closer to his as they walked.

"And what about that other one? That Tiger?"

Eve laughed. "A diversion. You have no idea how bored you get serving tea all day on silver platters."

"I take it he knew nothing of your work?" Ryuk stopped beneath a streetlamp and stared at her.

She shrugged again. "Of course not. I told you, I took care of everything before I came here."

Ryuk sighed and continued walking. "Well, you know the director will ask questions. With the security guard, you can at least argue you were gathering intel. Trying to gain trust. But a sleazy punk off the streets? Come on, Ko. What's the director going to think of that?"

She ran her fingers up and down the sleeve of his suit. "Who's to say the director has to find out?"

CHAPTER 40

The water was warmer than Mee-Kyong expected and almost scalded her leg when she first stepped in. She gasped.

"Is it all right?" Mrs. Stern was out of her fancy chair and to the side of the tub in half a second.

"I'm fine." Mee-Kyong forced a smile, if only to make up for her comments earlier when Mrs. Stern had tried to help her get ready. She hadn't intended to lose her composure like that, but she was already prostituting her soul to the Sterns and their American God. There was no way she was going to do it looking like she just stepped out of the Round Robin Inn.

Mee-Kyong put her second leg over the side of the tub. Mr. Stern was already waist deep in the water. "Well, we all know why we're here today, don't we?" He talked as if he were addressing a room full of witnesses, but it was just his wife and their newest religious convert. Not even Benjamin had come to her baptism. Did he refuse to participate since he knew it was a farce?

"Sister Mee-Kyong." Mr. Stern put one arm on her shoulder, and Mee-Kyong forced in a deep breath to keep from squirming away. "Because of your confession of faith and your desire to accept Jesus as your Lord, Savior, and Master, it is my privilege to baptize you today."

Mee-Kyong clenched her jaw shut. Yes, she would submit to this strange ritual. She would let Mr. Stern submerge her in water and congratulate himself on yet another Asian convert. Why should it matter to her? She had been conceived behind bars. What right did she have to think she might one day be free?

Mr. and Mrs. Stern both watched her expectantly. Realizing

she had missed something, Mee-Kyong glanced from one to the other, trying to pick up some sort of cue. "I asked if you believe that Jesus died for your sins and came back to life," Mr. Stern prompted.

"Oh." Mee-Kyong placed a stray wisp from her hair behind her ear. Mrs. Stern could make her own blond curls perform staggering stunts that defied physics, but she obviously had no experience with fine, straight Korean hair. "Yeah, I believe that."

"And do you want to live your life from now on in obedience and submission to him?"

"Sure." The word tumbled out of Mee-Kyong's mouth before she could correct it. "I mean, yes. Yes, that's what I want."

Mr. Stern frowned slightly, but he cleared his throat and went on. "Well then, Sister Mee-Kyong, it is my pleasure to baptize you in the name of the Father ..."

His hand was on her shoulder. His other held her wrist. Mee-Kyong locked her knees in place.

"... and of the Son ..."

He moved her hand and covered her mouth. She opened her lips to try to suck in a breath of air, but he clamped his palm down over her. She shut her eyes and braced herself.

"... and of the Holy Spirit."

He pressed down on her shoulder. She opened her eyes, her pupils screaming although her throat couldn't. She wasn't even under the water yet, but she needed air. *Air.* She gulped a mouthful of nothing. A vacuum. Her lungs made the motion of inhaling but didn't suck anything in. She thrashed both arms out wildly and scratched at whatever she found. The motion startled her restrainer. She pushed him back. "Get away from me." The water seared her skin. She lifted one red leg out of the tub, flinging her hands behind her to keep him from grabbing her again.

The woman was standing now, blocking her path. With a worried frown on her adipose face, she reached her arms out, groping, grabbing. Mee-Kyong wrestled free, flinging her abductors aside and racing out the room, dripping water as she scrambled toward the hallway and down the stairs.

***

Benjamin wiped his brow. It was so cold he could actually see the sweat steaming off his forearms. He jabbed the shovel into the ground that would soon be hard from frost. Why should he care if Eve left? What did it matter to him? He had already evicted her from his heart. He should be glad at least now he didn't need to live with the walking, breathing witness to his shame and guilt.

When it came right down to it, the Party was to blame. His superiors were the first ones to introduce Benjamin to voyeuristic pleasures, back when he was young enough he should have stayed ignorant. They liked taunting the boys they trained. *"This is how you'll be rewarded once you've risen through the ranks."* And Benjamin had worked harder than any of his peers.

He cursed the Party. He cursed the day the head recruiter arrived at his school to "ask him some questions." He cursed the tears he shed when the man told him he couldn't say good-bye to his family. *"Your training is top-secret. It's a matter of national security."* Benjamin plunged the shovel blade into the earth once more and thought about all the men and women he had buried so deep they would never be discovered. That was the problem working at the Sterns'. All he wanted was to forget, but haunting reminders lurked in every shovelful of dirt.

A commotion from inside made him turn once toward the house. A few seconds later, the back door flew open. Mee-Kyong stumbled past him and collapsed near the mound of soil. Doubled over, she gasped noisily, her shoulders heaving with each breath. The shovel dropped to the earth, and Benjamin knelt down beside her. "You okay?"

She glanced up at him. The only part of her that wasn't wet was the messy braid of hair on top of her head. He placed himself in front of her and laid his hands on her shoulders.

"Look at me," he ordered. She raised her gaze up once before retching onto the ground. "Look at me," he snapped again. Mee-Kyong shut her eyes for a moment and then opened them slowly. He nodded. "Better." He got up and closed the door behind him. If he knew the Sterns, they would be coming after her soon. "Let's go back here. It's quieter."

***

Mee-Kyong wrapped Benjamin's sweatshirt around her shoulders, hugged her knees, and prayed to whatever deity might exist the Sterns wouldn't follow her. Benjamin sat down next to her on the bench, keeping a considerable distance between them. "Want to tell me what happened?"

Mee-Kyong glared at her bare toes, the cold bite of winter stinging her wet skin. "I couldn't do it," she whispered.

"The baptism?"

She nodded. "I thought I was ready. But I was there in that huge tub, and he was about to dunk me ..." She glanced around and heard Mrs. Stern calling her name. *Please let them just leave me in peace.*

Benjamin frowned and adjusted the sweatshirt so it covered a little more of her shoulders. "Nobody made you."

Mee-Kyong shook her head and rocked slowly back and forth on the bench. "It wasn't supposed to be such a big deal."

"Maybe that's your problem."

Her teeth started to chatter. "What do you mean?"

"Baptism is a big deal. Supposed to be, at least."

She shrugged. "I didn't see it that way."

"Then you probably weren't ready."

229

Mee-Kyong was shaking too hard to argue with the security guard who got drunk every weekend. "I was at least hoping to make it through the whole winter."

Benjamin wrinkled his brow. "What?"

"I don't want to be on the streets again. Not with winter coming." She glanced at the fence that shielded them from the road and wondered how long she had before the first snowfall. Oh, well. Her reprieve had been nice enough while it lasted.

"Nobody's turning you out, Mee-Kyong." The way he spoke her name made her turn toward him again. "Stay as long as you want."

"That's nice of you to say, but last time I checked, this wasn't your house." She rubbed her legs and found she could barely wiggle her toes.

Benjamin leaned in just slightly toward her. "Don't have to get baptized just to stay here."

She shrugged. "Isn't that what you did?"

He looked down into his lap. "Maybe at first. But I've learned more now."

"How nice for you." She stood up, trying to figure out if there was a way to sneak back to the house for some clothes without running into the Sterns.

He reached out for her wrist. She tried to pull away, but his grip was too strong. "Please." He loosened his hold just enough so it stopped hurting. "Go in with me. We'll talk to them. Together. Nobody's sending you away."

***

Juliette yanked the barrette out of her mess of hair and slammed it on the counter. "I can't believe I let you talk me into baptizing her." She ran her fingers through her curls, but they only made it halfway before catching in the tangles.

230

Roger came up to hug her from behind, his breath warm on the side of her neck. Her sweater scratched against her skin. He took in a deep breath. "I guess she just wasn't ready."

Juliette rolled her eyes. That was so like her husband. No matter what the problem was, he'd find a way to understate it. If she had only listened to her gut and never mentioned baptism to Mee-Kyong in the first place, today's fiasco would have never happened. She jerked her glasses off her face, and pointed them at Roger's reflection in the mirror. "I hope you're impressed with yourself. I really do. Guilt-tripping a traumatized little girl ..."

Roger sighed. "She's not a little girl."

She threw up her hands. "Not a little girl? Oh, that's right. She's not a little girl because you found her in a brothel. Is that what you're saying? That because she used to sell tricks to earn money for someone else she's corrupt? Disgusting? Un..." Juliette's face was hot. Her throat failed her. She swallowed and tried again. "Un..." Roger was there, his hot breath smoldering her shoulder as he wrapped his arms around her from behind. Juliette flung her glasses aside and tried one last time to swallow away the cry that threatened to betray her. "Unredeemable." The word came out as a whisper, and with it came a torrent of fears and frustrations. Her husband didn't say a word, but held her in his arms while she sobbed.

***

The cool breeze stung Mee-Kyong's skin. She craned her neck and looked behind her. The Americans' outer fence extended all the way around the perimeter of the yard, but she could scale it in five seconds or less. Still, she wished she had some shoes. It was time to go, though. Staying any longer was just a waste of daylight. She jumped up, refusing to look back when Benjamin called out after her. She started to sprint, knowing his instinct would be to reach out toward her. "Thanks for the sweatshirt," she called back to him.

She was halfway over the fence before Benjamin grabbed her by the waist. "Get down." He tugged, and she landed on the lawn on the pads of her feet. Benjamin held his hands up. "You're soaking wet. You can't wear that out there."

She tilted her chin up. "I've earned a living in even less."

He lowered his eyes for a moment. Mee-Kyong didn't waste the opportunity and clambered to the top of the fence, poised to kick him if he reached up for her. He put his hands on the railings, his eyes pleading. "Nobody's going to make you do anything. Stay here. Keep up your studies with Mrs. Stern. Or tell her you need a break. Just talk to them."

"They'll keep trying to convert me like they've been doing this whole time."

Benjamin shrugged. "Maybe. But they've been good to you. Better than you'll find on your own."

Mee-Kyong scowled. "And what if I'm never ready to convert? What if I never get baptized? What then?"

He took his hands off the fence. There was a softness in his dark eyes Mee-Kyong had never noticed before. "At least you won't go hungry."

"I know how to take care of myself."

"You leave the Sterns' and you'll be back in the hotel district by nightfall. You know that, don't you?"

She narrowed her eyes. "I'll starve before going back there."

He reached up slowly toward her. "Please." She had never heard him sound so concerned. She was used to pity — Mrs. Stern doled out enough of that to last Mee-Kyong a lifetime — but this felt different. "Please come back. I'll go with you. We'll talk to them. Together."

She looked down at him and realized she was at another crossroads, forced to decide her fate in a single instant. No wavering. No second guesses. It was as though the way had been paved for her years ago, before Pang, before her escape from Camp 22, before the Round Robin, before Sun. Mee-Kyong knew the path she was going to take.

She just hoped she wouldn't live to regret it.

PART 5

CHAPTER 41

Several years later

She clicked up to the front desk, precariously balanced on her high heels. The man behind the counter raised his head from his computer screen. His eyes went first to her face but then traveled quickly to her business suit and designer handbag. He curled up his lips. "How may we help you today?" He laid both hands in front of him and sat perfectly still.

She looked around and appraised the double chandeliers, the large mirror hanging in its ornate mahogany frame, the hand-designed rugs splayed out for all to see. Once satisfied, she nodded at the proprietor and extended her card. "I am the president of Morning Pleasures. We plan and promote parties for some of the most prominent local businessmen, whose tastes extend to the … more delicate members of the hotel district." She didn't give him time to respond. "I'd like to hire thirty of your girls for a gathering this Saturday evening at the Glorious Dynasty Hotel. You're familiar with the venue, I presume?"

The proprietor nearly dropped the credentials she handed him. She smiled and tapped a perfectly-manicured fingernail on the marble countertop. "I've been told you have a wide selection of girls in the following age ranges." She turned the card over, pointing with her blood-red fingertip. The man coughed once and cleared his throat. She raised an eyebrow. "I assume you have what we're looking for."

He scratched at his neck, which had reddened against the white starchiness of his shirt, and dabbed his forehead with a pocket handkerchief. "Of course, we have just what you need. Shall we choose the girls for you, or do you want to select them yourself?"

She raised her chin until she was staring down slightly at the balding manager. "At Morning Pleasures parties, we guarantee each patron receives nothing but one-hundred-percent satisfaction." She leaned forward as she said the last word. "We don't leave anything up to chance. We examine each girl and personally ensure she is the proper fit for our clients' needs."

The man reached into a desk drawer, fumbled with a key, and hustled around the counter. "In that case, if you'd be so kind as to follow me, I'll introduce you to our young ladies right now. If … if now is quite convenient."

In her heels, she stood several centimeters taller than he. "Quite." She followed him to a winding staircase, and the clicking echoes of her footsteps sounded off the gaudy wallpaper.

***

"Hold still," Sang-Hee admonished as she brushed her little sister's hair. Girls were scattered across the large dormitory like rags tossed haphazardly into an open bin. Some rested on flimsy cots. Others sat looking out of the only window, huddled together to share the tiny view. A few sat in a corner playing marbles, using earrings instead of balls. In the opposite corner, two girls argued over a doll made of rolled-up fabric.

When the door flung open, the chattering stopped and was replaced by the sound of rushing feet and rustling cloth. Sang-Hee picked up her sister and hurried her along with the others. "It's all right," she whispered. When she reached the line-up, she propped Min on her crooked feet and leaned her against the wall. The girls each stood in their proper places, their arms at their sides, except for the one who had forgotten to put down the doll, which she hid behind her back. Sang-Hee hoped the innkeeper wouldn't notice.

He marched in as proud as a peacock, followed by a lady, a very rich one. She had thick hair the color of starless midnight and wore a tailored suit made of stiff maroon fabric that didn't wrinkle when she walked. Her shoes sparkled subtly and made her even taller than the innkeeper. She entered the room with a severe frown. Sang-Hee instinctively put one leg in front of Min's, both to help her sister withstand the weight on her crippled feet and to shield her from the woman's attention.

Without waiting for the innkeeper to invite her, the woman strode to the start of the line and inspected each girl in turn. Every so often, she'd instruct one of the girls to open her mouth or turn around. She examined several heads of hair and cleared her throat more than once. When she got to little Min, she leaned over. "What is your name?" Her voice was distant, almost bored.

Sang-Hee trembled inwardly. "She doesn't talk, ma'am." She stared at the woman's spiked heels.

"Silence," the innkeeper roared. Sang-Hee squeezed Min's quivering hand.

The woman straightened up and tilted her chin toward Sang-Hee. "And you are?"

"Her sister, ma'am. I mean, *adopted* sister." The word tore at her throat. She shut her eyes for a moment. "I just help take care of her."

The innkeeper had closed the distance between himself and his client, and he placed a hand on the woman's waist and led her further down the line. "A speechless idiot," Sang-Hee heard him mumble.

She held tight to her sister with one hand and dug her fingernails into the palm of the other. Once the innkeeper passed by, she leaned toward Min and whispered that old, familiar lie she had long ago ceased to believe:

"Everything's going to be all right."

***

The innkeeper's pen scurried to record her selections as Mee-Kyong singled out the girls. "That one there, with the short hair and freckles." She despised this part of the job, having to make such snap-second choices, but she refused to show any indecisiveness. "The one next to her who's trying to hide that little dolly behind her back." She thought, as she did every now and then, about the promise she made to Benjamin to never return to the hotel district. Well, at least she was on the right side of the industry now. She adjusted one of her dangling ruby earrings, a gift from a generous benefactor.

"Her. In the white blouse."

The innkeeper grunted his assent. Mee-Kyong crossed her arms and shifted her weight to one hip. She studied the small one with the mangled feet. The older girl beside her put a defensive arm across the cripple's chest. "I'll take the silent one, too." She hadn't spoken very loudly, but the teenager visibly tensed. Mee-Kyong scrutinized her next. She hardly ever requested anybody that old. The teen met her stare, and Mee-Kyong shrugged her shoulders. "I'll take the older one with her, too. The sister."

"Adopted sister," the innkeeper corrected.

"Just put her name on the list," she snapped and continued to scan the line of children.

***

The innkeeper tried not to let his excitement bleed through his words. Assuming the woman's finances cleared, this would be his biggest deal of the year. "You're sure that this will be enough girls to meet your client's needs?" He licked his top lip as he left the children to their lazy leisure time and walked down the winding staircase.

She ignored his question. "The girl with the crippled legs … what's wrong with her?"

"Ahhh, the idiot." The manager smiled. "Yes, some might turn away from the sight of a deformed beast like that. But I see you know your business well." He turned and added conspiratorially, "Of course, many show preferences for such … creatures."

The woman cleared her throat. "How much assistance does the cripple require?"

"Just help walking, just help walking," the innkeeper hastened to explain. "The rest … well, you know. Her customers always leave quite content," he added when he noted the woman's severe scowl. The expression didn't change, so he quickly continued. "I assure you that all our girls will surpass your guests' expectations. They are well-trained, willing to oblige." He realized he was rambling, but he couldn't stop himself. "As you can see," he prattled, gesticulating with both hands, "we keep our girls clean. Clean and well-kempt. Not like other establishments in the hotel district."

The president of Morning Pleasures gave a curt nod and interrupted his jabber. "They're adequate." Disgust dripped from the word.

She was several paces ahead, and he scurried to catch up. "It's early in the day still, you see. They're tired. They work best at night, of course. You won't be disappointed at all, I assure you."

She didn't slow her pace. "I'll judge their quality when my client is satisfied. Before that, we have your fee to discuss."

The proprietor held up a hand. "Not now, not now. It's still morning. You should come back this evening. Allow me to treat you to a dinner, perhaps. Money is such a bore to talk over unless there's good food … and pleasant company … involved."

The woman halted and turned so abruptly the innkeeper nearly bumped into her. "We will settle the payment now," she declared. "Half today. Half when I return with my driver to pick up the girls Saturday night."

The innkeeper opened his mouth once but didn't have a chance to interject.

"If all goes smoothly," she continued, "you can expect us to call on you again after this weekend. Good day." She waved a check, and he struggled to catch it with both hands before it fluttered to the ground. When he saw the amount was already filled in, he scampered after to thank her for her business, but she had already left. The gold-plated door swung inward behind her, and the innkeeper barely scurried back in time before it hit his nose.

CHAPTER 42

Sang-Hee hadn't let go of her little sister's hand for the entire bus ride. She rested one cheek on the young girl's head and whispered sweet senseless musings: *"It's going to get better." "One day, this will be over." "Life won't always be so hard."* When the bus slowed down in front of a hotel, she took a deep breath. At least the building looked fancy enough to have an elevator. The last time Min had been taken to entertain at another establishment, Sang-Hee had to carry her up three flights of stairs.

The businesswoman, now wearing a low-cut dress with beads swirling from its short skirt, stood up in the bus aisle next to the driver. "This is where you will work tonight. The party begins in forty-five minutes, which should give you time to freshen up in your rooms upstairs." She furrowed her brows, and Sang-Hee blinked as she stared at the mascara caked onto the woman's eyelashes. "You'll go right to your assigned rooms. Hurry up."

The girls filed off the bus. "Let's go now." Sang-Hee hoisted her sister up on her back and made her way down the aisle. She stalled once at the top of the steps and did what she could to shift their center of gravity to make the descent safely. The businesswoman was on the curb, but she put one foot up on the lower bus step and supported Sang-Hee by the elbow as she made her way down.

Sang-Hee and Min would share a room with two other girls. They had each spent over an hour primping before the bus ride, and there was little left to be done now but wait. Once they were settled in their suite, Sang-Hee lay down next to Min, carefully ensuring neither of their dresses would get crumpled on the soft hotel bed. "It's all right," she whispered. "You can rest for a little bit. Nobody's coming to bother us." She sighed with weariness. "Not yet," she added, quietly enough only she could hear.

Sang-Hee woke up to the sound of quiet knocking several hours later. A tiny smudge of drool moistened her cheek. She shivered once with the chill. One of the other girls in the bed next to her snored slightly. She looked at the clock and sucked in her breath. They had missed the party. She sprang out of bed. How would she explain her mistake to the innkeeper? She was several years older than the other girls. She should have known better. She threw on the lights, fluffed her curls once in the mirror, and flung the door open.

"Shhh." It was the woman from the bus. She had taken off the evening dress and now wore casual black leggings and a dark hooded sweatshirt with the same pointed heels. She glanced behind her once and slipped into the room.

"I'm sorry, ma'am," Sang-Hee whispered. "It's my fault."

The woman shook her head. "You didn't do anything wrong. There's no party. I came to bring you these." She held up four small backpacks, two draped over each arm. "Wake the girls up. Tell them to get changed. We leave in fifteen minutes."

A chill raced its way up Sang-Hee's spine. "Leave?" The word caught in her throat like a desperate gasp for air.

The woman met her gaze. "Leave. I'm getting you out of here." Sang-Hee thought about the borders she had already crossed, the miles she had already traveled. Was it starting all over again, then? "I'll explain more on the bus," the woman whispered. "Just wake everyone else up, and tell them to be ready. I'll knock once when it's time."

Sang-Hee's legs were heavy as she made her way to Min. The child was cherubic, her porcelain cheeks shining with a babyish radiance. Sang-Hee nestled her nose into the side of her little sister's neck. "Come on," she whispered. "We've got to get dressed."

Half an hour later, thirty sleepy-eyed girls stumbled down a back staircase to the bus that waited for them in an alleyway. Sang-Hee hadn't been able to fully rouse Min but had managed to dress her and carry her downstairs. The woman in heels was at the bus waiting. "What's going on?" Sang-Hee asked.

"We've found safe homes for you. Away from here. You'll never have to go back." She placed one hand on Sang-Hee's shoulder, and with the other, gestured to the girls behind her to continue boarding. She lowered her voice. "I made sure that you two would stay together." She swept a strand of hair from Min's forehead. "She'll need someone like you watching over her."

"Where is it you're taking us?"

The woman shook her head. "There are parts to the puzzle I don't see. When I get off this bus, the less I know, the better. It's enough for me that you'll be safe."

Safe? Sang-Hee balked. "Why? Why are you doing this?"

The woman's melancholy smile was as enigmatic as her response. "I like to think of it as repaying a debt." Min squirmed in her sleep. "You better find seats," the woman said.

Once everyone was settled, she spoke to the girls in a quiet, simplistic manner. "I know it's late, and it's a little chilly. There are blankets in some of the backpacks, but you'll have to share them. You're going on a drive. It will take all night. Try to sleep if you can. When you stop in the morning, you'll be taken to homes. Nice homes. Not like the one you're leaving. There will be mommies there. Maybe not as good and kind as the mommies you might have had when you were younger, but they will love you and care for you just the same. After that, some more nice people will take you to other homes. Even better homes. Far away from people who want to hurt you. But you have to be brave. You older girls need to help the younger ones if they get tired or scared." Sang-Hee saw the woman wipe the side of her face, smudging some of that extra mascara from the corner of her eye. "I'm sorry for what you've had to go through. Just …" Her voice caught for a moment. "Just remember nothing that's happened to you is your fault. Nothing. I promise you, from this moment on, it's going to get better."

From where she lay cuddled on her big sister's lap, Min stirred with a pitiful whine. The woman in the sweatshirt walked down the aisle of the bus, her steps brisk and noisy in her impossibly high heels. She knelt down and tucked Min's stray bangs behind her ear. She put her face close to the child's. "It will be all right," she whispered. The woman leaned forward and kissed the squirming girl once on the cheek. Min blinked her eyes open and drifted back off to sleep.

"Safe journey, little cousin," the woman breathed. Her clicking heels pierced the silence as she clacked down the aisle, descended the stairs, and hurried out into the dark night.

***

When she was a safe distance from the hotel, Mee-Kyong turned toward the late-night cafe and plucked her cell phone out of her pocket.

"They're all off," she told him.

"Congratulations," he responded. "Another job well done. Where are you now?"

"Right where we agreed."

"On my way." She stood waiting, thinking about the girl with the crippled feet and her older sister, two more nameless faces to add to her ever-growing prayer list. A moment later, she sensed his presence even before he came up behind her for a hug. "You did it," he whispered into her ear.

"That didn't take you long," she remarked. "What were you doing, stalking me the whole time?"

"Maybe." He rested his cheek on the top of her head and inhaled deeply. "Just because I love you."

"Careful." She nudged him with her elbow. "I thought bodyguards were supposed to remain professional at all times."

He held up both hands. "Guilty." She didn't return his smile, at least not soon enough to keep him from noticing. "What's wrong?" He put one arm around her and led her down the sidewalk.

"I was just thinking about the girls we left behind. There were so many of them."

"Always will be," he reminded her.

She sighed again. "I just keep thinking about her."

She knew he understood which *her* she was talking about. "I know." A trace of playfulness crept into his voice. "But the past ..."

"... is a closed book," she finished, and she laughed with him, even though her heart was burdened by a sadness no amount of inside jokes would ever erase. "I'm ready," she sighed.

He took her by the hand. "Then let's go, my love." Together they walked through the darkness toward the safety and shelter of home.

ACKNOWLEDGEMENTS

There are many people I'd like to thank for the encouragement, prayers, and practical support they poured out while I was working on *Slave Again*. My husband continues to be my biggest inspiration. Thank you so much for letting me bounce so many different plot ideas off you. Thank you also for teaching me that Eve should be holding a revolver, not a gun, and that she can't use a concealed holster if she's wearing a skimpy outfit.

I'd also like to give a shout-out to my buddies from the Christian Indie Authors forum, a community of online friends and encouragers. Thanks especially to those of you who pray for me when I send out S.O.S. prayer requests. The author friends of mine who live or have lived in East Asia (you know who you are), thanks for fielding all of my strange, random questions, like what kind of delicacy a fat innkeeper would eat. I'd like to especially mention Precarious Yates and thank her for teaching me more about the sex-trade industry worldwide and sharing her passion with me.

Slave Again went through more rounds of edits than I could ever care to relate. I'd like to thank my story editor, Nat Davis, and my troop of beta readers (you also know who you are!) for all the advice you gave. Kate and Annie get the prize for finding the most typos. A big thank you Mary for the thorough copy edits, and a shout-out to all my WIPpet blogging friends. I could also devote an entire page thanking Regi McClain for just about everything she's ever done, but she hates sap, and so I'll just mention here that she did a ton of behind-the-scenes work to help me when carpal tunnel slowed me down, and she is an invaluable sounding board. (As of now, she also happens to be the only person in the entire world who knows how the series is going to end!) What's amazing about Regi is she knows all my characters by name and keeps them all straight. Thanks for your friendship, Regi.

Krystine Kercher helped prepare the cover image, which was designed by Damonza, and I think they did a great job. I was also very encouraged by those who pledged their support for the *Slave Again* Kickstarter project and who patiently waited for my novel to come out. A huge thank you to all the bloggers and book reviewers who agreed to help with my launch, as well.

There were times, especially as I struggled with carpal tunnel, when I really wondered if this book would ever get published or not. God, You brought me the healing when I needed it, and You taught me to rest even though I was kicking and screaming the whole time. Thank You for letting me write another book. May it bring You glory.

Liberty in North Korea estimates that seventy percent or more of all females who escape from North Korea into China fall victim to sex slavery. *Slave Again* is dedicated to these girls and women. May God bring you freedom and deliverance.

"For you did not receive a spirit that makes you a slave again to fear, but you received the Spirit of adoption."
Romans 8:15

Liberty in North Korea (LiNK) runs an underground railroad that helps North Korean refugees like Mee-Kyong find freedom in safe countries. Visit alanaterry.com/link to donate, learn more, or start up a rescue team of your own. All money is donated directly to LiNK's field expenses. Please join me so girls like Sun and Mee-Kyong can experience true freedom.

Books by Alana Terry

North Korea Christian Suspense Novels

The Beloved Daughter

Slave Again

Torn Asunder

Flower Swallow

Kennedy Stern Christian Suspense Series

Unplanned

Paralyzed

Policed

Straightened

Turbulence

See a full list at www.alanaterry.com